MOONLIGHT, MURDER, AND SMALL-TOWN SECRETS

A Katy Cross Mystery Book One

K.C. HART

Also by K.C. Hart

Music, Murder & Small Town Romance

Memories, Murder & Small Town Money

Merry Murder & Small Town Santas

Medicine, Murder & Small Town Scandal

Marriage, Murder, & Small Town Schemes

Praise For The Katy Cross Cozy Mystery Series

Moonlight, Murder, & Small Town Secrets

"K.C. Hart knows how to grab your attention and keep you guessing."

"This is my first book by KC Hart and she is a great writer!" Normally, when I think of a cozy mystery it's easy to figure out who done it. Not this book. Y'all will enjoy to the very end. I like her characters, atmosphere, delicious food they ate. Like, I'll take a bag of boiled peanuts please! So get the book and start reading.

Music, Murder, & Small Town Romance

"If you loved Nancy Drew as a kid, you need to meet K.C. Hart!"

"A simple band competition turns into murder involving the local Casanova. This keeps you moving from one suspect to another without giving away the true villain. The dependence on God of the main character flows through the storyline in a very authentic way."

Memories, Murder, & Small Town Money

"I think this might be the best book in the series so far. The mystery is great, as usual, and kept me guessing until the end. I also really enjoyed seeing Katy's character grow and watch the sweet, honest friendship between her and Misty reach a new level. I highly recommend this book and the entire series."

"This is the most awesome series I've come across yet! I have been looking for a good Christian cozy mystery series and this is exactly what I have been searching for."

Merry Murder & Small Town Santas

"A great murder mystery that will pull you in from the beginning. So fun trying to figure out who is the killer. The author keeps the reader on a rollercoaster ride with clues and suspects. The town and characters are great fun

and a little quirky. Katy is bold and gets herself into some situations that make her an excellent main character. I love reading this series and I'm looking forward to the next book. This is a clean book that doesn't have gore, but mystery and humor a plenty!"

"I loved this story, it was different. I never once gave the ending a thought, so it was a complete surprise. I love surprises! As always, the love between Katy and John was great, and the spiritual aspects were good also. The humor is always much appreciated."

Medicine, Murder & Small Town Scandal

"KC Hart gives hands and feet to a Christian way of life. KC Hart did it again. I love how her characters connect to my actual daily life. (Poor Katy, the struggle between chocolate pie and cholesterol!) I also love the way KC Hart makes belief in Jesus Christ an every day, every hour, every minute way of life, not something pulled out and shown off on "church" days or holidays.

If you need some down time, something to grab your attention and lose yourself for a few hours, get a KC Hart cozy mystery."

"Lots of twists and turns, and I had no clue "who done it" 'til the end! Loved the medical aspect too. Katy Cross keeps it interesting."

Marriage, Murder & Small Town Schemes

"I have really enjoyed these Katy Cross mysteries. This one is no exception with plenty of red herrings, and further development of some of our favorite characters."

"You'll get engulfed in this awesome Christian cozy mystery by the very talented author, KC Hart. I loved it and would highly recommend this book and the entire series."

Dedication

This book is dedicated to my mom and dad
who believed that small-town country life was the
best life.
Love you Mom. Love you Dad.
Wish you were here.

PHILIPPIANS 2:4-8

CONTENTS

Moonlight, Murder, and Small-Town Secrets   xiii
Book Blurb   xv

Chapter 1   1
Chapter 2   11
Chapter 3   22
Chapter 4   29
Chapter 5   38
Chapter 6   47
Chapter 7   60
Chapter 8   68
Chapter 9   78
Chapter 10   90
Chapter 11   99
Chapter 12   111
Chapter 13   123
Chapter 14   135
Chapter 15   143
Chapter 16   150
Chapter 17   162
Chapter 18   169
Chapter 19   180

Chapter 20 — 192
Chapter 21 — 201
Chapter 22 — 204
Chapter 23 — 213
Chapter 24 — 222
Chapter 25 — 236
Chapter 26 — 246
Chapter 27 — 255
Chapter 28 — 265
Chapter 29 — 273
Chapter 30 — 287
Chapter 31 — 303
Chapter 32 — 312
Chapter 33 — 325
Chapter 34 — 342
Chapter 35 — 353
Chapter 36 — 359
Chapter 37 — 372
Chapter 38 — 381
Chapter 39 — 391
Coming Soon — 399
40. Chapter One — 400

Acknowledgments — 417
About the Author — 419

Moonlight, Murder, and Small-Town Secrets

A KATY CROSS COZY MYSTERY

Book One

K.C. HART

Book Blurb

Katy Cross is more than Skeeterville's favorite home health nurse. She's also lead guitarist for her band, *The Moonlighters,* a wife to her goofball husband, and a friend to Skeeterville's colorful elderly community.

When *The Moonlighters* land their biggest gig yet at the annual Peanut Patch festival, Katy can't wait to cover her favorite songs on stage for her friends and family. However, things hit a sour note when she stumbles across a body during a mic check. The open-and-shut case strikes a wrong chord with Katy, and she is worried that an innocent man is being framed, leaving the real killer to roam free. Can she solve the murder before anyone else is forced to join the heavenly choir?

This debut cozy series from K.C. Hart follows amateur sleuth Katy Cross as she solves crimes in her small southern town with the help of her husband, her elderly patients, the vocal locals of Skeeterville, and, of course, her band mates, *The Moonlighters*.

Chapter One

Katy rushed home from her last patient's house to change from her nursing uniform into a pair of jeans and the Peanut Patch tee-shirt that all the members of her band, *The Moonlighters*, were wearing to the festival. After a glance at her reflection in the mirror, she grabbed her guitar and a folder with the songs for tonight's performance. She jogged back to her car to drive the short distance to the festival grounds on the outskirts of town.

The Moonlighters had opened for *The Wildcats* last night and would again tonight. This was the biggest event Katy's cover band had ever played, and she loved it. True, most of the people were only half listening as they walked around eating boiled peanuts, drinking Cokes, and looking at the vendor booths, but that didn't matter. Katy and her friends were on the stage playing to an audience who, for the most part, were not close family members, which was a step up. No, while they were on that stage, they weren't a home health nurse, a florist, a phlebotomist, a college student, and a single mom. When Katy was playing lead guitar, and her best friend Misty was rocking a drum solo, they got to imagine they were musical stars like Alison Krauss or even Dolly or Emmylou. Not that they were fighting aspirations of greatness, but being in the spotlight doing something you loved right here in Skeeterville did feel good.

Katy turned on the air conditioner full blast and began running over the setlist in her head. *The Moonlighter's* music was a sharp contrast to *The Wildcats. The Wildcats* were old country-rock with fast tempos and great drums. They made you want to put down your cup of peanuts and grab a dance partner. Even though she didn't care too much for their lead singer, Jessa Williams, Katy had to admit their band knew how to perform and put on a good show. *The Moonlighter's* bluegrass and gospel music made you want to pull up a lawn chair and sing along. Mixing the two kinds of music had worked out well. Last night's crowd did a lot of smiling and lingered around until midnight when the lights were finally turned out.

The car knocked and bumped along the rough, homemade road that cut through the hayfield. Only a handful of people showed up this early, so she would be able to park much closer than she had last night. Todd—Skeeterville's youngest deputy sheriff, as well as Katy's favorite nephew—was already parked in the usual place upfront reserved for security. He wouldn't mind helping her make sure all the equipment was set up on the flatbed trailer which served as the stage.

Katy pulled into a spot beside Jessa Williams' Mustang and stepped onto the trampled grass. She bet Jessa wasn't here yet. She had probably just left her car last night and rode home with someone else. Katy heard Marissa Holmes, another member of *The Wildcats,* complaining that Jessa acted like a diva. All she ever did was show up and sing. Katy could definitely believe it. One thing she loved about her band was that everyone got along well. That did not seem to be the case with *The Wildcats.*

Katy lugged her guitar from the back seat of her car and slammed the door. She turned just in time to catch a sliver of movement disappear on the other side of Jessa's Mustang. Suddenly a head popped up again at the back of the car near the trunk. *That's strange,* she thought.

"Uh, hello, can I help you?" Katy glanced back over her shoulder to make sure Todd was nearby in case there was trouble. Skeeterville was a safe town, but purses still had a way of disappearing out of back seats at festivals and fairs.

"Hey, Mrs. Katy." Laney Finch, the wife of the high school football coach, jolted upright like a rubber band had popped her in the backside. "I didn't see you over there." Her face flushed bright red with either surprise or guilt, Katy wasn't sure which. "I just dropped my purse and was trying to gather all my stuff back up. Don't pay me any mind."

"Sorry I surprised you, Laney. For a minute there I thought someone was breaking into that car."

"No problem." Laney stretched a taut smile onto her face and made a point of looking under the edge of the car one more time. "I think I've found everything. I better be going." She dug around in her monstrous designer handbag. "Mom has my kids and is waiting for me to get home."

"Good seeing you," Katy said as she turned and made her way toward the stage, guitar in tow. She would have bet a bag of peanuts that Laney had been trying to sneak off without being seen. And why in the world would she leave the festival before it even began? It sure seemed like the woman was up to something.

Katy smiled as the sound of whistling drew nearer from the food vendors' section. Todd's sandy brown head and lanky frame appeared from that direction just as she reached the edge of the stage, lips still puckered from his slightly off-key tune. A much-needed breeze brought the smell of freshly boiled peanuts and fried turkey legs along with her nephew. She laid a hand across her stomach to smother the growling.

"I'm happy to report that all the food booths are secure and ready to start serving the crowds," Todd said as he made his way across the grassy field towards Katy.

"It's nice of you to be looking out for our hard-working vendors." Katy held her hand up to her forehead to shield out the setting sun. "I love this festival, but I've got to be careful this year."

"Why, did something happen last year?" Todd asked, concern in his voice. "I didn't hear about any trouble, but if I need to check up on somebody I can."

"I'm the only one you need to check up on," Katy laughed. "I've got to be careful and only eat one bag of boiled peanuts tonight. Last year I ate too much festival food and made myself sick as a dog. It was so bad I missed church that week. It would be awful if I got too sick to perform."

"You're on your own with that one," Todd said, patting his flat stomach. "I ain't coming between any woman and her boiled peanuts. Momma raised me better than that." He turned back from the food vendors and glanced around the stage. "Can I help you set anything up? I can't believe Uncle John isn't here to help you."

"You know he'd be here if he could. He's in Missouri on business. Besides, I can handle this." She climbed up the rickety wooden stairs at one end of the stage, then leaned over and hoisted up her guitar. The six-string acoustic wasn't terribly heavy, but Katy stifled a groan as she pulled it up. "But if you have time and don't mind, I guess I could use a little help. It looks like some of the others have already been here."

"Show off," Katy grinned, watching Todd hop over the hay bales and onto the stage, completely skipping the stairs. "I could do that too if I was still in my twenties and six foot tall."

"Yeah," Todd said, flexing his lanky bicep, "I have extra energy from that fried Oreo I sampled a while ago." He looked around at the mics and wires. "Mike and Misty were setting up stuff when I got here. You must've just missed them. They said they were going home to put on their nut shirts and were coming right back." He eyed Misty's drum set. "What can I do? Drum solo while you tune-up?"

"Maybe later," Katy said, "but you can help me make sure everything has power."

"No problem, and you know I work for peanuts."

"Wow, so original, Todd. You should write a song or a book or something," Katy said, laughing sarcastically as she began flipping on switches and checking power cords and connections. "Let's see, for some reason this amp isn't getting power. I've checked these connections up here. Would you mind making sure everything's plugged in at the shed?"

"Sure thing." Todd hopped off the stage and trotted over to the shed.

She wasn't sure what it was used for the rest of the year, but during the Peanut Patch festival, the flatbed trailer was backed up to a metal shed where extension cords could reach the electrical outlets to power the show. If it started to rain, the equipment could quickly be moved indoors. That happened a few years ago. It only rained for about thirty minutes, but for the rest of the afternoon the bands played in the shed's garage door opening.

Luckily, *The Moonlighters* didn't perform that

year. You could see the heat devils rising off of the garage floor while *The Bluegrass Babes* were playing. Mrs. Ella Johnson, the Babe's seventy-year-old fiddle player, had to go to the emergency room at the end of their set to be treated for heat exhaustion. Her children wouldn't let her play the festival anymore. It was a shame. Katy enjoyed watching the women. They were all in their seventies, had matching silver beehives, and wore red silk shirts with enough fringe and sequins to impress a group of Elvis impersonators.

"Everything seems to be okay here, Aunt Katy." Todd wiggled all the cords that were plugged into the outlets. "Maybe it's in one of the connections. I'll check them while I'm down here."

He followed the wires from the shed to the base of the flatbed. They disappeared under the bales of hay, then reappeared in the crack between the base of the trailer and the top of the hay bale where they were duct-taped to the metal trailer frame to hold them secure. Todd began checking each cord while Katy continued to check the equipment.

"Here's the problem," Todd called. "This one's not taped to the frame, and the connection has slipped loose." He reached down to pull more of the power cord from under the hay bale. "Oops... dropped it," he said. The cord slivered between the crack of the hay bale and trailer and disappeared underneath. He shoved his arm down and tried to blindly fish it back out from the hay. "That's not working," he said, pulling his arm back out of the crack.

"Just pull the bale out and pick up the cord," Katy instructed. "There's some extra duct-tape in the shed. You can re-tape it. Then we won't have to worry about it coming undone again during the show."

"Sure thing, boss lady," Todd said, grinning as he pulled out the bale of hay. He moved the hay bale, then squatted down to retrieve the cord but bounced right back up. He glanced at Katy then went right back down. The image of prairie dogs coming in and out of burrows flashed through her mind. Todd popped up again, this time his brows were pulled together in a frown.

"What is it, a snake? There's a hoe in the shed. I'll fetch it real quick." The wooden stairs swayed as she bolted down to get the hoe.

"Uh, wait, Aunt Katy, it's not a snake." Todd's voice was strained. "Just give me a second to think." He got down on all fours and crawled halfway under the trailer.

Katy shifted her head from side to side, trying to see through the three-foot section where the bale of hay had been. She quickly gave up and dropped to her knees, crawling into the dark narrow space beside her nephew. What had caught his attention so quickly? She sure hoped it wasn't a rat. She could handle snakes, but man, she hated rats. Those long, hairless tales just made her skin crawl.

Todd pulled out his flashlight from a loop on his belt and flashed a beam through the pitch black, crowded space.

"Good gravy and biscuits!" Katy's voice climbed several decibels as her pupils focused on the figure in the dark opening. "That's Jessa Williams."

Jessa lay on her back with her arms flailed to either side. Her blond hair was scattered across her face in a way that made Katy want to rake it out of her eyes. She shuddered as her eyes adjusted to the dim light. Jessa's eyes were stretched wide open, fixed, and staring at the bottom of the dirty trailer that was covered in spider webs hovering a couple of feet from her face. The woman still had on the leopard-print mini-skirt, thigh-high black leather boots, and black silk shirt she had performed in the night before. Katy leaned in closer and placed her finger on the side of Jessa's neck, trying to find a pulse.

"Todd, she's dead."

Chapter Two

"Yeah, I know," Todd said. "Don't touch her. I have to call it in." He backed out from under the trailer and pulled out his phone.

Oops, too late. Maybe just touching her neck didn't hurt anything, Katy thought. A little more sun was shining in now that Todd had moved out of the opening. She looked around the cramped, damp area where the woman lay. Once Todd called the station, he would probably run her off so he could do his job.

It seemed so undignified to see Jessa lying there under the flatbed. Katy had seen a lot of people die in her line of work, but that was always in the hospital or either with dignity in their own homes with their loved ones around them. This was different. No one deserved to die like this.

Katy's eyes roamed carefully over the body of the young woman, assessing her from top to bottom just like she would one of her patients. She tucked her hands close to her side so she wouldn't be tempted to touch her again. The large, dark sticky-looking spot under Jessa's head was probably blood. Her blue eye shadow looked cyanotic against the death pale that had settled on her skin, but there was nothing unexpected on her face, like swelling or bruising. Katy leaned in a little closer to look at the small scratch at Jessa's collar bone where the button-up shirt flared open a bit and revealed cleavage. Jessa had seemed to love attention related to her looks, and she certainly had the looks to get the attention.

Katy hurriedly finished her assessment. Todd would be off the phone any minute and shoo her away. Jessa's shirt was still tucked in at the front, but from what she could see without flipping her over, it appeared to be untucked and wadded up in the back. It almost looked like someone had picked her up from a lying position and moved her here.

Jessa's fake corral colored nails looked just as beautiful on her long fingers as they always did. Katy couldn't wear the fake ones because the policy at her job didn't allow it. She couldn't play half of her guitar chords when she wore them either. This was probably why she always noticed every other woman's nails... and why she suffered from chronic nail envy.

Jessa's hair was tangled and messed up. A bright red fake fingernail was hung up in a knot of the long blonde tresses. This nail definitely didn't come from Jessa's hands. There were also a few strands of hair tangled in the giant gaudy pink diamond ring on Jessa's right ring finger. Katy squinted her eyes in the muted light. Most of the strands of the tangled hair were blond or silver but mixed in were also a couple of strands of a bright, bright blue.

She placed the palms of her hands on the soft, cool earth to steady herself and leaned even closer to take one quick last look at the woman's body. At least Jessa died smelling nice. Her perfume was heavenly, soft and clean smelling, which really seemed out of place right now. The heel of her left boot was missing, but everything else looked normal.

It was a good thing they'd found her. Even though she was lying on the ground in the shade, it wouldn't take long for her body to start decomposing in this Mississippi heat. She backed out from under the trailer, rear end first, and leaned against the hay bale.

"Looks like you won't be playing tonight, Aunt Katy," Todd said, putting his phone back in his pocket. "The sheriff 's on his way over, and I'm supposed to keep everybody away from this area until he gets here. He doesn't want to mess up the crime scene."

"Yeah, that sounds like what they do on TV. I never thought we'd be doing that here in Skeeterville. Do you want me to guard the body while you secure the perimeter?"

"I don't think so," Todd said, scanning the field. He turned back towards Katy. "I appreciate your offer of help, but I'm going to need you to clear out from here too."

Katy arched one eyebrow and tilted her head to the side. "Now Todd, I don't think I'm the 'everybody' that Sheriff Reid is talking about keeping away. I practically discovered the body. I checked her pulse to make sure she was dead. The sheriff won't mind me helping you out until he gets here." She tried to stare him down, hoping she could bluff him into letting her hang around.

"I don't think he'll see it that way, and besides, I told you to not touch the body," Todd said, looking Katy in the eye. "What if you messed something up already?"

A fresh cloud of dust appeared across the field as a small parade of cars made its way toward the make-shift parking area. "Hey, here comes Misty and the rest of your crew. The best thing you can do for me is go head them off before they get any closer. And Aunt Katy," Todd paused as he scanned her face, "don't tell anyone what you saw."

Todd ran his hands through his hair and rubbed his stubbly chin. "We don't know what happened here, and we don't need to start any more rumors than necessary," he said, glancing around the back of the stage. "Heaven knows this will be the main topic of conversation in every Sunday school class tomorrow without you or me fanning that flame."

Katy poked her lip out but didn't argue. Todd knew she wasn't a gossip, but guessed he was just trying to do his job. She grabbed her guitar and folder and quickly headed to meet her band, who had parked their cars and were walking down the dirt path. She needed to write down everything she'd noticed about Jessa before it got fuzzy in her head.

The sheriff's car turned into the makeshift path with sirens blaring and blue lights flashing just as Katy reached her friends. They quickly moved to the side to keep from getting mowed over. "What's gotten him in such an all-fired hurry?" Misty asked, coughing as the dust flew up in all their faces. "Somebody stealing the peanut money, or worse yet, somebody stealing the peanuts?"

The other three women, Sarah, Heather, and Vickie looked to Katy for an answer. Everybody would know what had happened within the hour, but she knew that she did not want to be the one to let the cat out of the bag. Oh well, she would just give them the short answer. Maybe they would be satisfied with that. "Todd found a body under the stage," she said. "They don't want anybody going up there to muck up the crime scene."

That was all it took. The women all began talking at once, like a bunch of excited chickens, each one trying to be a little louder than the other. Two more cars came racing by, probably some of the sheriff's people. One was Ted Morse, the coroner and owner of the funeral home. She didn't recognize the other car. The sheriff's car then came back from the crime scene with Todd dri-ving. He parked the enormous Crown Victoria sideways at the entryway to the festival and turned back on the flashing blue lights. Katy shook her head as she stared at the car. The lights would at-tract more attention to the field with all that com-motion instead of keeping people away. She turned and looked back toward the stage. The sheriff and a couple of the other men were putting up the crime scene tape and shooing away the ten or twelve vendors who had walked up when they heard the sirens.

"Come on, ladies," she said, "we won't be playing tonight. Let's head over to the Burger Barn and get out of this heat." She threw her guitar and folder in the back seat one more time and led her small caravan of cars into town to the local hangout. The Burger Barn's parking lot was empty, but she figured that would change once the news got out that the Peanut Patch festival was canceled for the night.

Skeeterville had a fast-food chain restaurant, a fish house, and the Burger Barn for the locals to gather, and that was about it. If you didn't want to watch high school football, basketball, or baseball on the weekend for entertainment in this town, then you were going to be pretty bored. That's why the Peanut Patch festival was such a success every year. To go to the movies you had to drive forty-five minutes into the neighboring big city.

The ladies crowded into a booth, and Diet Cokes were ordered all around, except for Sarah. She still drank the real thing. She probably weighed one hundred pounds soaking wet in her birthday suit. Katy pulled out the little green notebook she kept in her purse that she used for writing her grocery list. She began jotting down all the details she had gathered from her assessment. The skin on her neck grew warm as everyone stared at her. She ground her teeth together without looking up and continued to write. They could wait for just a second while she got her thoughts on paper.

"Well, Katy." Vickie leaned across the table and tried to read the upside-down writing. "Don't think you're going to sit there and write down your to-do list after what you told us a few minutes ago." She looked around the nearly empty restaurant and whispered loud enough for the whole group to hear. "What do you mean Todd found a body under the stage? Was it a human body? I bet Sarah a burger that it's just a big dog or cow or something and has the place all stunk up and that's why they're calling off the concert." Sarah and Vickie had ridden to the hayfield and then to the Burger Barn together and apparently had already started exploring scenarios for the Peanut Patch festival's cancellation.

"I told you it had to be more than that," Sarah exclaimed. "When has the coroner, or the sheriff, for that matter, ever come out with lights flashing for a dead cow? Come on Katy, you might as well tell us what's going on. Everybody will know in a couple of hours." The other three women nodded their heads.

"Katy, you know as soon as the coroner gets home and tells his wife who it is, she's going to blab it to every person who'll listen," Misty said. She paused and took a quick sip of her Diet Coke. "I'm not being mean, but the woman just can't help herself. She loves to tell folks about who died, why they died, when they died, and then give all the details about how the family reacted. If Mr. Morse had any competition for business with the dead folks in this town, his wife would have done caused him to lose his income. People just don't have any other way to bury their dead around here, so they have to put up with her mouth."

"I guess you're right," Katy sighed. She looked around as the restaurant door swung open. Probably half the town already knew about it anyway. The Burger Barn was starting to fill up and people were talking. "Okay, ladies," she said, "but don't spread around what I'm going to tell you. I promised Todd I wouldn't add to the gossip." Four heads bobbed up and down in agreement. "Todd found Jessa Williams' body under the stage while he was helping me check a loose plug connection."

Katy watched as the women digested the information. Misty and Sarah both opened their eyes wider than Katy thought possible and began shaking their heads back and forth in unison, kind of like trained seals. Sarah's hand went over her mouth, and tears began forming in her eyes.

"Bless her heart," Vickie said, speaking first, as usual. "I just can't believe it. Bless her heart."

"Shhhh, Vickie, not so loud." Katy reached across the table and squeezed the younger woman's arm. "Remember, keep this to yourselves."

Katy began to slide out of the booth. She needed to be alone to mentally digest what she had observed. She could see that she was not going to be able to write anything down while she was here. If she didn't get away from her friends, they would continue to pick her bones until she told them everything. They didn't mean anything by it, that's just the way it was in a small town. Everybody felt they had the right to know everybody else's business.

"Oh, sorry," Vickie said, looking at the other ladies and again whispering, "bless her heart."

"Where are you going, Katy?" Misty grabbed Katy's hand as she started to stand up. "John's out of town, so why don't you stay and eat dinner with us? Mike will be here in a few minutes and we can try to sort this out."

"Thanks, but I'm going to head on home," Katy said. "I need to just sit and think for a while. Besides, we have church tomorrow, and I need to make sure I'm ready for my class. You know I'll have a hard time trying to talk about Jesus walking on the water with all of this going on."

Katy said her good-byes and walked to her car. The parking lot was almost full of people who had planned on eating a supper of fried festival food but now would have to settle for fried fast food. She jumped in her car and pulled out before anybody could come over to quiz her down. Being a nurse in a small town meant she knew everybody. Over the years she had gone into a lot of these peoples' homes to care for their sick. She just couldn't imagine any of them killing someone.

Lord, please help me not to get all worked up and scared over this while John's out of town. I know I'm in your hands, Lord, but you know how big my imagination is, and sometimes I get a little carried away. Katy turned into her drive as she finished her prayer. *Oh, and Lord please be with the Browns and whoever the rest of Jessa's family are as they deal with this situation. Be with our little town too, Lord. Protect us from whoever this is that has hurt one of our people.*

Chapter Three

Katy fluffed up the throw pillows behind her back. She had showered, fixed hot chocolate and cranked the air conditioner down to North Pole level. Now she was ready to think. The foot of the recliner eased her legs up as she pulled the lever. She looked at the new yellow legal pad she found in John's office. Her tiny green note pad was always getting lost in her purse. She wanted to keep up with this information a little bit better than that.

The first thing on her list was the pool of blood behind Jessa's head. She thought back to the last time she had seen Jessa alive... Friday night. *The Moonlighters* had finished their last set at ten-thirty and *The Wildcats* had returned to finish up the night. Jessa had been having a rather heated conversation with Marissa Holmes, one of *The Wildcats'* guitarists and back-up singers, and the only other female in their band. Katy hadn't bothered to speak to the women. Both were very focused on their conversation. She had been focused on getting a Diet Coke.

No, that's not right, she thought. She had seen Jessa on stage right before starting home later that same night. That would have been about midnight. She had left at eleven-fifty before *The Wildcats'* last song was over so she could beat the traffic out of the field. She jotted this down. *That means Jessa was killed sometime after eleven-fifty, probably after midnight on Friday night,* she thought. *Well, that's not much, but it's a start.*

For some reason, writing this stuff down on paper helped to make what happened seem real. It also made it feel personal. Goosebumps popped up on her arms as she pulled the afghan off the back of the recliner and put it across her legs. She would be snuggling deep under the covers tonight. Even if the light bill was three hundred dollars, it would be worth it if it helped her sleep alone in their house until John got home on Friday.

The breath caught in her throat as "Hello Darlin", John's ringtone, blared from her phone. She glanced at the screen. Ten-thirty-five. John was calling thinking they had just finished their last set at the festival. She answered the phone and began to fill her husband in on what was going on.

"So, you and Todd were the first people to see her body?" John asked.

"Yep."

"And she was under the flatbed and the hay bales had been put back in place?"

"Yep," Katy answered again.

"Well, one thing is for sure, she didn't get there by accident," John said. "Somebody put her under there, or she put herself under there. They've kept the bottom of that stage closed up tight for the past several years. I guess it's been done that way ever since those junior high boys set off firecrackers under there during the mayor's speech that time on the opening day of the festival." John paused, concern evident in his voice. "Look, why don't you fly on up to Kansas City tomorrow and spend the rest of my trip with me. I don't like you being home by yourself with all this going on. What if some serial rapist or murderer has wandered into town? You don't need to be there alone."

"Oh, John, I'll be fine. I really don't want to leave town tomorrow." Katy pushed back the yawn rising in her throat. "I have lab results to follow up with on Monday and band practice. Besides, you know I hate flying." She adjusted the afghan on her legs. "I don't think Jessa was raped anyway. Her body was not just thrown under the flatbed, it was kind of placed there very neatly, and she didn't look like she had been molested." She paused, "I mean, I haven't seen a lot of rape victims, but Jessa's make up was still neat, and her clothes were straight except for her shirt being a little rumpled." Her eyes roamed around the empty living room, and a shiver ran across the back of her neck despite her brave words.

"But you're right," she sighed, "she didn't get under there by accident. If that big, shady spot under her head was blood, and I'm sure it was, that means she bled out from a head wound after she was placed under the stage." Her eyes roamed toward the front door. The chain was in place, and the lock was on. "Somebody must have knocked her out and then put her under there. Maybe they thought she was dead and left her body there and then she died from blood loss. Or maybe they didn't think she was hurt that bad and were trying to scare her... and she died from blood loss. Either way, I don't think the person who put her there thought the whole thing through."

"That doesn't make me feel one bit better," John said. "So, the guy was kind of dumb, or drunk, or high, or whatever. I still don't like you being by yourself."

"Honey, I'm fine. I just feel so sorry for that woman. If we hadn't found her tonight, her body would have stayed there until Monday when the county cleans up the festival site. By then she would've started to have an odor. I'm glad that didn't happen." She stopped and began to mumble, half-way talking to herself. "If the killer didn't want her body found, he, or she, picked a sorry place to stash it. But if they did want the body found, then why there? Nobody looks under the stage, so she would not have been found until three days later. No, I don't think the person who put her there thought this through."

"Katy, listen, this isn't CSI Mississippi." John's voice became a little deeper, stern. "This really happened, and I don't want you by yourself until the law figures this out. I think I can wrap things up early and be home by Monday or Tuesday at the latest. I'm gonna call Todd and see if he can come sleep in the spare bedroom until then."

"Oh no you're not. Todd's going to be too busy with all of this to have to babysit me." Katy stopped. *Maybe that's not a bad idea after all,* she thought. *If Todd stays here, I can find out what he knows without being an obvious nosey old aunt.* John took her silence to be second thoughts, which it was, but the thoughts were motivated by curiosity, not fear.

"Look," he said, "I'm going to call Todd. Don't buck me on this. I won't get any sleep, or any work done because I'll be worried about you."

"Well, alright, if it'll make you feel better, give him a call. But if he can't do it, don't make him feel guilty," she said. "I don't think I'm in any danger. If there's a rapist or crazy woman-killer roaming the streets and backroads of Skeeterville, I don't think I'm his type." She looked down at the worn afghan laying over her lower body. "My wrinkled Peanut Patch tee-shirt and varicose veined legs are a far cry from Jessa Williams' miniskirt and low-cut blouse... uh, bless her heart."

"Yeah, bless her heart," John chuckled. "Don't be talking ill of the dead, sweetheart, it's not nice. Let me give Todd a call and I'll call you back."

John was right. That did sound sort of catty. Oh well, she would ask forgiveness in a little bit when she said her prayers. She studied over her notes while she waited for him to call her back. "Hello Darlin" sang out again in about five minutes.

"Todd sounded a little shook up," John said, when she answered the phone. "He said he was already planning on offering to come over after he got off work. I guess that's probably the first dead person he's ever seen that wasn't in a casket. It'll do him good to have you to talk to, and will do me good knowing you have someone in the house with you until I can get home."

"Poor Todd, of course, he can stay with me," Katy cooed. "I'll get the spare bedroom ready."

She got up and walked down the hall. Sometimes John would use the extra bedroom as a storage room for his hunting and fishing gear until he could get it put back up in the den closet. Sure enough, there was a tackle box on the bed and a pair of waders propped against the footboard. She straightened that up then turned the air conditioner back up to seventy. There was no need to freeze Todd out tonight, and if she was honest, she would sleep better knowing he was there with her.

Todd came in looking exhausted around one that morning. He looked much too tired to grill for information when he obviously just wanted to go to sleep. She needed sleep too. After all, she had to be sharp for church tomorrow. Teaching the seventh, eighth and ninth grade girls in Sunday school would be trying. They would be much more interested in what she knew about Jessa's death than what she knew about Jesus. She was determined to not let her teaching hour be a gossiping hour.

Chapter Four

A glazed expression set on Katy's face as she walked to her car. Thoughts of the past twenty-four hour's events tumbled loosely around in her head. The Sunday school lesson had gone smoother than expected. Victory Jones had to be put back on track several times, but that was every Sunday. Poor Victory could be an ADD poster child.

The preacher's sermon had really stepped on her toes. He spoke about treating everyone with love and respect. After all, we never know what the other person is going through. She had tried to not squirm in her seat. Jessa Williams' death deserved to be treated with dignity and not judgment. She again had to ask God for forgiveness during the prayer time at the end of the service.

"Hey, girl, you must be in some deep meditation," Misty said, tugging on the back of Katy's shirt. "I've been calling your name ever since you left the church steps and you just kept on walking. Come have lunch with me and Mike. I'm not taking no for an answer this time."

"Sorry," Katy smiled softly. "I was just thinking about what the preacher said. I didn't get enough sleep last night, so I'm probably sleepwalking a little too."

"That's okay. You've had a busy weekend," Misty said, hugging Katy's shoulders. "Come on, let us take you to lunch. We insist."

"I probably need to get to the house," Katy said. "Todd's bed was empty when I got up this morning. He's staying with me until John gets home. I want to get back so I can talk to him about last night." She stuck the tip of her fingernail in her teeth. "But I don't even know if he'll be back home yet." She looked at Misty and then Mike as they waited for her answer. "I guess it would be nice to visit with friends instead of going home to an empty house. I just wish John was here to go with us, but work is work. He'll be jealous tonight when I tell him that I ate lunch with y'all."

"We'll have to do it again next weekend when

he's home," Mike said. "How does Fred's Fish House sound?"

Soon they were being seated at the locally owned seafood restaurant. On the way over Misty and Mike had talked about church activities, work, the band, the upcoming holidays, and general chit chat, but they had made a point to avoid the topic of Jessa's death. Katy knew she had given Misty the impression that she didn't want to talk about it last night before she left the Burger Barn.

The lighting in the restaurant was low. Even though the place was quite full of the after-church crowd, there was only a low murmur of conversation heard as they walked into the dining area. The effect was very calming, and it made Katy realize how hungry she was. She had overslept this morning and skipped breakfast. "I'll have the fried oyster po-boy with hushpuppies and fries," she said to the waitress, sticking the menu between the salt and pepper shakers in the center of the table.

"So, how're you feeling?" Misty asked as she looked over the menu. "Did you get any sleep? I should've invited you to stay at our house last night, but I honestly didn't think about it until around midnight when we got home."

"Actually, I did get some sleep with Todd there." Katy smiled as she watched Misty twist her lips into a pout trying to decide what to order.

"He's planning on staying at the house until John gets home later this week. I don't think he needs to do that, but I did sleep better just knowing I wasn't alone." Katy paused as the waitress set a sweaty glass of ice water on the napkin in front of her. "What in the world kept you two out so late last night? Everybody knows y'all are a couple of homebodies. I figured our little group would have broken up after I left."

"Normally I'm sure it would have, but things were crazy at the Burger Barn, and got a little crazier after you left." Misty took a sip from her water glass. "Amy Phobs came in right after you left to talk to Vickie and Sarah. You know she's only a few years younger than those two, nineteen I think, and of course, Vickie had to find out if she knew anything about Jessa's death."

"She must have said something mighty interesting if y'all talked past midnight," Katy said.

Misty waited while the waitress sat the appetizer in the middle of the table. "That conversation went on for about an hour. Then Mike and I rode back by the festival site just to be nosey. Mr. Grover was parked by the entrance giving away bags of free boiled peanuts. He said he didn't have room for all them in his refrigerator and he didn't want them to go to waste." She tapped her finger on the table. "Don't let me forget, I have you a bag at home in my fridge. Anyway," she continued, "Todd was still there blocking the entrance when we left, but the field was mostly deserted except for the sheriff's crew and the coroner. They still had all the lights on around the stage, but I couldn't see anything else from the road."

Katy put a piece of piping hot blooming onion in her mouth. "I hate I had to cut out so early, but I needed to be by myself so I could wrap my head around everything I saw. It was quite a shock to find Jessa like we did."

"Girl, don't apologize. You know I'm a florist. If I'd just found a dead body, I would've been at the emergency room getting some Xanax or Valium or something to calm me down. I was amazed that you were acting like it was no big deal. I guess you see dead people all the time, so it didn't bother you."

"I probably do see a lot more dead people than most folks, but I can't say that it didn't bother me. That poor woman lying on the ground like that was just horrible. Leaving her under that flatbed was so inhumane. I can't imagine what kind of person could do something like that."

"I can't either," Mike said, "but I think John was wise by getting Todd to stay with you. The scary thing about all of this is that the killer could be anybody, maybe even somebody we go to church with or work with and see every day."

"Yeah, you're right," Katy nodded looking from Mike to Misty. She pulled off another piece of the fried onion and dipped it in the come-back sauce. "By the way, what in the world could Amy Phobs have known about Jessa's death? Jessa is what? Ten years older than Amy? I can't imagine them two being great friends."

The waitress brought the rest of the food, and they stopped to say a blessing before continuing. Katy stretched her lips over the crusty French bread and bit into the piping hot sandwich. Her eyes closed as the taste and texture of the fried oysters took over her senses.

"Apparently Jessa has been dating Amy's older brother Joe," Mike said.

"I don't guess I know him. Did he go to school with any of my girls?" Katy's asked, wrinkling her brow. "One of them Phobs boys was in Kelly Ann's class, but there were six kids in that family, so I might be thinking of the wrong one. If I'm right, that would make him about twenty-eight years old."

"According to Amy, Joe works offshore and lives in the trailer park off Highway five-eighty-seven." Misty pointed over Katy's head in the direction of the highway, "He started dating Jessa right after she moved to Skeeterville last year."

"Is he the Phobs kid that got kicked in the head by a cow when he was young?" Katy asked. "I know it sounds cruel, but I just can't imagine Jessa dating him. His hair never did grow back on the left side of his head because of that scar, and I can't see Jessa with somebody who didn't look, well, a certain way."

"No, that's Josh, a younger brother," Mike said, setting down his tea glass. "Joe's older, in his thirties, I think. He's a little older than any of your kids. That's why you can't place him." Mike picked up his fork and stabbed a piece of battered, fried catfish. "He's a big guy, not fat, just a bulky, muscled up fella. He drives that silver monster truck with the giant tires that you see parked in front of The Pig sometimes. Amy says she drives that big tank to work when Joe is offshore for his seven days. I've met him a couple of times at the bank. He's a nice enough guy, just not good with his money. But there are plenty of people in that shape." Being the president of the bank, Mike knew most of the people in town.

"Amy said that Joe and Jessa had a huge fight Friday night after the Peanut Patch festival." Misty's eyes stretched wide, and she leaned across the table toward Katy. "She said they were yelling and screaming at each other right there behind the shed where everybody could hear."

"Really?" Katy set down her sandwich.

"Amy said she had been embarrassed and wanted to just get in the car with her boyfriend and leave, but when she talked to us last night, she looked worried," Misty said. "She said everybody there saw them yelling at each other and heard her brother threaten to do Jessa in if she didn't straighten up and act right. She said she had never liked Jessa. The woman always talked down to their family like she was better than them. Amy was so upset." Misty shook her head. "She didn't want to see Jessa dead, just out of Joe's life." She paused and looked at her husband and then at Katy. "Do you think Joe had something to do with Jessa's death? Amy sure acted nervous last night, like she was even unsure about her own brother and what was going on with him and Jessa. Poor girl, I felt sorry for her."

"Don't jump to any conclusions," Katy said as she dipped a hushpuppy in ketchup. "I'm beginning to think there are a lot of people that have had words with Jessa Williams. I heard her fighting with Marissa Holmes that night too, but that doesn't mean anything. I *would* like to hear what both of those fights were about though." Katy smiled as she got an idea and looked at Misty.

"How about you and I make a trip to the Nail Palace tomorrow?"

"Girl you have a date," Misty said, returning Katy's smile.

Mike looked from one woman to the other. "Wait, what am I missing here? You two just said something to each other that I didn't hear, and I was listening to every word both of you said."

"Mike, The Nail Palace, and the beauty shop are the two very best places in this town to get any information you need," Misty said, patting Mike's hand like he was a confused little boy. "By tomorrow afternoon we'll know all about those fights or my name isn't Misty Maleficent Morgan."

Katy laughed, "And I'm afraid it is."

Chapter Five

"Stop your squawking," Katy called to the oven timer as she hurried to the kitchen to get out the peach cobbler. After Misty and Mike dropped her back at her car that afternoon, she decided that the right thing to do would be to express her condolences to the Browns. She wasn't sure how the Browns were related, but Jessa had been living with them for the past year. As far as Katy knew, they were the only family Jessa had in town. She would drop the peach cobbler by their house tomorrow and express her sympathy.

Peach cobbler was the only thing she could bake that tasted good almost every time she made it. She could get elbow deep in some nasty wound care and start IVs in anybody's home. She could detect the signs of heart failure with a quick assessment and rattle off teaching on hundreds of medications without blinking an eye, but most days following a simple cake mix recipe seemed to be beyond her skill set. She didn't chance it anymore. If she needed to fix a dish for a church function, a death, or illness in the family, she had dibs on the peach cobbler. Everybody expected her to fix it and were nice enough not to bring one themselves. Several of her cooking failures had been experienced by her friends and neighbors in the past, and they supported her in the peach cobbler success by calling it Katy's special peach dish. She knew that it was their polite way of saying, "at least we can eat that," but she didn't care. When they needed somebody to drop by on a Sunday afternoon and check on their ninety-year-old momma who had a stomach ache because her bowels hadn't moved in five days and they didn't want to take her to the emergency room, Katy was on their speed dial list. Everybody had their place in life.

She pulled the cobbler out of the oven and looked at the crust's very pale shade of tan. It should be a little crispier, but the last time she stuck one back in the oven the house had smelled like burnt peaches for a week.

"Aunt Katy, you home?" Todd called as he came through the foyer. "It's just me, letting myself in."

"I'm in the kitchen fixin' to get some tea," she called back. "You want me to get you a glass?"

"That would be great." Todd stepped through the doorway to the small, but tidy kitchen. "I'm going to go put on a tee-shirt and get out of these work clothes. I'll see you in a minute."

Katy poured two large glasses of sweet tea and returned to the living room. When Todd worked on Sunday mornings, he was usually at church on Sunday night, but he hadn't made either service today. He would probably be working all kinds of hours until they figured out how Jessa died.

Todd walked in and flopped down in one of the oversized recliners. John had surprised Katy with the matching set last Christmas. At first, she had not been thrilled. They had needed new living room furniture for years. She had wanted to shop around and find something with a little more modern feel, but now she loved the chairs as much as John did. They blended well enough with her sofa and love seat and were great for kicking back to read, cuddle with a grandkid, or taking an afternoon nap, even if her living room didn't look like a picture out of *Southern Living*.

"Looks like you've had a busy day," she said, handing him the glass of tea.

"You have no idea." Todd pulled the lever on the side of the chair to let his feet up. "I used to think I wanted to move to a bigger town with a little more exciting workload, but not anymore. I'm exhausted and I need to be at the station right now doing paperwork."

"You can't work twenty-four hours a day, Todd. And after all, the girl ain't going to be any deader tomorrow than she is today."

"I guess dead people don't fluster you as much as the almost dead do, huh?" The corners of his mouth turned up in a small smile that contrasted with the dark circles under his eyes. "There are just some things that need to be checked up on and straightened out, and I don't want anything to get missed. I sure would hate for that girl's killer to go free because I overlooked something."

"I know that's a huge responsibility." Katy reached over and patted his hand, "but you aren't the only one working on this, are you?"

"Oh, no ma'am. As a matter of fact, I'm the low man on the totem pole and I'm mostly doing the grunt work." Todd tilted his head from side to side to loosen his stiff muscles. "The sheriff and the coroner are doing all the really important stuff and all the other guys are on it too. I just don't want to overlook anything. This is the first murder this town has seen in years."

"They're sure it is murder?" she asked. Her forehead puckered in thought.

"Yes ma'am. We have Joe Phobs locked up at the station. A lot of people saw him and Jessa fighting Friday night, and he even threatened her right there in front of everybody. But you know that guy must not be very bright."

"Why do you say that?"

"Well, the thing that sealed the deal is that we found a bloody monkey wrench in the back of his truck this morning when we went to his trailer." Todd shook his head. "He was drunker than Cooter Brown and swears he didn't do it, but it looks pretty bad for him."

"My word," Katy choked out the words as she forced down her swallow of tea. "She was beaten in the head with a monkey wrench? That would explain all the blood we saw on the ground under the stage."

"Yeah." Todd rubbed his hands across his eyes and then his mouth to stifle a yawn. "I imagine one good lick with that thing would do just about anybody in."

"But he must have struck her at a different location and then moved her body to under the stage." Katy paused and tapped her fingers against the cold tea glass. "Do you think he hit her in the head thinking he had killed her, then just threw her under the stage? As much blood as was behind her head, she must have still been alive after she was moved. It looked like she bled out while she lay there, hopefully unconscious, poor girl."

"Aunt Katy, you're pretty sharp," Todd said, suddenly becoming more alert with his surprise. "That's exactly what Mr. Morse decided when he examined the spot under the trailer. He looked at her head and told us that she had been struck and then moved. We turned that area upside down looking for more blood and sure enough, right there in the back of the shed was blood on the corner of a table and the ground. Somebody had covered it up with an old greasy tarp." The corners of Todd's tired mouth turned down. "Now you can't be telling anybody what I'm telling you. The sheriff has already pretty much told a news crew from Jackson most of what I've said, but he would have my hide if he knew I was talking about the case with a civilian. I'm not the official spokesperson, so I'm supposed to keep my mouth shut."

"I won't tell a soul, Todd, but do you mind if I ask you a question?"

"No, of course not."

"Is Joe Phobs dumb enough to threaten his girlfriend in front of a lot of witnesses, kill her, then leave the murder weapon in the back of his truck just waiting to be found? I mean, even if he killed her in a rage of passion, you would think he would be smart enough to hide the murder weapon. After all, he had enough sense to hide her body and cover up the crime scene."

"Like I said, I don't want to miss anything." Todd laid his head back against the recliner cushion and sighed. "It seems pretty simple to the sheriff, but I think there is more to it. And Phobs ain't helping himself one bit. He won't tell anybody where he was Friday night after he left the Peanut Patch festival. All he does is sit in that cell and blubber like a big ole two-hundred-pound baby."

"That doesn't sound like a cold-blooded killer to me."

"Me either, Aunt Katy, me either. And another thing that kind of bothers me is that we found a pack of Marlboro Lights with blood on them under the tarp in the shed, like maybe they fell out of the killer's pocket and he didn't notice it."

"That could be a good thing. Maybe you could get some DNA off of them or something like they do on CSI."

"Nah, none of that will work. This pack hasn't been opened. The only DNA would be from the blood on the package, and I'm fairly sure it belongs to the dead woman. There weren't even any finger-prints on it, and besides, Joe Phobs doesn't smoke." He paused and sniffed the scent of peach cobbler coming from the kitchen. "Says he has allergies and doesn't even let anybody smoke in his trailer or in his truck."

"I don't ever remember seeing Jessa smoke, but I only saw her when she was getting ready to go on stage, so I don't know," Katy said. "I guess they could have been hers."

She told Todd about seeing Marissa and Jessa arguing Friday night and what Misty had told her about Amy Phobs hearing her brother fighting with Jessa. *Joe Phobs killing Jessa just doesn't make sense,* Katy thought, shaking her head. *Not the way the sheriff thinks it happened anyway.*

Tomorrow she would attempt to gather a few more details about what was going on. She had to work in the morning but planned on taking the peach cobbler by the Brown's home then going and getting her nails done with Misty. Misty was in the Nail Palace about every other week getting a mani-pedi, but Katy had never had either. Misty assured her the place was a beehive full of gossip and in-formation.

Short fingernails were required at work. Fake nails and wound care just didn't go well together. She would go with Misty and try to gather infor-mation while she waited. Marissa Holmes was a nail tech there every Saturday, Sunday, and Mon-day. Hopefully, she could shed some light on what happened. She didn't tell Todd of her plans to nose around. He would try to stop her, and she decided that asking forgiveness later would be better than asking permission now. Besides, everybody in town was talking about Jessa's death, so she really wasn't doing anything odd.

That night she added everything she had learned to her yellow notepad. John called right before she turned out her bedside lamp and said he was finishing up early and would be home sometimes Tuesday. She was glad. She would show him her list and see what he thought about everything. John was a very practical, nuts and bolts kind of guy who didn't let his imagination run away with him like Katy sometimes did. He would help her reason out whether she was being realistic about what she saw and thought about Jessa's death, or whether she was making mountains out of molehills.

Chapter Six

Papa Dude, or Paul Swanson as the Medicare and the Social Security office knew him, had been running a low pulse and complaining of being dizzy. Katy grabbed the folder containing Papa Dude's digoxin level results that she had drawn during a visit over the weekend and headed into Dr. Roberts' office.

The doctor's office was already filling up with patients, a typical Monday morning, but the receptionist who knew Katy well waved her on back to the nurse's station.

Katy leaned on the corner of the tall bar that surrounded the work area and waited until Trudy Mae, Dr. Roberts' nurse, got off the phone. "Looks like you're already having a busy day," Katy said, looking back at the full waiting room.

"Honey, you know it's like this every Monday," Trudy Mae said, taking the lab results from Katy's outstretched hand. "These old folks think Dr. Roberts can fix anything and everything and they'll bust up in here if they burp a little too loud." She looked over Papa Dude's blood work. "Is he taking his medicines right? Looks like it's not the Digoxin making him dizzy. That level is normal. What did you say his pulse was Saturday, fifty-two?"

"Fifty-two and regular." Katy looked across the bar at the patient's folder. "Yeah, he's taking his medications correctly. I set up his pillbox and go over all of that with him about every other week. He didn't look dehydrated either. That's his vital signs from the last couple of week's visits written on the bottom of the page."

"Okay, give me just a minute and I'll get the doc to give you an order so you can be on your way." Trudy Mae turned toward the doctor's study, then turned back to Katy. "Oh hey, by the way, I read in the paper that you were with Todd Saturday night when he found Jessa Williams' body at the festival grounds."

"I'm afraid that's right. He was helping me with the amps when he discovered her right there under the flatbed. She had been dead for a while. Her body was as cold as ice."

"Well, I hate to speak ill of the dead," Trudy Mae whispered, leaning her full frame across the bar toward Katy, "but that girl was in here Friday to see Dr. Roberts, and she had this whole office in an uproar. She was pitching a big ole hissy fit."

"You don't say? Was she sick?"

"No, not unless you count morning sickness," Trudy said, rolling her eyes. "She was having nausea and insisted that we work her in to see the doc. You know we close at noon on Fridays and only do work-ins for the serious stuff, but she raised such a ruckus with the receptionist when she called that she told her to come on in. We did a pregnancy test and sure enough, she was pregnant. Doc figured she was about eight weeks. When he told her, she went to cussing and ripping and screaming like the crazy thing she was. I finally had to tell her to calm down or leave."

Katy bit her bottom lip to hold in the grin that threatened to creep out. Trudy Mae was probably one of the few women who could have put Jessa Williams in her place. She protected Dr. Roberts like she was a momma bear and him her baby cub. One time, a couple of years ago, a high school football player came in messed up on prescription pain killers with the crazy notion that he could get the doc to write him a new script for some more. Trudy Mae somehow managed to put a high school wrestling hold on him and walked him down the street to the sheriff's office where they called his daddy to come pick him up. Katy couldn't remember whatever happened to that boy. She would like to have seen Trudy Mae in action with Jessa Williams. "Did she calm down?" Katy asked, keeping a straight face.

"Oh yeah, honey. Turned all that craziness off like she was turning off a water hose, and then proceeded to ask for a referral to a gynecologist in Jackson." Trudy Mae raised one dark eyebrow and shook her head. "Said she wasn't sure if this was the best time for her to be pregnant."

Katy's eyes stretched wide. "Did Doc set her up with somebody?"

"Oh yeah, but not until after she got some intense counseling on responsibility and birth control. He told her that the doctor he was recommending could help her with getting the baby adopted too." Trudy Mae sighed. "Of course, I don't think she listened."

Katy waited while Trudy Mae disappeared into the doctor's study. *So, Jessa had been pregnant,* she thought. *Was that what she had been arguing with Joe Phobs about? No wonder he lost his cool, but would he strike Jessa knowing he was harming his own child? Of course, it might not have been his child. There was only one way to know for sure.* She needed to talk to Joe Phobs, but how could she arrange that with him locked up in the jail?

"Doc wrote a referral for Papa to see a cardiologist," Trudy Mae said, stepping back into the hall. "He needs to see one within the next couple of weeks, or as soon as he can get an appointment. I'll give their office a call after lunch and set it up for him."

"Alright, I'll run by his house when I leave here and talk to him about it. Is Doc thinking he needs a pacemaker?"

"Girl, you're good. I wish all them home health gals were like you. If my momma ever comes out of the Shady Acres you've got to be her nurse. I don't want none of them young know-it-alls looking in on her."

"When is she coming out?" Katy asked. She thumbed through the papers Trudy Mae handed back to her. "You know I'll see her."

"Probably next week if she behaves. I'll be giving you a call. She lives in that nice trailer park on five-eighty-seven, you know the one."

"Oh yeah," Katy nodded. "I've seen a patient or two down there. It's a nice community."

"Ain't it?" Trudy Mae grinned her big toothy smile.

"Just give me a call," Katy said, "or send a referral over to the agency requesting that I see her when you know for sure what day she'll be home."

⁂

The Browns lived in the garden district on the old side of town. The houses in that area were absolutely beautiful. Most of them were old plantation homes that had been updated with modern conveniences but still looked like Tara from *Gone with the Wind*. Even the newer homes that had been built in the last couple of decades were designed in the same style. She had been in and out of this neighborhood over the years seeing the occasional home health patient and knew that this area was just like all the others. Some of the people who lived here were as sweet as could be and very down to earth, while others wouldn't give you the time of day.

She pulled into the paved circular drive that led to the Brown mansion. It was a three-story sprawling white brick home with huge Grecian columns along the front, and balconies and decorative iron rails on every story. The yard was manicured to perfection with a mixture of maroon and white daylilies in the flower beds along both sides of the drive. Two large stone garden sculptures of English bulldogs set on either side of the walkway leading to the front porch.

Since maroon and white were Mississippi State University's school colors, Katy felt certain somebody in this house was loyal to that school. College sports rivalry was huge in this town. Even the people who couldn't spell the word alumni had their favorite college football team, and would defend their honor at the drop of a hat.

She rang the doorbell with one hand while balancing the peach cobbler she had picked up from home with the other. It was still warm where she had popped it in the oven for a few minutes while changing. A heavy-set, gray-haired woman in neatly pressed white scrubs opened the door.

"Hello, may I help you?" the lady asked with a slight smile.

"Yes, ma'am. My name is Katy Cross. I just wanted to drop by and pay my condolences to the family for the loss of Ms. Williams and bring them this dessert." Katy held the aluminum pan out to the lady as an offering. Hopefully, it would gain her entrance into the family's home.

"Who is it, Nelda? Is it the cable guy?" A voice called out from somewhere behind the woman blocking the door. "I'm going to miss my stories if he doesn't hurry up and get over here to fix that dad-blast-it TV."

"No, Mrs. Rita," Nelda called back over her shoulder. "It's somebody here to see Mrs. Evelyn." She took the cobbler from Katy's hand and motioned for her to follow her in and take a seat in the parlor.

Katy walked over and gently sat on the edge of a wing-backed chair upholstered in bright yellow paisley material. Nelda's tennis shoes squeaked on the shiny hardwood pine floors as she walked away.

Katy sighed and breathed in the feel of the beautiful room. The sofa, upholstered in a blue and yellow striped chintz, had dainty pillows neatly placed in the corners made of the same yellow paisley material as the winged back chair. Sunlight poured in through the white lace curtains covering the floor to ceiling windows across the front of the room. The delicate coffee table sitting in front of the sofa had a beautiful silver tea service in the center that probably hadn't seen a drop of tea in years. It was a gorgeous room, and she would love to see all the other rooms of the house, sure they would be just as stunning.

The Browns had one thirty-year-old son, Tripp. He was the same age as Penny, Katy's oldest daughter, and they had gone through school together. Katy had been twenty years old when she had Penny but knew that Mrs. Brown had been in her late thirty's when Tripp was born. Back then that had been considered old to have a baby. Now a day's women, especially wealthy women, were having babies in their mid-forties, but back then Mrs. Brown had been the topic of conversation in many of Skeeterville's different circles.

Katy's musings were interrupted as Evelyn Brown entered the room. Even though she knew the woman was in her sixties, she would have thought she was in her mid-forties at the oldest. Her silvery blonde hair was cut in a short bob with wispy bangs. Her periwinkle capris looked like linen and the sleeveless white blouse was silk. Katy glanced at the woman's thin ankles and noted there was no swelling or varicose veins in the calves. Yes, this lady had taken care of herself and could wear those cute little sling-back sandals without worrying about ugly feet. Her fingers and toes were both neatly done in matching French manicures.

"Hello, I'm Evelyn Brown." She extended her slender hand toward Katy. "Nelda said you are here to see me."

"Yes, ma'am, my name is Katy Cross." Katy stood and took Evelyn's hand, hoping her palms weren't sweaty. "I just wanted to stop by and tell you how sorry I am about the loss of your, uh, of... about the loss of Jessa." Katy didn't know how Jessa was related to the Browns. She had assumed a niece or cousin, but that was just a guess.

"Oh, please don't ma'am me, dear. It makes me feel old." She waved her hand at Katy as if she was shooing away a fly. "And just call me Evelyn. It's so sweet of you to stop by in person. Were you one of Jessa's friends?"

"No, not really." Katy paused, waiting for Evelyn to tell her how Jessa was related to the family, but she didn't. It would be rude to just ask her point-blank. She could probably find that out later today at the nail salon. "I knew her, but just in passing. I play in a band called *The Moonlighters,* and we opened for Jessa's band last week at the Peanut Patch festival. Other than that, I've just seen her a couple of times when she waited on me at your husband's dealership when I got my oil changed. We ran in different circles. I mean..." Katy paused and tried to discreetly wipe her palms on her pants leg. "I'm older than her and well, I pretty much just go to work, church and home." *My word. Just stand right here in the woman's house and insult the woman's dead relative. Yeah, we ran in different circles, alright.* Katy could feel the red heat taking over her face and neck.

"Oh, I see." Evelyn's polite smile continued, but her brow wrinkled slightly. "Well, we appreciate your thoughtfulness."

"I was with Todd Bishop when he found Jessa's body Friday night," Katy blurted out. "I just felt like I needed to do something for her after what happened."

"I remember reading that in the paper. What a horrible thing for you to go through. I just can't imagine how I would have reacted in that situation." Evelyn tilted her head to the side and studied Katy's face. "You look familiar. I'm sure we've met before. Do you work at the bank?"

"No, ma'am," Katy smiled and quickly corrected her faux pas. "I mean, no. I work as a field nurse for Magnolia Home Health here in town. You've seen me over the years at school functions and ballgames. My daughter Penny was in the same class as Tripp."

"Of course." Evelyn smiled, revealing a set of perfectly white teeth. "I see the resemblance. She was such a beautiful girl. Don't you have another daughter as well?"

"I have three more," Katy nodded. "Kelly Ann is just a little over year younger than Penny, and the twins, Mamie and Eudora are seven years younger."

"You know, I think Tripp might have gone out with Penny once or twice. I didn't realize she was Kelly Ann's sister. She is just as lovely, but they don't look a thing alike, do they?"

Katy smiled. Penny had gone out once with Tripp Brown and came home mad as a wet hen.

She'd described him as the rudest and most arrogant boy she had ever met and had made him bring her home before the movie was over because he couldn't keep his hands to himself. "Yes, Penny looks more like John's side of the family with that black curly hair. Kelly Ann favors me, and the twins are a mixture of both of us." Katy looked around the entryway and sitting room, or whatever the bright, delicate room was called. "You have a spectacular home Evelyn, and I love your flower beds."

"We bleed maroon and white here," Evelyn laughed, glancing toward the front of the house. "Miles and I both went to State and he is a diehard bulldog fan."

"Well, you do a fabulous job of making everything look beautiful. I'm sure it keeps you busy."

"It does, but I have lots of help. There's no way I could keep all of this up myself. We have talked about finding someplace smaller, but this is the house I was raised in and as long as we can keep it up, I imagine we will be right here."

"I don't blame you one bit for that. Family roots are such an important thing. It's so nice to be able to hand down your home to the next generation."

"Well thank you again for the cobbler." Evelyn

took a step toward the front door. "I'm sure we'll be enjoying it with dinner tonight."

Katy knew that was her cue to leave. The visit to the Brown's had not gone the way she had expected. Evelyn had been intentionally vague about Jessa's relationship with the family. Even stranger than that was how calm and unconcerned she had been about Jessa's death. Katy had dealt with a lot of family members mourning the death of loved ones over the years. She was fairly sure that there was not a lot of love lost between Evelyn and Jessa. This visit had brought up more questions than answers. Maybe this afternoon would shed some light on things. She said good-bye and headed to the Burger Barn to meet Misty for lunch and then go to the Nail Palace.

Chapter Seven

Katy searched the parking lot for Misty's Maxima as she pulled into the Burger Barn. Hopefully, she would have time to jot down some notes before her friend arrived. The cool air hit her face as she walked through the door. She looked around as the usual crowd of customers poured in for lunch. Luckily, she spotted an empty booth in the back. She pulled out the yellow pad and started scribbling what Trudy Mae had told her, then moved on to her impression of how Evelyn Brown was reacting to Jessa's death.

How was Jessa related to the Browns? If she wasn't related, why was she living with them? Did Joe Phobs know that Jessa was pregnant? Why were they fighting? Was he careless enough to leave the murder weapon in the back of his truck for everyone to see? Why were Marissa Holmes and Jessa arguing, and why did Jessa have electric blue hair tangled in the ring on her right hand? Did the hair belong to Marissa? She was the only blue-haired woman on the stage that night.

Misty slid into the booth as Katy finished up this last question. "Are you making your grocery list? I need to start keeping a notebook in my purse. I never remember half of what I'm going to the store to get."

"No." Katy flipped the notebook close and tucked it back in her bag. "I was just writing down what I found out today about the murder and writing some questions that I'd like to know the answer to. I can think better if all the information is in front of me in an orderly fashion."

"You and your never-ending lists," Misty smiled. "Sounds like you've been busy. What have you found out? I thought you had to work this morning."

"I did, but only for three hours." Katy paused as they gave their orders to the waitress. "I had to go by Dr. Roberts' office to drop off some lab results, and Trudy Mae told me something very interesting. Jessa had been in there Friday and found out she was pregnant."

Misty's mouth dropped open as she stared at Katy, speechless for a full three seconds. "I guess that could be why she was fighting with the Phobs boy," she finally said. "I heard on the news that he's been arrested on suspicion of murder." She paused again and rubbed her pointer finger across her bottom lip. "Pregnant, I never would have guessed that. Not that I thought the woman was a picture of virtue, I just figured she was sharp enough to take precautions against it."

Their orders arrived, and they took a few minutes to fix their plates. "Did you go by the Brown mansion like you planned? Have you seen their yard?" Misty stabbed her fork into a cherry tomato and looked across the table. "It's done up cute with the bulldogs and the maroon and white daylilies. Of course, we're Ole Miss fans at our house, but that really is a clever idea with the flowers in the school colors."

"I went by the Brown's after I left work and I agree. Their yard is fabulous. You should see the inside of their house," Katy said. "It's almost as pretty as yours." Misty's home was not as large or extravagant as the Brown mansion, but it could rival any home around Skeeterville with its style and décor. Misty just had a gift for putting things together and making them look beautiful. It not only showed up in her work as a florist but also in everything else she touched, including her home and personal attire.

"Do you think the boyfriend did it?" Misty popped the tomato in her mouth and stared across the table.

"I have my doubts about Joe Phobs being the killer," Katy said, taking a sip of her tea. "Something else was going on that night that hasn't been discovered yet."

"Look who the cat drug in." Both women looked up and smiled as Todd walked over to their booth. "Hello, ladies. Mind if I join you for a minute?"

"Not at all." Katy scooted over to let her nephew sit down. "Have you already ordered? If not, we'll flag down that fast-moving waitress."

"I can't stay but a second. I'm picking up a to-go order to take back to the station for the prisoner. I just saw you two and came over to say hello." Todd looked down at Katy's plate and grimaced. "I don't know why you ruin a perfectly delicious meal by covering it with all that slimy green avocado."

"Poor baby," Katy smiled and stabbed the fork into her salad. "You just don't know what's good. I hope you ordered a burger or something for you to eat too. You know when your Uncle John's not home I have cold cereal for supper. You'll starve to death at my house waiting for me to cook."

"Don't worry about feeding me," Todd said,

rubbing his stomach. "I'm like a snake, I can go for days without a meal if I have to."

"That's why you still have that schoolboy figure," Misty grinned. "And by the way, we missed you at church yesterday. Everyone assumed you were working, but our Sunday school class just wasn't the same without you." Misty and Mike taught the young unmarried class which also included Vickie, Heather, and Sarah. All three women had voiced their disappointment at Todd's absence. Misty strongly suspected it was because they wanted to get his take on who had killed Jessa.

"Yes, ma'am," Todd agreed, "that was it. I got home after midnight Saturday night, grabbed a couple of hours of sleep, and then was back at it all day Sunday. Hopefully, I'll be back with y'all this Sunday." Todd's answer was interrupted by the tune of "The Imperial Death March" coming from his trouser leg. "Excuse me, that's the boss. I better answer it." Todd stepped away from the table toward the restaurant's large front window and turned his back on all the diners for privacy.

"I never would have guessed Todd would have classical music for his ring tone," Misty said as she patted her lips with her napkin. "I imagined him to be more of a country or rock lover."

"Girl, that's *Star Wars* bad guy music." Katy

picked through her salad one more time to make sure she had eaten all the chicken and avocado. She looked over at Misty's confused expression. "You know, Darth Vader, 'Luke, I am your father,' stuff." She waved her fork around to the neighboring tables and booths. "You are probably the only person in this place who didn't recognize that ring tone. All the Cross family are sci-fi nerds. It's in the blood."

"You know the only place we go to is the football stadium. Mike gets season passes every year to Ole Miss Football, and that's about the extent of our outings." She paused as she dug around in her designer handbag for her lipstick. "I did go see *Nutcracker on the Bayou* with Mother last Christmas in Baton Rouge, but that's pretty much all of the entertainment I get. Besides, that sci-fi stuff looks kind of weird to me."

"Well, it is weird," Katy said, "but that's the whole point. I can see I've neglected your cultural growth. The next time John goes out of town, I'm going to borrow all seventy-five *Star Wars* movies from the library, and you and I are going to spend an evening in the stars. It'll be entertaining for me to watch you watch Yoda."

"If you say so, but I've never sat through seventy-five episodes of any television program. I don't think I can sit still that long."

"I'm exaggerating," Katy said, rolling her eyes and grinning. "There are only five, or six, or maybe seven movies. I'm not sure how many, really. I lost count when they started numbering them out of order, but I'll break you in slowly with the first two. Then if you're still weirded out by sci-fi, I'll never bring up the subject again. How does that sound?"

"That sounds great, but you have to do something with me in return." Misty tapped her silver lipstick tube against her chin. "Hey, I know. We could plan on seeing *Swan Lake* together this Christmas season. Have you ever seen it? It's beautiful, but Mike acts like the ballet gives him acid reflux or something."

"I've never been to any ballet except the twins' dance recitals when they were in elementary school. That sounds like a great plan. You set your date up and I'll set up mine. This ought to be fun."

"Joe will have to skip lunch today," Todd said, walking back up to their table. "There's been a wreck on the five-eighty-seven, and I have to get over there to direct traffic. Do either of y'all want a burger and fries? It'll spoil in my hot car before two o'clock. If not, would you mind canceling the order for me, Aunt Katy? I need to run."

"Why don't you let me take the food over to the station for you? Misty and I aren't pressed for time and that way you won't have to worry about coming back by later to get something for him."

"If you don't mind doing that for me," Todd said, "it sure would help out. Just hand it to Ms. Lois at the dispatch desk. It shouldn't take you three minutes to just run it in to her. It's already paid for. I need to go before the rubberneckers cause another wreck at the crash site."

They waved goodbye to Todd's back as he weaved between the café tables and left out through the double glass doors. Katy had taken care of Lois Davis' aunt a few years ago when the elderly lady had tripped over her wiener dog and fell, cutting her forearm. Katy remembered Lois as being overweight, very talkative, and a rather slow mover. Hopefully, she would have no problem with letting Katy do her the favor of walking the prisoner's lunch back to his cell.

Chapter Eight

Misty's pewter-colored Maxima pulled in front of the sheriff's office ten minutes later. The red brick building's flat roof, heavily tinted picture window, and one glass door in front, didn't look inviting. An American flag waved from the pole at the corner. This was Katy's first trip to the sheriff's office, but when she walked through the front door, she immediately noticed two things. The temperature was cold enough to hang meat, and the fluorescent lights gave everything a strange pale-yellow tint. What a depressing place to have to sit all day.

Lois' desk set immediately to the left of the entrance. She sat twirling the phone cord between her fingers as she listened to whoever was talking on the other end of the conversation. Katy stood directly in front of the large gray desk and fought the urge to tap the bell in the corner.

Two offices were on the other side of the front door across from Lois's desk, both with their doors closed. A couple of metal folding chairs set on the back wall facing the front door. Other than that, the room was empty. The walls were plain white sheetrock, and a Coke machine was stuck in the far corner of the room, off to the left from the front desk. A hall extended down that left-hand wall past the Coke machine. Katy assumed it went to the jail cells.

Lois glanced up from the phone. "I'm gonna put you on hold a minute, George. Somebody just walked in the office." She pressed the hold button and smiled. "Can I help you with something?"

"Hi, I'm Katy Cross, Todd's niece," Katy said. "He got called away to a wreck and asked if I would give this food to Joe Phobs. Do you mind if I run it back to him?" Katy held her breath, waiting for Lois to respond.

"Yeah, if Todd sent you, it'll be fine. Just take this dollar and grab him a Coke out of the machine on your way back." Lois reached in the desk drawer and pulled out a grungy one-dollar bill and passed it across to Katy. "I imagine Todd's going to be tied up all afternoon on that wreck. A big rig flipped over and has the five-eighty-seven completely blocked. All our people are out there, as well as an ambulance and the first responders from the fire station. If you don't take Joe something, he probably won't get a meal until tonight."

"Thanks." Katy quickly got the Coke and headed down the hall to the cell. She could hear Lois reconnect with George as she walked away. That had been simple enough. She walked down the dimly lit hall and ran directly into an alcove that contained two jail cells, each about eight feet square.

Katy stood back and took a second to study Joe before making her presence known. He sat with his broad shoulders slumped over on the edge of the cot, his elbows on his knees, his face in his hands. His grey tee-shirt stretched across his back and met his faded blue jeans. She looked down at his work boots with dried mud splattered all over them. She saw men dressed like this every day and had probably seen this fellow around town before too.

"Excuse me," she said, stepping forward. Joe lifted his head and a pair of silvery-blue eyes stared up at her from a face tanned to a golden brown like the crust on a pone of cornbread. His high cheekbones and strong square chin were enhanced with a slight five o'clock shadow. "Hi Joe, I'm Katy

Cross," she said, reaching through the cell bars and offered him the bag of food and the Coke. "Todd asked me to bring you your lunch."

"Thank you, ma'am." He took the bag and began scavenging through its contents.

She silently waited, hoping he would start some sort of conversation, but he seemed content to just eat his burger and fries. He was not going to be chatty, like Lois. Todd said he had refused to write out his statement and was only giving short yes or no answers to their questions. She turned to leave with a sigh. Maybe she would have better luck at the nail salon. This had suddenly turned into a dead end.

"I didn't do it."

Katy turned back around. He was still looking at his food, but maybe he did want to talk. She propped her shoulder against the wall, hoping she looked relaxed and waited for him to continue. He didn't. "I was with Todd when he found the body. I didn't know Jessa that well, but," Katy left the sentence open, not knowing what else to say.

"People saw us arguing that night, but people saw us arguing every night we were together," Joe said, looking up. "That was nothing new. You know, I've lived in Skeeterville my whole life. I don't go to church much and I get a speeding ticket every now and then, but I can't believe that folks think I could just up and kill somebody, especially my girlfriend."

"What were y'all arguing about?" Katy asked softly.

"The same thing we've been arguing about for months. Tubby Robinson told me back in the spring that Jessa was stepping out on me while I was off on the rig," Joe said, setting down the bag of food. "At first, I just blew him off. Tubby gossips worse than any woman. But then Jessa started acting differently. She's always had a smart mouth on her, but she used to direct it at other people, not me. Here lately, though, I couldn't do anything right. 'You're driving too fast, you're driving too slow,'" Joe's voice rose as he mimicked his girlfriend's badgering tone. "'Why you wearing that shirt? You never talk to me.' It was just one thing after another, and I knew something was up. Anyway, I was getting my oil changed last week at the dealership, and her cousin Tripp mentioned something about how I sure was a good man to not mind Jessa seeing other guys while I was gone. After that... I figured Tubby had been telling the truth."

"So, you were breaking up with her?" Katy asked.

"That's how it started. We were behind the shed having our usual yelling match. Man, was I tired of those. I told her it was time for us to part ways." He paused, rubbing his hand across the stubble on his chin. "I don't know why I'm telling you all this. I guess it's finally sinking in that if I don't get some help, I may be sitting in one of these places for the rest of my life." He shook his head again in disbelief. "That sheriff treated me like I was some kind of thug, and you know I have voted for that man every single time he's run?"

"I heard," Katy said, trying to sound casual, "that they found a bloody monkey wrench in the back of your truck."

"That's what they are saying, but if you can tell me how it got there, then we'll both know." Joe stood up from the cot, the half-eaten burger forgotten. "I don't know what's going on, but I didn't do this."

Katy shook her head, feeling his frustration. "After the conversation behind the shed, did you and Jessa part ways?"

"No, she wouldn't let it go that easily. I told her it was over, then she proceeded to tell me that she was pregnant, and I was going to pay for her abortion because she had her career to think about and a baby wasn't part of her plan, and a bunch of garbage like that." He paused and swallowed hard. "That's when she went stomping off toward the stage where her band and some other folks were hanging around. I followed her like an idiot and told her we needed to go somewhere and talk about this. She said that there was nothing to talk about, just give her a thousand dollars, and she would take care of things and be out of my hair. I told her I would see her dead before I would give her a penny."

"And everybody heard that, I guess."

"Oh yeah," Joe shook his head, "we were pretty loud by then."

"What happened next?" Katy watched as Joe's eyes lit up with emotion.

"She slapped me across the face. I decided it was time for me to leave before I did something I would regret, like slap her back, not kill her." Joe grabbed the cell bars and looked at Katy's face. "I got in the truck, went to Jiffy Mart, and bought a case of beer. I spent the rest of the night with Hank Williams Jr. in my trailer. I didn't get up 'til Saturday around noon. I mowed a little grass at Momma's, got drunk again and didn't wake up 'til the cops came beating on my trailer Sunday morning."

He went back to the cot and flopped his heavy body back down on the mattress then looked up at Katy. "Even if I did have it in me to kill somebody, which I don't, there is no way I would kill a pregnant woman. That poor baby is dead now too, and if word gets out about her being pregnant, I guess I'll be tried for murdering two people."

"Look, Joe," Katy said, leaning toward the cell bars, "I'm not trying to get in your business or any-thing, but I think it would be better for you if you tell the sheriff, or maybe your lawyer everything you just told me. At least then they'll have a place to start looking for the real killer."

"I know, and I plan on doing that," Joe said, staring at the ceiling. "I have just been too mad to put everything into words, and I can't write it down for them. I tried to tell them that, but when they wouldn't listen to me, I just clamped up." His voice grew quiet. "Do you think they will find out she's pregnant?"

"Yeah, I am pretty sure they will. Those things have a way of coming out." She paused and stared through the cell bars. "Why can't you write your story down? It doesn't have to be perfect English, just write down what you've told me."

"I can't. I want to, but I really can't." Joe sighed, "I'm dyslexic. They just thought I was stupid in school and passed me through every grade as special ed. When I graduated, I went to one of those adult learning centers in Hattiesburg on my own and asked them to try to figure out why I couldn't read or write. I wanted to, I just couldn't make heads or tails of what I saw." He smiled a sad smile and looked at Katy. "The lady running the place had pity on me and sent me to some kind of specialist. It took him about ten minutes to tell me what was wrong. I still can't write worth a flip, but once the doctor filled out some paperwork for me, I was able to get my driver's license with an oral test and get my job offshore. I've been working on it off and on through the years and I can get by with the reading now, but my writing's a joke."

"Dyslexia." Katy's eyes stretched wide. "Well, no wonder you didn't write down a statement. You're not trying to be uncooperative." She took a deep breath and looked down at the cot. "Look, Joe, you've got to get in touch with your lawyer and let him know this. I'm sure someone can dictate your statement or video it or something, but you've got to let them know what's going on." Her voice climbed with excitement. "I don't mean to sound cruel, but if you don't start helping yourself a little here, things are going to go from bad to worse quick."

"I know you're right," Joe said, sitting up. He took one step across the small cell and stood directly in front of her. "I've just been overwhelmed with this. Kind of in shock, you know. I'm sorry ma'am, but what did you say your name was? I've been spilling my guts to you like you're my momma, and I can't even remember your name."

"That's okay, you're under a lot of stress. My name is Katy Cross. I'm Todd's aunt."

"Mrs. Katy, would you do me a favor and have Ms. Lois call my lawyer and get him over here? She knows how to get in touch with him, and talking to you has lit a fire under me to start trying to get some help."

"I sure will." Katy smiled and patted Joe's hand as he squeezed the bars that separated them. "Joe, I know you said you don't go to church, but would you mind if I start praying for you? I think you're innocent, and you need all of the help you can get."

"Yes, ma'am, please do. I believe in God and Momma taught us to do right, even if she didn't take us to church. I guess I've just not given God much thought. I've been doing some praying on my own though since I've been in here. I think I need a miracle about now."

Yes, you do, she thought as she walked away.

Chapter Nine

"I can't believe how busy this place is. Their parking lot always looks full." Katy gawked, mentally counting the cars. "Am I the only woman in Skeeterville who doesn't get her nails done?"

"Nah, you're not completely alone," Misty laughed. She pulled into one of the few available parking spots in front of the salon. "I don't think Mike's ninety-year-old grandmother gets hers done anymore. It's too much trouble getting her wheelchair and oxygen tank in the salon door."

"Okay, okay, smart mouth." Katy raised an eyebrow. "Point taken. I realize most women like beautiful, nails and don't get me wrong, so would I. It's just that I can't have those long fake nails with my job, and then I think about how much money it costs and how busy I am, and well, I just don't ever get it done." She looked at her hands in disgust. The nails weren't bitten, but they obviously didn't get any attention either. The right thumbnail was long, with a jagged edge resembling a rickety staircase. The other nine weren't quite as bad. She needed to buy a nail file to keep in her purse. She slipped her hands between her knees and looked over at Misty's hands resting on the steering wheel. The short, even manicure with glossy pink nail-beds spoke volumes to Katy's bruised ego.

"Don't act like your money's so tight that you can't afford to get your nails done." Misty pulled the key from the ignition. "There's nothing wrong with not getting your nails done, it's your choice. I just think you deserve to pamper yourself a little, that's all. You're always running around doing this, that, and the other for everybody else. Why don't you do this for yourself?" She reached and grabbed her purse from the backseat. "It really is nice. I get mine done about every two weeks along with my eyebrows. It's just part of my life."

"They do eyebrows too?" She glanced at Misty's perfectly arched brows before looking out the windshield. She knew that their appearances were a sharp contrast of a well-groomed, attractive woman and a rather sloppy friend who could be easily overlooked.

"Girl, they'll wax any body part you stick in front of them. I get my chin waxed too, but if you tell anybody, there'll be another murder in this town before sundown."

"You mean to tell me grown women go into that building and get their uh... stuff waxed right there in front of their friends and neighbors and the UPS guy if he happens to be walking through?" Katy's mouth dropped open. "I can't believe that. You might have to go in and snoop around without me. There're some things about the women of this town that I just don't want to know."

"You're cracking me up." Misty swatted at a tear trickling down her cheek. She took a deep breath to control the laughter bubbling up after Katy's rant. "To be so smart, you sure are ignorant about some things." She dabbed a tissue under her eyes to prevent her mascara from running. "I don't even get my eyebrows waxed in front of anybody else, and I sure wouldn't be going in there if bikini waxes were being done in the parlor."

She flipped down the visor and checked her face. "Let me fix my mascara real quick before we go in. I look like a gothic princess." She repaired the damage with swift accuracy. "Hey, Marissa Holmes is a waxer. She doesn't do me. I go to Jaylynn, but everybody says she's good. Why don't you get your eyebrows done? That way she'll have to take you into the little room in the back. Y'all will be alone, and you'll have a chance to ask her some questions."

Katy pulled down her visor and looked in the mirror. She turned her head from side to side, looking at one brow, then the other. She hadn't plucked in over a month, and a small briar patch was growing over her eyes and across the bridge of her nose. "My girls have been trying to get me to wax my brows for years, but I know it has got to hurt." She leaned closer to the mirror. "I don't know."

"It's not that bad, and don't you want to find out why Marissa and Jessa were fighting? If she's working on other people, I probably won't get a chance to talk to her. She usually stays pretty busy." Misty opened her car door. "It's up to you but if you really want to find something out, I recommend manning up and getting them bad boys done."

"You're right." Katy snapped the visor shut. "John's coming home today, and boy will he be surprised." She opened her door and slid out. "What the hay, I might even get my nails done while I'm at it."

"Whoop, whoop!" Misty pumped her arm in

the air as she stood up. "I like this sleuthing stuff. We're going to make a girly girl out of you yet, Katy Cross."

"I'm girly, sort of. I'm just practical, and uh, understated."

"Sure girlfriend," Misty laughed, locking the doors as they started across the parking lot. "Anything you say."

Ninety minutes later the women were back in the car headed towards home. Katy pulled the visor down again and looked at her new, perfectly arched brows. The skin between her lids and the artistically shaped line was puffy and an angry shade of hot pink. "I almost wet my pants when she ripped that wax off. I cannot believe I paid somebody money to inflict that kind of pain on me." She dabbed the angry skin above her nose with her finger. "Forget waterboarding, waxing should be the mode of extracting information from terrorists. I'm sure it would be way more effective." She cut her eyes across the car. "I thought you said it wouldn't hurt."

"Now I never said it wouldn't hurt. I just said that it's not that bad." They stopped at a red light, and Misty turned to examine her friend's new look. "They are fantastic and I'm jealous. Did you get your chin done too?"

Katy grinned as she took one last look in the

mirror before flipping the visor back into place. "They do look good, don't they? I've always wondered how women got their eyebrows to look so pretty." She rubbed her fingers across the lower half of her face. "Yeah, she did my chin, and lip too. It's a little numb. I guess I had an old lady mustache going on that I didn't know about."

"It wasn't that noticeable. I would look like Magnum P.I. if I didn't take care of things like that. Let me see your nails."

Katy held out her hands for inspection. Her cuticles had been soaked and pushed back, making the nails appear longer even though they didn't extend past her fingertips. She had chosen a very pale shade of pink called Champaign Blush. For the first time in so long that Katy couldn't remember, she was not ashamed of the way her hands looked. "What do you think?" she proudly asked.

"Gorgeous, and you can still play the guitar and wear your nursing gloves to do all that disgusting nursing stuff you love." The light turned green, and she moved the car forward. "Now do you see why the parking lot is so full all the time?"

"I guess so. I have to agree," Katy conceded, "this is very nice. I can see why you would want to make it a habit to keep looking like this, even with the pain of having your face ripped off."

"Good, because I scheduled us appointments again for two weeks from today."

"Oh really," Katy looked at her friend and smiled. "You were that sure that I would want to come back?"

"I was sure hoping you would. I think maybe next time you can get your toes done too. I'll get one of the technicians to explain how they make sure you don't get the golden toe like you are so scared of catching."

"We'll see," Katy said slowly. "I'm going to have to ease into this or John will go into shock, bless his heart. He ain't going to know what to think now with these new eyebrows."

"Do you think he'll notice?" Misty asked, glancing quickly at Katy then back to the road. "Mike is a sweetheart, but he never notices things like that."

"That's because he's always used to you looking so perfect." Katy sighed. "Poor John. Yeah, he'll definitely notice. I have sort of let myself go." She looked again at her new and improved hands. "Maybe this is the start of something good."

"And speaking of something good, did you learn anything about Jessa's fuss with Marissa? That blue hair has to be hers. Who else around here has electric blue highlights?" Misty reached up and unconsciously rubbed her lip. "And did you notice those red marks on her neck? I heard her telling one of the women that a tree branch scratched her while she was mowing grass this weekend."

"I saw that," Katy said. "She also has the end of her pointer finger on her right hand bandaged up. I asked her what happened, and she said she accidentally tore off a nail while pumping gas." She looked down at her fingers. "Are those fake nails that secure? Will they damage your finger if they get hung in something like that?"

"Sister, please," Misty's hand fluttered up from the steering wheel. "That stuff they use to stick on those nails is stronger than crazy glue. It takes a force of nature to get them off. Usually, if someone chips one, or cuts it down, or just wants it off for some reason, they go in and have it soaked off with acetone, or whatever they use."

"I would bet you good money that was her nail I saw tangled in Jessa's hair." Katy pursed her lips. "You know, Joe Phobs said that Tubby Robinson knows about Jessa's personal life and that he loves to talk. Since Marissa is also a member of their band, I bet he knows all about how they got along. He could probably tell us if they had a fight over the weekend." She raised her new fingernail to her lips, then self-consciously dropped it to her lap. "I don't know this Tubby Robinson fella, or I would go ask him what happened between those two women. I've seen him with *The Wildcats*, but I've never spoken to him."

"He's Jenny Faye and LeRoy Robinson's youngest boy. You know that family. LeRoy owns Robinson Logging. Tubby works for his daddy."

"They don't sound familiar. Maybe John knows them."

"His wife is a teller at the bank, Emma Robinson. She's short and blonde and wears a lot of makeup." Katy continued to shake her head and Misty tried to think of how to further describe her. "You'll know her when you see her. She sells About Face Make-Up and Skincare and if you compliment her, she tries to sell you something. She's the teller at the bank's first window."

"Oh yeah," Katy finally nodded her head, "looks like a Barbie Doll."

"Exactly. That's Tubby's wife."

"That beautiful girl is married to a big ole guy like Tubby Robinson?" Katy's eyes stretched wide. "I never would have put them two together. She's so put together, and he looks so country looking, you know, with the flannel and beard and all." She leaned her head back against the seat. "That doesn't help me, anyway. I don't know her either, except for seeing her at the bank."

"I don't know," Misty's voice tilted in a sing-song rhythm. "I think she's just about as gossipy as

Tubby. Mike says that she's always coming in telling some kind of tale about different folks. He has to remind her not to be gossiping to the customers. People don't want the person handling their money to be spreading around their affairs. I bet her and Tubby are just fountains of information."

"I wish we could go knock on their door and just ask them to tell us everything they know about Jessa Williams' and Marissa Holmes' catfight," Katy said. "I couldn't be a cop. That kind of power would go to my head."

"I have an idea if you're willing to go along with it." Misty pulled her car into the Burger Barn parking lot to drop Katy at her vehicle. "Tomorrow I'll go by the bank and casually tell Emma how much I love her lipstick, or eyeshadow, or something. It will be true because she always looks perfect. This time when she asks me to host a party, I'll take her up on it. Then, when we have her at my house all excited about selling her stuff, we can quiz her down."

"How can you be sure that she'll ask you to have a party?" Katy asked. "She's never asked me to have one."

"That's because you're a customer, and she can't solicit. For some reason, she has it in her head that Mike and I are loaded with money." Misty's chin jutted forward. "She drops little hints about how nice it must be to have money to blow, or how nice it is to be married to a rich man. That's why I've never offered to host one of her parties, she gets on my nerves."

"And you don't have to have one now," Katy said, turning down the offer. "I'll figure something out. Just give me a little time."

"I want to do this," Misty insisted. "It won't be a lick of trouble to get *The Moonlighters*, Mama, Aunt Virgie, and Pickle to come over to the house for a party." She counted the women off on her fingers. "I'll make a couple of snacks, and we'll have a good time while we figure out why Jessa and Marissa had a throw down. Plus," she dragged the word out slowly. "Once she's in my home, and I'm free to talk to her, I'll set the record straight on being married to a rich man. I worked my behind off waiting tables to put Mike through school. It's about time she knows that."

"Okay," Katy said. "If you're sure you don't mind."

"It's no trouble, I promise." Misty smiled, her voice returning to its normal happy tone. "I'm getting kind of excited about it. I hope that stuff she sells is good because she'll expect everybody to buy a little something."

"Let me know when it is." Katy opened the car

door. "Don't forget about band practice tomorrow night. Oh, and are you going to Jessa's funeral? I need to find out when it is."

"She'll be at the funeral home tomorrow from four until nine and the service is Wednesday morning at eleven." Misty rattled off the schedule. "They're doing everything at the funeral home. I guess she didn't go to church with the Browns since they aren't having it at the Methodist church. I'm dropping by on my way to practice. I have to work at the shop all day Wednesday."

"I might do the same thing. I feel like I need to at least stop in." Katy looked at her hands as she pushed the key fob to open her car door. *That looks so much better. It's a shame it took somebody dying to get me to pay attention to how raggedy they had become.*

Chapter Ten

"Hello, are you in here?" John dropped his bag by the front door and headed through the house to the bedroom.

"I'm back here." Katy turned around and bumped into John as he walked up behind her. Her arms wrapped around his neck, as always, when he came home in the afternoon. Over the past thirty-plus years of marriage, she had learned that few things felt as good as a hug from her husband.

"I'm glad to be back." John's full force hug followed by a heartfelt kiss showed how much he meant it. "I know I just left last Thursday, but it seems like I've been gone a month. After talking to you Saturday night about that girl being killed, I really wanted to get home." He looked down at

Katy's face, then stepped back and held her at arm's length. "Well my, my, don't you look nice. I would've told them folks in Missouri to take a flying leap and came on home Sunday if I'd known you were going to meet me like this."

Katy's throaty laugh was something she only did when John teased her. He had called an hour ago to say he would be there soon. She decided to use the time to fix up a little, which, according to his response, had been a good idea. Putting on make-up, fixing her hair, and changing into something besides her grey sweatpants and wrinkled, green John Deere tee-shirt must have been a good idea. "I decided to do a little experiment. Looks like it was a success." She showed him her hands. "Look at this. Don't they look nice?"

John examined Katy's manicure and smiled. "Okay, you look like my wife and sound like my wife, but my wife does not believe in fancy girly fingernails."

"I'm not that bad." Katy slapped him on the chest. "I can be a fancy girl too. I went with Misty to The Nail Palace, and she talked me into having them done. Look." She turned her face to the side and wiggled her forehead. "I got my brows waxed just for you."

"Well, look a there," John grinned. "I thought you looked different, but I couldn't be sure with the paint you have on. They look nice. Since you're all dolled up, why don't you give me a minute to wash up, and we'll go out for supper? Ain't no use wasting all this updo on just me."

"We can if you want to," Katy said. "I have grilled pork chops ready. I thought you might want a home-cooked meal."

"Stick 'em in the fridge. I'm gonna show off my woman." He patted Katy's backside as he went into the bathroom. "Of course, everybody's gonna be jealous, but that'll be okay."

Katy heard John whistling through the closed door as she went to the kitchen to put up the pork chops. She sighed as she stuck the field peas in the refrigerator. It was a shame that she had let herself get into such a rut over the years. He had never stopped telling her she was beautiful, never treated her any differently, but gauging from his reaction, he did appreciate the small effort she'd put into her appearance today. *I'm going to do better,* she thought. *For John, but also for me.*

They decided on Fred's Fish House and were soon sitting across from each other drinking sweet tea and waiting on their orders. Katy ordered crawfish étouffée, and John the seafood platter.

"I guess people don't eat at home much like they used to." He looked around at the nice-sized crowd. "There are a lot of folks in here for a

Tuesday night. I remember eating out on three occasions the entire time I lived at home. Now, most people eat out at least once a week."

"You have four sisters and three brothers. If your family had eaten out once a week, your dad would've had to file for bankruptcy."

"That's true. Even eating at home was a big ordeal. Momma would sometimes bake three pans of biscuits and two skillets of tomato gravy at one sitting when me and the twins were older. For a while, she had three teenage boys and two teenage girls along with the little ones to try to keep full. That woman spent a lot of time in the kitchen."

Their food arrived, and John said the blessing. "That's some good-looking shrimp." He took a bite of the deep-fried delight, then reached for another. "What have you found out about the murder since the last time we talked? I know with Todd staying at the house you've been able to quiz him down to see what the police know."

Katy pulled out her little notebook and caught him up to speed on everything she'd found out, and how she had come upon the information.

"You went to the jail and interrogated a man accused of murder? I don't think I like that very much," John said.

"It wasn't like that." Katy lifted a spoonful of étouffée from her bowl. "Todd needed me to deliver this guy's lunch, and while I was there, I just asked him a few questions. I'm sure he didn't do it." She brought the spoon to her lips and blew the steamy liquid. "Once you go home and look at my big notebook and think about everything I've said, then you won't think he did it either."

"That's not the point I'm trying to make here, Katy. I don't like you getting involved in this thing. What if that guy had done it? What if he had a friend who didn't like you asking all those questions and decided to do something to hush you up?"

"Nothing like that has happened. Joe Phobs is just kind of pitiful. He was in a relationship with Jessa that was coming to an end. They had a fight over her wanting to give up her baby. Somebody saw the fight and decided to get rid of Jessa and pin it on him."

"I'm not doubting that you're right. I'm saying that you must be more careful before you jump into these kinds of situations. If you're right, there's someone in our town who thinks they have gotten away with murder. If you mess that up for this person, he won't be happy." He picked up the third shrimp and pointed it across the table. "If he killed one person, he might kill again."

"I understand what you're saying. That's why nobody but you and Misty know about everything

I've found out. I haven't even told Todd yet. I wanted to discuss it with you first."

"That's good. Don't tell the rest of them women in your band. They probably wouldn't mean to, but they would spread every bit of what you just told me all over the town." He paused and took a deep breath. "I think you'll have to tell Todd. Just make him promise to not mention your name to anybody. He might already know the stuff you know, anyway."

"Okay. I guess he'll come by tonight and get his things since you're back home. If I'm back from band practice, I'll tell him then." Katy looked at her watch. "Do you mind if we run by the funeral home for just a second when we leave here? I want to pay my respects. We don't have to stay. I have practice at Sarah's at seven."

"Might as well. You're neck-deep in this mess, and I know why you're going to the funeral home, so don't even try to kid me. You want to see who all will show up, and you want to talk to Tubby Robinson if you get a chance."

"You know me too well." Katy cocked her head to the side and smiled. "I figured that since you know Tubby, maybe you could start up a conversation with him if he happens to be there. Then I could ask him about Jessa and Marissa. That way Misty won't feel like she needs to have that ridiculous party just so we can talk to Tubby's wife." Katy leaned across the table and kissed her husband lightly on the lips. "You sure know how to treat a girl right. Taking me out to eat and then a trip to the funeral home all in one night. That's why I love you so."

"Yeah, right," John laughed, "we're going to have to do this more often."

❧

Katy's shoes clicked with each step as she walked across the ceramic tiles of the large funeral home foyer. She'd been in here many times to see the families of patients who had passed away, but she was always in scrubs and quiet work shoes. The clicking echoed and caused several people to turn to look as they walked past.

Mr. and Mrs. Brown were standing together near the casket when they entered the parlor. Tripp was sitting on a pew near the back, talking with Marissa Holmes. Their heads were together, and they appeared to be laughing over something she was telling him. Katy guessed that really wasn't strange. People grieved by telling funny stories of things that had happened to their loved ones. Still, they did look mighty chummy. She noticed another member of *The Wildcats* walking up to view the body, but she didn't see Tubby.

She peered into the casket. Jessa looked like she was sleeping, but Katy knew if she touched her hand, the skin would be as cold as ice. A tear appeared on her lashes, and she swatted it away. The poor little baby nestled in Jessa's womb being buried along with her mother would not be mourned.

John looked at Katy's face as she wiped her eyes. "He's not here. Are you ready to go?"

"I guess so. Let me look at the flowers. Misty does such pretty arrangements." They spoke to the Browns as they passed by the end of the casket. A huge spray of yellow roses standing nearby was the most prominent arrangement in the parlor. Katy looked at the tag. 'With our deepest sympathy from the Brown Family Motors employees. That was nice. There were a few other plants and arrangements, but none half the size of the prominent yellow roses display.

Katy looked at a beautiful spray of wild daisies and sunflowers that had just been brought in and placed near the rest of the flowers. "No tag," she said, stepping closer to the arrangement. "That's odd. I've never heard of someone sending flowers to a funeral without sending a card to show who it was from." She looked at the label on the stand.

"They're from Misty's shop. Maybe they forgot to place the card on the arrangement."

"That is strange," John nodded. "I'm sure Mrs. Brown will contact Misty's shop and find out who they're from."

"Yeah, you're probably right." Katy glanced around the room one more time. "We might as well go. I've already talked to Mrs. Brown and Marissa. I don't guess talking to Mr. Brown or Trip would do any good." She looked back into the parlor one last time as they headed out of the room. Mr. Brown was pulling out a handkerchief to wipe his eyes while he was talking to *The Wildcats* member that Katy didn't know. Mrs. Brown had left the casket and was talking to Mr. Morse, the funeral director and coroner. It looked like she wouldn't learn anything new tonight. She did plan on asking Misty about the flowers that didn't have a card. Was the card left out by mistake or had someone sent flowers and didn't want anyone to know who they were from? She would find out shortly in band practice.

Chapter Eleven

Katy dropped John by their house, picked up her guitar, and headed to Sarah's house. All the ladies oohed and aahed over Katy's change in appearance, which boosted her ego, but also embarrassed her about how she normally looked. She didn't give it much thought; however, once they started tuning up the instruments and looking over their song list.

Playing with *The Moonlighters* was her favorite pastime. Their next engagement was their monthly Saturday afternoon session at the nursing home. They had played for weddings, church gatherings, family reunions, and parties, along with the nursing home gig, and even some elementary school functions. She knew they would get together and play, even if nobody ever called inviting them to perform.

"Sarah, why don't you play a turnaround between the verses for 'Unclouded Day'? That'll give us a chance to catch our breath. Plus, it will give your pawpaw something to brag about during the bingo game after we leave."

"Sure will, Mrs. Katy, but he doesn't need encouragement to brag. I know the nursing home staff are sick of him telling them about our band and how he doesn't understand why we've never made a song for the radio."

"My Aunt Geraldine's the same way," Vickie laughed. "I heard her last time telling one of the other women at her table that the only reason we hadn't made it big was because we were all good Christian girls and didn't want to get involved in that seedy music industry. I liked to have choked on my Coke, trying not to laugh. If we were half as good as the nursing home crew thought we were, we would be something special."

"That's one of the perks of playing there," Katy said, pulling her guitar pick from the corner of her mouth. "Not to mention being told how young I look by all the residents." She looked at her watch. "We've got time for a couple more songs, then we need to wrap it up."

"Mrs. Misty, I got your text inviting me to your

party Friday evening," Vickie said, closing the tab on her mandolin case when the final song was finished. "I should be able to make it, but I'll be a couple of minutes late since I'll be coming straight from work."

"That's fine. It's going to be informal and fun. I hope the rest of you are coming." Misty glanced around the room at Sarah and Heather.

"I'm coming," Sarah said.

"Me too." Heather picked up her phone and read the name of the make-up from the texted invitation. "About Face… I've never heard of that. Is it what you wear, Mrs. Misty?"

"No, I've never used it myself, but Emma Robinson at the bank sells it and has been asking me to have a party for quite a while. She always looks nice, so I thought, why not? I think it'll be fun."

"I know her," Sarah said, hoisting up her electric bass guitar with a breathless grunt. "She lives in Pecan Acres Mobile Home Park near my cousin. I like going to those kind of parties. I love playing in make-up."

Misty smiled, "Well here's your chance."

"See," Misty said as they walked to their cars, "I told you this would work. By nine o'clock Friday night we'll know all about that squabble between Marissa and Jessa." She tapped a drumstick on

Katy's shoulder. "By the way, did you go by the funeral home? And how did John like the eyebrows?"

"John loved the eyebrows and the nails." Katy spread her hands out in front of her, admiring their new look. "I did go by the funeral home but didn't find out anything. I have a question for you, though. There was a beautiful arrangement of daisies and sunflowers from your shop that arrived without any information from the sender. Do you think that was an oversight?"

"I don't know. I guess it could have been." Misty's eyes narrowed in thought. "Mother did a couple of arrangements while I was working on that huge spray of yellow roses. I'll ask her about it, but if there wasn't a card, I bet the delivery boy knocked it off because you know my mother. She's OCD about those cards. She makes the people write everything down themselves when they place an order, and then she reads back every line. She even makes people let her double-check the spelling when they are called in over the phone." She unlocked her car and tossed her purse into the front seat. "Now I'm curious. I would call Mother tonight, but she would drive herself nuts if a card got knocked off and give that poor delivery boy the what for. I'll look into it first thing in the morning and let you know something."

"Alright, be safe going home." Katy backed out of Sarah's drive and turned her car toward home.

⚜

John and Todd sat in the living room eating chocolate chip cookies and drinking coffee. John was one of those rare people who could drink two cups of coffee at ten pm, chase it with a Mountain Dew, and still sleep like a baby all night long. Since Katy wasn't wired that way, she opted for a bottle of water instead.

"Have you told John about the wreck yesterday on the five-eighty-seven?" Katy asked Todd. "I heard an eighteen-wheeler with an empty trailer flipped over blocking both sides of the road for almost two hours."

"He just got through telling me about it," John said, taking the last sip of his coffee. "I came through that way today, coming home, and there were skid marks all over the road. That truck must have been flying."

"He wouldn't admit to it, but I'm sure he was going pretty fast," Todd nodded.

"You've had a busy week," John said. He looked at Katy. "You about ready to tell him your little bit of information?"

Katy set down her water bottle. "I guess so. Let

me get my notebook." She ran into the bedroom and returned with her yellow notepad. "You know yesterday when I took Joe Phobs' lunch by the station for you? Well, Ms. Lois was busy, so I just took it back to Joe myself, and we talked a little." Katy looked at Todd and waited for his reaction. After all, he hadn't told her that she couldn't talk to Joe Phobs.

Todd's forehead wrinkled into a crease, and he ran his fingers through his short, sandy hair. "Uncle John, you know that she's doing all this on her own, right?" He looked from Katy to John. "I'd never have asked her to take Joe his lunch if I'd known she was going to go back there and talk to him." He turned to Katy, clearly aggravated. "Aunt Katy, you know that's not what I meant when I told you to take that man his lunch."

"We've already had a very similar discussion and I promise you, I know you wouldn't ask her to do anything that would put her in danger," John said. "That's one of the reasons why I wanted you to come over while I was out of town. I wanted you to be around to help look out for her." He looked at his wife and smiled. "You can't seem to grasp how dangerous this could be with your snooping around."

"Excuse me, you two," Katy glared from one man to the other. "I'm sitting right here, so please quit talking about me like I'm a child who cannot take care of myself." Both men stared at Katy. "Okay, Todd, I knew you hadn't intended for me to talk to Joe Phobs, but don't you want to know what I found out? I also found out some other things yesterday afternoon at the Nail Palace. And for the record, I'm not a snoop."

"Yes, ma'am." Todd took a deep breath and slowly blew it out. "Tell me what you found out."

She looked triumphantly at both men and flipped the page on her yellow notebook. "Well, first of all, Joe Phobs didn't do it." Todd started to speak, but she held up her hand to silence him. "Just hear me out, Todd. I don't know who did this, but somebody set up Joe Phobs."

She then told him about Jessa being pregnant and that she and Joe were arguing about this. "It makes no sense to think that he would kill Jessa while she was carrying his child," she said. "He didn't want to harm his child." She then told him about the scratches on Marissa Holmes' neck and the missing fingernail from her right hand. "Oh, and I talked Joe into giving a statement to his lawyer. Did he follow through and do that?"

"Yes, ma'am, he did." Todd brushed a cookie crumb from the front of his shirt. "When Sheriff Reid read Joe's statement, he looked at the autopsy report and sure enough, Jessa was pregnant. We ain't letting that news out right now though, because the sheriff ain't sure how it will affect Joe's sentencing."

"Todd," Katy's voice grew tense, "I'm telling you that boy's being set up."

"Aunt Katy," Todd held up his hand and raised his voice a couple of decibels, "I'm not saying that he is guilty or he ain't. I do know that until the sheriff gets a better suspect, he'll be hanging onto Joe Phobs. If the murder weapon hadn't been found in the guy's truck, then he might be more inclined to listen. But as it is, he's pretty sure of the man's guilt." He broke off and took a deep breath. "He figures Joe killed her, threw the monkey wrench in the back of the truck thinking he would have time to get rid of it before anybody found her body, then got drunk out of his mind. When you look at it that way, it's pretty convincing."

"I disagree," Katy said, shaking her head. "The whole thing was planned out. Jessa and Joe's fight just gave the killer the opportunity he needed. I can't prove it, but you've got to keep looking into this."

"I will. Don't worry. I have to admit that I've had a tough time picturing Joe killing somebody. I'll go talk to the Holmes woman tomorrow." He paused and looked down at the notebook in Katy's hands. "Now, is that all you know?"

"Well, yeah, I guess, except maybe you might just want to talk to Tubby Robinson." She looked down at her notes, then back up. "Joe said Tubby saw the fight Friday night and was always keeping up with band gossip. I don't know if he knows anything, but he might since he spent a fair amount of time with Jessa between the band practices and gigs and all."

"I'll look him up tomorrow. He's usually at the Wacky Pack every morning getting a Coke and cigarettes. I go in there after all the morning school traffic." Todd looked at Katy with a gleam in his eye. "Guess what kind of smokes he's always buying?"

Katy's eyes opened wide. "Not Marlboro Lights?"

Todd nodded slowly. "Aunt Katy, you may have stumbled onto something. After all, he lives in the same trailer park as Joe." He suddenly jumped up from his chair. "Thank you for the coffee and cookies. I'll clear out my stuff tomorrow. I need to go home and think about all of this." His eyes crinkled in the corners as he looked down at Katy. "Now I don't mean to sound disrespectful, but please let me handle all of this. From now on, if you think of something or notice something, just call me and I'll come a running. You've got some good ideas, and I appreciate the insight and your thoughts on this stuff, but things could get dangerous."

Katy started to protest, but before she could say anything John answered. "Don't worry Todd, from now on Katy's going to leave all the snooping to you. If she accidentally hears or sees anything, she'll just keep her mouth shut until she contacts you." He looked pointedly at Katy. "And I do mean accidentally."

"I guess you have your answer, Todd." Katy stood and closed her notebook. "I obviously don't need to add anything to that." She glanced at her husband, fire snapping from her eyes. "Y'all forget that I've been going into stranger's homes all over this town seeing patients for years. I've been in all kinds of houses in all areas of this town, the good side and the not so good side, so I'm not an idiot. I don't go looking for danger and I can take care of myself. I've been doing just fine for years."

"I know, Aunt Katy, but you have to admit that having a murderer running around loose kind of ups the ante a little bit."

"You bet it does." John put his arm around her shoulders and gave her a squeeze. "Katy knows it too. Now you don't worry about her and just look out for yourself."

"Don't worry about me. I'm pretty cautious." Todd grinned. "I think I can outrun ole Tubby even on a bad day."

John walked Todd to his truck and Katy began turning off lights and preparing for bed. *So Tubby Robinson smokes the same kind of cigarettes as the bloody pack found at the crime scene, and he lives close enough to put the monkey wrench in the back of Joe Phobs' truck without much trouble,* Katy thought. *That certainly was unexpected news.* She sat on the edge of her bed and jotted everything down. *One thing is certain. The make-up party on Friday should be interesting if Todd talks to Tubby tomorrow. Emma Robinson hopefully won't cancel it if they arrest Tubby or bring him in for questioning. Maybe she will still want to make the money from the sales.*

John walked in as she was finishing her notes. "I need you to think about something for me," she said.

"What is it?" John asked, leaning against the door frame.

"When I got through talking with Joe Phobs, I asked him if I could pray for him and he said that would be good and he would be praying himself."

"I'll pray for him too." He walked over and took Katy's hand. "You know I will."

"Thank you. Do you think maybe you could go by and talk to him?" She looked up at John's face.

"Not about the murder, but just to let him know that we're praying for him and want him to know that God hasn't forgotten about him. He needs some friends right now."

"I guess I can do that. Maybe he'll let me pray with him."

"I'm so glad you said that," Katy smiled. "He needs that."

She climbed into bed with a lot of questions and confusion about Jessa's murder. *The flowers without a tag probably don't mean anything,* she thought. *How many people in this town smoke Marlboro Lights? Probably a lot more than just Tubby Robinson. Do either one of these things mean anything? Somewhere there's a clue about who killed that girl. Somebody knows something. How can I continue to investigate this without being on Todd's snoop radar? I'll figure this out, I have to.*

Chapter Twelve

“The admission is a ninety-two-year-old woman that fell during the night,” the nurse on the other end of the phone explained. “She has this nasty skin tear on her leg from the fall. The family took her to the emergency room, and it turns out she had a low blood sugar.”

Katy looked at the clock on the stove. “It's seven now. I'll get ready and run out and get it done before lunch.” She got up and walked to the sink with her empty coffee cup. “Just have the orders and supplies ready for me to grab when I get to the office in a bit.”

Katy placed her brain on autopilot as she drove to the patient's home, following the directions given by the GPS with the voice of a cultured British woman. *Do people in England have women with American accents guiding them through their country with these devices? It would be nice if a GPS had a southern girl telling her where to turn,* Katy mused. *Honey, you just missed your turn! Now if you don't want to be late, just take the next left on Albritton road and I will figure out how to get you there on time darlin'. Dolly Parton could voice a GPS and make another million.*

She looked at the familiar antebellum homes and manicured lawns as the Brown's long paved drive came into view. She checked the address on the home health folder against the GPS address to make sure she had put it in correctly. Yep, this was the place. The patient's name was Rita Tellman. Maybe that had been the voice of the lady from the other room during her visit to the Browns earlier in the week.

She hoped the Browns wouldn't think she was stalking them when she showed up as the nurse this morning. She hadn't seen Mrs. Brown since their kids were in high school years ago and didn't really know her at all. Now she had seen her three times in three days. If Evelyn Brown gave off an uncomfortable vibe, she would explain that another nurse would be seeing the patient after this visit.

She pulled up the long curving drive adorned

with the maroon and white daylilies and parked her little car out of the way. Rob Clay, the local radio personality, said the temperature would get into the nineties again today. It was still early enough for the air to not be the choking, wet heat that would arrive by mid-morning. Carrying the nursing bag, the wound care supplies, and the computer bag made her feel like she was bringing in groceries or luggage or something when she first came to a new patient's home. She balanced her computer bag on her foot and rang the doorbell.

"Hello, dear," said the neat lady in scrubs. "We've been waiting for you to come."

"Hello." Katy shifted the nursing bag on her shoulder. "I didn't realize I'd be coming back to the Brown residence when I talked to you this morning on the phone. It's nice to see you again."

The lady who introduced herself as Nelda brought them in through the sitting room with the cheerful yellow chair, and silver tea service to the back of the house near the kitchen. "Mrs. Rita's rooms are here in the back," Nelda said. "The family moved her downstairs years ago when she first started getting a little unsteady on her feet."

Nelda led Katy into a large bedroom with soft white walls and thick pale green carpet. The wall that faced the back yard was a ceiling to floor window with French doors in the center leading to a covered patio. The drapes, which were a deep purple, were pulled to both sides of the windows letting in the warm morning sun. The room had a beautiful cherry wood queen sized sleigh bed, along with matching furniture, arranged in one section of the spacious room.

Above the bed hung a large black-and-white photo of a man, woman, and little girl dressed in their Sunday best. The woman sat in a wingback chair while the child sat on the ground at her feet. The man stood beside the chair with his hand casually lying on the woman's shoulder. The woman's hairstyle and the clothing had Katy guessing that the photo was taken during the early sixties or maybe late fifties. The woman in the photo was stunning, and the man was very handsome. Katy wondered if this was Mrs. Tellman and her family.

Across the room from the bed was a sitting area with a television, a small couch, and a couple of dainty chairs arranged around a coffee table along with a sturdy recliner. Katy noted more family photos of different sizes scattered along the other walls. Some of the pictures were of the Browns taken over the years, but some were older, probably other family members of earlier generations. She glanced around at the photos and realized there was not a single picture of Jessa Williams among all the photos, even though some were of large groups that looked like family gatherings.

"Where does Mrs. Tellman like to sit?" Katy asked, following Nelda to the couch and chairs. "I usually like to sit across from the patient if that's possible, so she can see what I'm doing while I'm gathering her information."

"This is her spot here in the recliner. You just sit anywhere you want." Nelda waved her hand toward the furniture. "We got this TV tray out for you to use as a little table, so you wouldn't have to try to reach across to the coffee table with your stuff."

"That was so thoughtful of you," Katy said. She glanced around the room, wondering where her patient was. As if on cue, she heard a flush coming from behind a door off to the left of the bed on the other side of the room. Shortly afterwards the door opened, and a very petite elderly lady stepped through, followed by Evelyn Brown.

The older lady was still in her nightgown and robe, both a light powdery pink satin with lots of lace around the collar and sleeves. She already had on her makeup and her short silver hair was neatly brushed so that the loose curls charmingly framed her face. She stopped in the doorway, holding onto the door frame as her daughter gave her instructions from behind.

"Mother, your cane, you forgot your cane. That doctor said you should be using it whenever you get up."

The little woman paused and looked over her shoulder at her daughter, then turned back to Katy and smiled. "Don't get old dear, it's the pits. You have one little spill and they start trailing you around like a bloodhound. Even have to watch you go to the bathroom." She shook her head as if aggravated, even though her smile told Katy she was thankful for the care her daughter was giving. She took the silver cane with the large rubber tipped end from her daughter and shook her head again.

"Well, Cane, if you're going to be my new side-kick, I guess I'd better quit leaving you lying around all over the place." She leaned on the silver stick and started walking to her chair. "But I'm going to give you a new name. Since Cane killed Able, I don't like having a partner named Cane. I think I'll call you Sam, short for Samson, since I'll be leaning on you and expecting you to carry my weight." She patted the cane on its silver head and continued across the bedroom to her chair.

Katy smiled. Rita Tellman might be ninety-two and unsteady on her feet, but she seemed to be pretty sharp. She waited until the patient was settled in her recliner with her feet elevated and Sam at her side before she sat down to begin her usual admission procedure.

"Mrs. Tellman, the doctor called and ordered our home health to come out and teach your caregiver how to dress the wound on your leg and about dealing with low blood sugars. Is this something you think will help you?"

"Well, sure honey, if the doctor thinks I need it," Mrs. Tellman said, "but only if Medicare pays for it."

"Yes, ma'am, it does." Katy pulled out the papers and showed the patient where to sign.

"Evelyn is my official power of attorney, dear, but I want to do as much for myself for as long as I can," Mrs. Tellman said as she signed her name multiple times on the forms. "You can't ever tell, I might outlive her and then Tripp will ship me off to the nursing home for sure."

"Please don't take everything my mother says to heart, Katy," Edna said, shaking her head. "She loves to pick and cut up." She reached over and patted the elderly lady's hand. "Mother, you know that nobody is ever going to send you to the nursing home. Tripp wants you around just as much as the rest of us do."

Mrs. Tellman handed back the signed papers. "Well, if that's true Evelyn, I've certainly misjudged things. But I know I'm going to kick the bucket way before anybody else in this room, so I'll just let you believe what you want and keep my mouth shut for appearance's sake."

"Would you like a glass of tea or coffee or maybe a Coke?" Mrs. Brown said as she stood up, her smile forced. "Mother has a little kitchenette right next door to her bedroom, and I would love to get you something."

"No, thank you, but I do need to look at all of Mrs. Tellman's medications if you would get them for me." Katy could see that the patient was embarrassing her daughter and tried to get the conversation back on a neutral topic. This kind of thing happened all the time in her line of work. Once the elderly reached a certain age, most of them tended to speak their mind whenever they pleased, often making the ones closest to them uncomfortable.

Mrs. Brown stepped into the bathroom adjoining the bedroom and quickly returned with three bottles. Katy took the bottles and typed in the prescriptions, a blood pressure pill, a fluid pill, and an antibiotic. "Okay, I have these. If you'll just show me where the rest are, I'll put them in the computer."

"Well, that's all I take, honey," Mrs. Tellman said, her toothy smile showing a pearly white set of dentures. "And that big horse pill is new, but I only have to take it a week. The doctor said last night that I have a urinary tract infection. I'm not sure he's right on that because I don't feel like I have one."

"You mean this is all the medications you take? There's no vitamins or sleeping pills or pain pills or anything else?" Katy asked.

"No, that's it." Mrs. Tellman's smile stretched even wider. "I take less medications than anybody under this roof. I don't believe in taking medicine unless there's just no other way around it, so if you plan on starting me on any, we're going to butt heads." She paused and turned to her daughter. "Speaking of butting heads, Evelyn, tell that little cleaning woman of yours that I don't want her snooping around in my rooms. Nelda doesn't mind picking up after me and you know I don't like people going through my stuff."

"Now, Mother, I've told you before, Laney only comes in here to clean your bathtub and toilet. She's not interested in anything else in here." Evelyn smiled apologetically to Katy. "Besides, we can talk about that later. Right now, we just need to help Katy get everything she needs to know so she can take care of you."

"She thinks I'm going to tell you something that would embarrass her." Mrs. Tellman snorted. "I'll be good, Evelyn, don't worry." She reached over and cupped her hand over her mouth, pretending to whisper to Katy but talking loud enough to make sure her daughter could hear. "As long as you don't try to make me take a bunch of dope, we'll do just fine. I don't believe in taking all that stuff."

"No, ma'am," Katy laughed, "you seem to be doing quite well with that philosophy. Most people your age have to take several medications, so you just caught me by surprise. It sure does make my job easier." Katy finished up the visit, teaching Nelda and Evelyn how to do the daily wound care and blood sugar checks.

"Another nurse will be by tomorrow to watch one of you perform the wound care." She looked from Evelyn to Nelda. "We just have to make sure you're doing everything correctly, but I don't think you'll have any problems." Katy smiled and looked at the three women. "Mrs. Tellman won't be needing home health very long."

"Won't you be the one coming?" Evelyn asked. "When I spoke to the nurse at the hospital last night, I told her to make sure that they sent you."

"I guess I can if that's what you want, but usually I just do the admission."

"I'd really appreciate it if you could come to see mother," Evelyn said, as she walked Katy back to her car. "We just never know what she's going to say or do, and with Jessa's unusual death so recent, we would all be more comfortable with you seeing her. Sometimes she gets the craziest ideas and I'm afraid that she might, well..." Evelyn stopped and looked at Katy as tears began to well up in her eyes. "Oh, dear, I'm sorry. It's been a rather hard week."

Katy set the computer bag on the back seat of her car and took Evelyn's hand. "I don't mind coming to see your mom at all. As a matter of fact, I think I'll enjoy the visits."

"Thank you so much." Evelyn smiled, wiping a tear away with the back of her hand. "That will give me much more peace of mind. I'm sure all of the nurses are very good at their jobs, but since I met you Monday, I just feel that I can trust you to not, well, let's just say I think you won't take mother too seriously." She stepped away from the car as Katy got in the front seat.

"Evelyn," Katy said, before she closed the car door, "I plan on praying for you and your family tonight when I say my prayers."

"Thank you, dear." Evelyn paused and stared at Katy. "That would be very much appreciated."

Katy thought about the visit as she drove toward her home. The elderly lady seemed to be completely oriented, just very outspoken. Evelyn had definitely been uncomfortable and seemed overly concerned about having other nurses in her home with her mother. She sighed as she turned the air conditioner on full blast. The day was heating up just like an oven. She turned the vent to blow the icy air directly into her face.

Maybe Evelyn was just a little sensitive because of Jessa's death. Having a family member murdered would probably make anybody cautious about having a bunch of strangers coming into their home. That made sense. Katy turned at the stop sign and headed toward the other side of town.

Chapter Thirteen

Katy snapped the laptop shut and pulled the lever on her recliner, moving it back to an upright position. She slowly rotated her head around on her shoulders. It had taken an hour to finish the new admission, and she was a little stiff from sitting still so long. She fixed herself a glass of tea, then rummaged in her purse for her phone and punched in the number.

"Deep South Florist. This is Misty. What can I do for you today?"

"Hey," Katy answered. "I was just checking in to see if you have found out anything about the cardless flowers."

"I meant to call you before lunch, but my counter girl called in sick," Misty said. "Her baby has the chickenpox and can't go to daycare so, it's just me and Momma, and you don't rush Momma, if you know what I mean."

"Aww, poor Brittney." Katy set her icy glass on the bar and wiped the moisture from her hand onto her pant leg. "Is it her two-year-old or the little one? I don't guess it matters because they'll both have the pox before it's over."

"I think it's the baby. Either way, I'm going to be down a counter person for a while, but yes, I did find out about the card," Misty said. "Momma said that Jake Finch, the high school football coach, came into the shop and ordered those flowers. He paid with cash and did not want a card."

"That sounds odd. Does that happen often?"

"No, never at a funeral. We've delivered some arrangements without cards to offices and a few to people's homes, but usually that's a husband or boyfriend surprising their mate on their anniversary or birthday or some other special occasion." Misty paused. "Sometimes it's not, and you can only guess what the flowers are for then, if you catch my meaning."

"Anyway," she continued, "Momma said she asked him if he meant he wanted a card with just his name, or the family's name with no words of condolences, and he kind of got irritated and said no card period. I had to laugh when Momma told me about it because she said he was just as rude off the football field as he was on the football field. Like Momma would know how he is on the football field."

"Well, he does have that reputation of being a smart mouth," Katy said. "Some of the girls in my Sunday school class have him for Mississippi History or PE, and they all say he's on the obnoxious side. Celeste's mother said that when he first came here, he got in trouble for cursing the players, but I guess he straightened that out. It's been four years, and he's still here."

"That's because we're still having winning seasons," Misty laughed. "These mommas might hate a potty mouth, but these daddies love to win. Anyway, he sent the flowers and put my momma in her place."

Jake Finch, Jake Finch. Something about Jake Finch is familiar, Katy thought. *What is it?* "So, what do you think it means?" she asked. "It seems a little shady to me."

"I've watched enough "Young and the Restless" back in the day to have my suspicions. I bet you a Burger Barn salad that he was fooling around with Jessa. You said that she was fooling around on Joe Phobs with somebody, why not him?"

"Because he has three kids and a wife and teaches school and is supposed to set a good example and, oh man!" Katy pulled in a deep breath. "I just remembered why his name is ringing bells in my head. I totally forgot something that happened on the day of Jessa's murder." She rubbed her forehead with the tip of her finger. "That Saturday when I was walking through the field to the stage, I passed Jessa's Mustang and guess who was snooping around it?"

"Jake Finch."

"No, but close, his wife, Laney," Katy exclaimed. "She tried to hide from me when she saw that I had noticed her, then acted like she had spilled her purse and was picking up her things, but she was doing something to Jessa's car and I completely forgot about it until just now."

"Maybe she found out that they were fooling around and was keying it. You know like that song by Carrie Underwood." Misty started to sing, "I dug my keys into the side of his something, something, something. Oh, you know the one."

"Yeah, I know which song you're talking about... maybe so. I didn't pay enough attention to what she was doing to even think about looking at Jessa's car, and then I forgot all about it when we found her body." Katy shook her head. "This whole week is turning into a "Young and the Restless" playbook."

"I know, right?" Misty puckered her lips. "So, what are you going to do next?"

"I guess I'll talk to Todd after church tonight. Maybe by then, he'll know something about Tubby Robinson." Katy filled Misty in on the discussion she had with Todd and John the night before. She didn't know if this was a lead, but it sure did sound suspicious to her. Hopefully, Todd would be willing to share what he'd found out about Tubby after she shared her information.

Katy pushed the red button ending their call and pulled out her yellow notepad and wrote down what she had learned. First, there was Evelyn Brown and her being overly cautious about letting anyone around her outspoken mother. That probably wasn't anything, but it was going on her list. If something strange happened later that related to the Browns, she wanted to have all the details on paper and not have to rely on her memory. Next, she added everything she'd found out from Misty about Jake Finch, and what she had forgotten about Laney Finch on the day Jessa's body had been found. That had to mean something.

Laney and Jake Finch had three young kids. Laney worked at the daycare in town next to the dentist's office. Katy wondered if that was the same daycare that Misty's counter girl, Brittney, sent her kids to. If so, then chicken pox would probably be in the school soon. Her Sunday school girls would let her know if that happened

Katy came out of the church doors smiling. She enjoyed the Wednesday night services. They would come in and have a devotional led by their pastor, then break up in their groups to pray. She had prayed for Joe Phobs and asked the other ladies to pray for him as well. They had agreed, and Katy felt better about his situation in jail, and his spiritual situation now that several people were praying for him.

She looked across the parking lot at Todd, talking to some of the older, silver-headed crowd who had him cornered. They were always interested in what was going on at the sheriff's office and would pick him for information. They also loved to joke with him about his love life and tried to set him up with any new woman they had discovered in the area. She stepped close enough to be within hearing distance of their conversation.

"Ladies, I assure you that you're all perfectly safe in your homes," Todd explained. "I'm pretty sure Jessa Williams' murder was an isolated incident."

"Now Todd, you make sure you take care of

yourself when you're out there looking for that killer." Maureen Case, a feisty widow in her seventies who had worked as a second-grade teacher for over forty years until she finally retired, reached up and patted Todd's cheek. "Do you wear a bullet-proof vest?"

"No, ma'am, Mrs. Case," Todd smiled, "but I don't think that's necessary. The only time I fire my gun is at the shooting range, and remember, this was not a shooting."

"Now you listen to me. There's always a first time for everything," Mrs. Hopper, one of the deacons' wives said, shaking her finger in his face. "And it would only take one bullet to do you in."

"Just because he didn't shoot that girl doesn't mean he won't shoot you." Mrs. Case bobbed her silver head up and down. "Especially if he finds out that you are hot on his trail. I think you should be wearing a bulletproof vest." She looked at the other ladies for support. They all chimed in their agreement at once, sounding a lot like a pack of hungry squawking hens.

Todd threw up his hands, holding off their well-meaning verbal attack. "Now ladies, I don't own a bulletproof vest and they're expensive. I don't think I'll be getting one anytime soon. I appreciate all of you looking out for me, but I promise that I'm very careful. I just need all of y'all to continue to pray for my safety. Besides, we already have a suspect behind bars."

The group began to break up just as Katy joined them. She could hear Mrs. Case talking to Mrs. Hopper as they were walking off. "Gloria, you need to have your husband talk to the deacons about the church buying a bulletproof vest and giving it to Todd. If we have money to buy new pots and pans for our kitchen, then we have money to save his life."

Katy smiled to herself as they walked out of earshot. They might have to do a bake sale and sell some spaghetti plates to come up with the money, but she was pretty sure that the golden girls class would be getting Todd that vest in the very near future.

"Whew, Aunt Katy. You just missed it. I feel like I've just gotten off the trial bench," Todd said, laying his hand over his heart. "Those ladies have quizzed me down. They won't let you dodge a question either. They hound you until they get a direct answer."

"I know," Katy chuckled, "I have been there. They used to pin me down about my home health patients. It has taken a few years, but they've finally decided that I'm not going to tell them anything. Every once in a while, Mrs. Case still tries to wear me down."

"Yeah, she's kind of the leader of the pack." Todd looked around to make sure no one could hear them talking. "I checked out what we discussed last night on Tubby Robinson, and it didn't pan out. He does smoke the right kind of cigarettes and lives right next door to Joe Phobs, but he has an alibi. After he witnessed the fight between Jessa and Joe, he came home and went to bed. His wife was with him the whole time and they drove through a gas station together right before midnight to get a Coke. He knows it was ten 'til midnight because the place closes at midnight and they were rushing to get there in time."

"I would've been surprised if he was the killer anyway," Katy said. "From what I've heard, I think he just likes to stay up on everybody's business. How is Joe doing?"

"I guess about as good as he can, sitting in a jail cell. Uncle John came by and talked with him this afternoon. I don't know what they talked about, but he seemed to be in a good mood when I left him his dinner tonight."

"John just went by to pray with him and let him know that he had our support and prayers. We wanted him to know that he's not in this alone. I'm glad it helped."

"You know, you have a good heart," Todd said. He wrapped a lanky arm around her shoulders. "I just never know what to expect from you, but I'm glad you're on my side."

"My heart could use a little more aerobic exercise every day, but I do try to keep it in the right place." Katy placed an arm playfully around her nephew's neck. "And while you seem to have a high opinion of me, I need to fill you in on a few things."

She told Todd about Laney Finch being around Jessa's car on the day the body was discovered and also about Jake Finch sending flowers to the funeral without a card. "Did Jessa's car have any kind of marking on it, like Laney had keyed it?" she asked.

"No, ma'am, it was fine." Todd shook his head. "It's locked up over behind the station. Jessa's cousin came by yesterday and asked when he could get it. We told him it'll have to stay where it's at until we've gone over it. I started that today but didn't get very far." He stroked the whiskers on his chin absentmindedly. "I had to go out to those apartments on Mars Circle to deal with a domestic dispute and that took all afternoon." He paused and lowered his voice to a whisper. "You reckon Coach and Jessa were fooling around?"

"Kind of sounds like it to me, but I don't want to assume anything." She patted Todd on the back.

"Poor boy, it sounds like they're working you into the ground."

"Nah, not really. Once we get caught up with all the details related to this murder, then I can have some breathing room again," he said. "There's just so much stuff we have to go through and so many people to talk to at the beginning. The sheriff's doing a lot of the questioning, but that leaves a lot of the other things to me. I don't mind though. I'm learning a bunch of new stuff."

"Did he question the Browns?"

"Oh yeah, did that early Sunday morning. Mr. Brown seemed to be taking it the hardest. Mrs. Brown was upset, but she held it together better."

"What about Tripp?" How's he doing?"

"He wasn't there when the sheriff questioned Mr. and Mrs. Brown," Todd answered. "They said he was out with some friends. He seemed alright when he stopped by yesterday. He was just irritated with us because he couldn't get the car."

"Do you know for sure how Jessa was related to the Browns?" Katy's forehead wrinkled as she looked at Todd. "I find that situation a little odd."

"I thought she was their niece, but I don't guess I know that for sure." Todd looked down at Katy and frowned. "That's just what I've kind of thought. Why? Do you know something that I don't?"

"Well, no, not really," Katy said. "I admitted Mrs. Brown's mother to home health today, and I just noticed that there were no pictures of Jessa anywhere. There were tons of pictures of different family members on the walls in the old lady's room, and not a single one of Jessa. Just seems odd to me."

"I guess that is strange. I'll talk to the sheriff tomorrow and nail their relationship down."

Katy left Todd and got in her car to go home. John had to work late, then came straight to church in his truck. She was glad he'd taken time to go by and talk to Joe Phobs. Maybe he would see why she didn't think he was the killer. She smiled. John was a deacon. She would give him a heads up about the bulletproof vest thing tonight, so when Mrs. Hopper's husband brought it up, he would be prepared.

Chapter Fourteen

Katy rubbed the sleep from her eyes as she breathed in the smell of coffee brewing and bacon frying. John frequently got up before her and cooked their breakfast. She took a quick shower and got dressed. By the time she reached the kitchen, John had set out two plates with bacon, fried eggs, grits, toast, and coffee. He would probably eat again at lunch, but when she had a big breakfast like this, she usually skipped the noon meal. Her eating habits needed some improvements, but she would save all those thoughts until January with the rest of her New Year's resolutions. They said the blessing. She added creamer to her coffee and dug into the huge meal.

"How did the visit go with Joe Phobs last

night? Todd told me you stopped by the jail, but I didn't get a chance to talk to you about it." She picked up the salt and added a few shakes to the grits. "I got too caught up in the bulletproof vest story and filling you in on Laney and Jake Finch."

"Poor fella. He said the only people who've come by to see him have been me, you, and that other woman from *The Wildcats*."

"Who?" Katy looked up from her egg, "Marissa Holmes?"

"Is she the blue-haired one?"

"Yep."

"Then she's the one." John raked his fork through the flesh of the fried egg. "He said she came by and told him that she was there for him, and if he needed a shoulder to cry on, hers was available."

"Hmmm. Well, I guess that was nice."

"I guess so. He didn't say much else about it. He mainly just needed somebody to listen to him talk." He paused to scoop up the bite of egg and dip it into the runny grits. "Poor guy. I think he really loved that woman. Not being able to go to the funeral or talk about the loss of his baby is rough on him."

"So, now do you see what I'm saying?" Katy asked. "I just don't think that man killed anybody."

"Yeah," John swallowed his bite of food. "I

can see where you have a hard time picturing him as the killer, but I'll be glad when they find out how that monkey wrench got in the back of his truck."

"I told you that the Tubby Robinson lead was a bust, didn't I?"

"Yeah. I asked Joe what he thought about Tubby and he said that Tubby was an alright guy, just a busybody."

"That seems to be the general consensus of everyone in town." Katy laughed. "Poor man. I wonder if he knows he's listed as one of the town gossips."

"Who knows, but he probably doesn't care. I imagine if he minded too much about what people thought about him, he wouldn't spend so much time nosing in other peoples' business. Of course, you and I seem to be doing an awful good job of snooping around in folks' business ourselves here lately too."

Katy leaned over and kissed him on the nose as she picked up their empty plates to load in the dishwasher. "But dear, we are snooping for a good cause. It seems like we might be the only hope Joe Phobs has for clearing his name."

"I sure hope not." John drained his coffee cup, then set it on her pile of dishes. "A semi-retired home health nurse and an engineer don't sound like too much hope for a guy falsely accused of murder."

"But we have people praying that this is going to work out," she said.

"That's true."

"So, don't write us off yet." Katy picked up her pile of dishes and walked to the sink. "Now I have to call and set up a time to see my patient and figure out when I'm going to buy groceries. If I don't get that done, we'll have to eat peanut butter sandwiches for supper."

"Do you have band practice tonight?"

"Oh yeah, I do, and I have that make-up party tomorrow night. I sure am busy to be semi-retired."

"That's what keeps you young and beautiful, honey." John wiggled his eyebrows and kissed her on the cheek as he headed out the back door. "See you tonight."

Katy pulled out the yellow notepad. She was beginning to think of it as the clue book. She added a note about Marissa Holmes visiting Joe Phobs. She now had several pages of notes, but she didn't feel like she had found any answers to all the questions. She sent up a prayer that God would help her find something that shed light on what had really happened to Jessa Williams.

The Pig was a little crowded, but Katy wheeled her car in a spot just a couple of spaces from the buggy return. Hopefully, she could get in and out in less than an hour. She dug through her purse, searching for her grocery list. Half of the time she forgot it at home, but today she'd remembered to put it back in her purse after taking inventory of the fridge and cabinets.

She picked through the buggies until she found one that steered easily and didn't squeak, then set out to the back of the store. She always shopped in the same order, starting with the canned goods and ending with the fresh produce. Occasionally, the store would decide to move stuff around, and she would spend an extra thirty minutes searching for what she needed. She read that stores did this on purpose, so customers would have to go all over the place and discover new things to buy. All it did was aggravate the daylights out of Katy. Luckily, today aisle four seemed to still have the canned vegetables and tomato sauce.

She pulled the items off shelves and marked them off her list with determination. She moved through canned goods, rice and noodles, and was turning the corner toward the breakfast aisle when an alluring and vaguely familiar scent caught her attention. The smell reminded her of spring flowers and the clean, crisp air after a shower, all at the same time. She followed the scent up the aisle like a coon dog on a trail. The heavenly aroma grew stronger as she made her way to the lone woman on the aisle who was bent over intently studying the different brands of breakfast pastries.

"Excuse me, ma'am. Do you mind telling me the name of the perfume you're wearing? That scent is gorgeous."

The woman jerked the name brand blueberry and the off-brand strawberry boxes to her chest as she sucked in a breath of air. She stood up completely straight, startled out of her sugary breakfast debate.

"Gracious, I didn't mean to scare you," Katy said, squinting her eyes as she looked at the woman's face. "Oh, hello Laney. I'm so sorry I startled you, but your perfume drew me over here like a moth to a flame. It's heavenly."

"That's okay, Mrs. Katy. Little Gunner is at Momma's with the chickenpox, and I'm trying to pick up a few things to keep him happy. I took off half a day from the daycare to get everything he needs so he'll be easier for her to deal with."

"I heard the chickenpox was going around. I hope he doesn't get a bad case."

"I just found a few bumps on his arms and body

this morning," Laney said, pointing her finger to the body parts she was describing. "I think it's too early to tell. I probably wouldn't have known they were chickenpox, but a kid at the daycare came down with them this week too, so I was kind of expecting it."

Laney lifted her wrist to her nose and sniffed. "I guess I have it on a little strong if you could smell it around the corner, but I love the smell too. It's called Heart's Desire. Jake started giving it to me when we began dating years ago, and it's all I've ever worn since then. He always gets me a new bottle for my birthday."

"I don't think it's too strong," Katy said, smiling. "I think it's wonderful. I love perfume, but I can't wear it while working and I forget to put it on half the time on the days I'm off."

"I'm glad you are enjoying mine," Laney smiled back. "Some people don't care for any perfume at all. I don't wear but a dab to work at the daycare. Nobody has complained about it yet and I've been there for a couple of years."

"Our agency has it in their policy that the field nurses cannot wear perfume." Katy glanced down at her watch. "Well, speaking of home health, I'd better get back to my shopping. I have to be at a patient's house after lunch."

She left Laney with her pop tarts and moved on

down the aisle to pick up a box of grits. That was the same perfume she had smelled on Jessa Williams. She was sure of it. Was Laney involved in Jessa's murder? She'd been snooping around Jessa's car that day. She hoped Laney had better sense than to kill a person over that puffed-up airbag coach.

Chapter Fifteen

"That's perfect, Mrs. Nelda. You've got this." Katy watched as the sitter put the final piece of paper tape on the gauze dressing.

"I sure do appreciate you writing out those instructions for us. I was so scared I'd mess this up, but it wasn't too bad with your steps written down for me to follow."

"That's just part of the job." Katy turned her attention to Mrs. Tellman while the sitter put up the wound care supplies and went to wash her hands.

"If the wound care gets too uncomfortable, remember that you can take a couple of regular strength Tylenol about thirty minutes before she starts to help ease the pain."

"Oh, it wasn't bad at all. Nelda has a real gentle touch. It would take a lot more than a scratch to make me pop a pill. I delivered Evelyn in my own bed with a little help from the doctor and not a drop of medicine." She rolled her eyes. "People just want to take a pill for everything nowadays. It's plumb ridiculous."

"You're definitely a trooper," Katy said. She patted the elderly lady's hand with genuine affection. "How are you doing with the antibiotics? Are they causing any nausea?"

"Not a bit. I'm taking one with my breakfast and the other with my cookies and milk at bedtime. I have Evelyn break those bad boys in half so I can swallow them, but that's the only problem we've run in to."

"That's great. You're truly blessed to have a family to care for you so well."

"Evelyn's a good girl. Now I wouldn't give you a plug nickel for that husband of hers and not much more for my grandson." She shook her head. "Part of that is my fault. He was such a cute little fellow. We just spoiled him rotten, but once you get to be a teenager, all that fit throwing and meanness needs to stop." She shrugged her shoulders and reached over and patted Katy's cheek. "That's enough bellyaching. I need to do like you said. I need to remember how blessed I am."

"That's okay." Katy smiled. "Sometimes we need to just talk about things that bother us. I don't mind listening."

"I imagine you hear all kinds of stuff from all kinds of people doing this job," Mrs. Tellman said as she reached down and smoothed the tape on her bandage.

"Yes, ma'am, I do. Sometimes it's entertaining and I enjoy my patients." Katy looked down at her laptop screen. "Let's see, all we have left to do is record your blood sugar. Did you remember to check it before you ate breakfast this morning?"

"We did, honey. I think it was seventy-eight, but ask Nelda when she gets back in here. I was watching the weatherman while she was checking it, so seventy-eight might be my blood sugar, or it might be the low temperature for the week."

"Okay," Katy chuckled. "I'll check. I just love your sense of humor."

"Oh, honey, you should have known me in my heyday. I was what my husband called 'a force to be reckoned with.'" She turned in her chair and pointed to the large portrait above her bed. "That's me and my husband, and of course little Evelyn at my feet. I was in my late twenties or maybe thirty there. There are some smaller pictures of me along that wall from when I was in my young twenties and teens. That's when I was at my best in some ways and my worst in other ways."

Katy walked over to the bedroom wall covered in pictures. They were different sizes and in an assortment of frames. She walked slowly down the wall, examining the photos, attempting to pick out the younger version of the elderly lady behind her. One black-and-white photo in an expensive-looking silver frame caught her attention. A very attractive young woman with long, black, curly hair was posed on the hood of a stretched out white car. She was propped on her elbows against the windshield of the vehicle and the way she was smiling made you think she was enjoying having her picture taken very much.

Katy turned to her patient, who was watching her intently. "Is that you on the enormous white car?"

"That's me," Mrs. Tellman said, her eyes twinkling. "I was eighteen and had the world by the tail."

"That's a big ole car," Katy said, turning back to the photo.

"That was a nineteen-forty-one Packard. Amos had just bought it. Cost him about eight hundred dollars, the shirt off his back and one pants leg." Mrs. Tellman's eyes gazed lovingly into the past. "It was his very first car, and we thought we were something."

"Amos was your husband?" Katy asked.

"For sixty years, bless his sweet, patient soul. He was the most easy-going man that ever walked this earth. He had to be to put up with me." She grabbed a tissue from the box in the side pouch of her recliner and blew her nose. Her eyes sparkled with the tears on her thin lashes. "He was too good for me."

Katy walked back to the chair and sat down. "You have a lot of lovely pictures. Sounds like you and your husband had a good life."

"We did," she nodded. "Not always easy, but good."

"Mrs. Tellman, can I ask you something?"

"Of course."

"I see all kinds of pictures of old and recent people on your wall, but I notice you don't have a single picture of Jessa Williams."

"No, I don't." Mrs. Tellman's tone suddenly turned sharp. "There's no reason why I should and plenty of reasons why I shouldn't."

"Mrs. Katy," Nelda said as she walked into the room, "did I hear you ask about her blood sugar? It was seventy-eight. I'm going to keep track of them in this little book." She handed Katy a small pink notebook. "I wrote down the date, the blood sugar results, and how much she ate. Mrs. Evelyn wants me to start making little notes about how she's doing every day so we can look back on them if we need to."

"That's a good idea. I kind of expected Mrs. Evelyn to be here today so I could check her off on the wound care too."

"She had to run down to the dealership." Nelda took the notebook back from Katy. "They are short a person now until someone is hired, and Tripp said they needed her help."

"I didn't realize she ever worked there," Katy said as she typed the blood sugar results into her computer. "That's where I get my car serviced and I've never seen her there."

"She hasn't in a long time," Nelda said. "She only does it now when they're in a big pinch, but she used to work there pretty often before Mrs. Tellman moved downstairs."

"Just go ahead and say it, Nelda," Mrs. Tellman snorted. "She used to work down there before her mother almost broke her neck on that ridiculous staircase. After that happened, they moved me downstairs and Evelyn wouldn't leave me alone anymore. It was the beginning of the end of my freedom."

"Now Mrs. Tellman, it's not that bad." Nelda patted Mrs. Tellman's shoulder. "Me and you get out and go for a ride whenever you want to if the weather permits. I don't think Mrs. Evelyn minds not having to work at the car place one bit either."

"No, Nelda, it's not bad at all." Mrs. Tellman reached up and put her hand on top of the sitter's. "I'm just mourning the loss of my youth today. Anyway, Katy, I don't imagine Evelyn will be doing any wound care. She's pretty squeamish."

"That's right," Nelda said, "I'm going to be doing it all. I think I have got it down, so you don't worry about that place on her leg."

"Oh, I'm sure it's going to heal just fine," Katy said. "I don't imagine I'll be seeing y'all very long."

She wrapped up the visit and was soon back home, pulling out her clue book. What had Mrs. Tellman meant about not having a reason to put Jessa's picture on her wall? If she could be alone with her for just a few minutes, she could probably find out how Jessa was related to the Browns and why they were keeping her relationship hush-hush. Nelda had stepped in like a protective setting hen and steered the conversation away from that topic just when it was getting interesting.

Chapter Sixteen

“You sound like you’re straining a little when we get to the chorus, Sarah,” Katy said, as the band finished the first verse of “Wayfaring Stranger.” “Why don’t we drop down a key and try it again in D minor?”

“That will probably work,” Sarah said. “It’s a little high in some parts.”

The band started the song again on the second verse, but this time in the lower key which worked well, and the different harmonies blended in perfectly.

“Let’s call it a night,” Vickie said, laying down her mandolin. “Mrs. Katy, you look kind of tired.”

“I feel a little worn around the edges,” Katy

said with a yawn. "Y'all don't forget that the party is still on for tomorrow night."

"We won't forget," Sarah said. "You just go home and get some rest."

"You were right about the chickenpox spreading through the daycare," Misty said, as they walked to their cars. "Brittney came by to pick up her check today and said over half of the kids were absent. There are already a few cases at the elementary."

"I'm not a bit surprised." Katy clicked her car fob and opened her back door. "I saw Laney Finch at the grocery store today, and one of her kids is home with it. I imagine his older siblings who are in school will have it by the weekend. It's probably that way with a lot of the daycare kids."

"I had the chickenpox at six. Have you had them?" Misty asked.

"Yeah." Katy nodded. "I was three. I don't remember them, but I had them."

"Aren't you glad that you don't have to deal with those problems anymore? Poor Brittney looked kind of frazzled."

"So did Laney, but at least she smelled nice." Katy propped against the door of her car. "By the way, have you ever heard of a perfume called Heart's Desire? It smells wonderful."

"Heart's Desire?" Misty let out a low whistle.

"That's the good stuff. You're going to give over a hundred bucks for a little bottle of that."

"Oh well, that's too rich for my blood," Katy said, shrugging her shoulders. "No wonder I've only smelled it on a couple of people."

"It does smell nice," Misty agreed. "I've sampled it at the Macey's counter when Momma and I were Christmas shopping at the mall in Baton Rouge. I'd love to have a bottle, but it's like wearing liquid gold."

"Laney Finch says she's been wearing it ever since Coach Finch bought her a bottle when they first met. She must not mind spending the money on it." Katy puckered her lips. "That seems kind of odd, though. She doesn't look like the type that would blow a lot of money on something so frivolous."

"You never know, Katy." Misty swatted at a June bug trying to land in her hair. "Everybody seems to have their own ideas about what's important and what's worth splurging on. Mike's about as tight as a person can get, but he only wears these expensive socks that I have to buy online because the seams don't bother his toes. He'll wear the same pair of khakis until there's a hole in the seat, or I sneak around and throw them away, but he makes sure he has plenty of them seamless socks."

"I guess you're right," Katy said. "We only eat Blue Plate mayonnaise and Heinz Ketchup. Heaven knows they cost a little more, but John can tell when I buy anything else and acts like he's having to eat prison food if his sandwich is made with any other brands."

"That's probably how Laney is about the perfume. That might be her one big splurge. You know they can't afford too many over the top things on their salaries. Who else wears it?"

"I'm pretty sure I smelled it on Jessa Williams Saturday night under the flatbed," Katy said. "I remember thinking how bizarre it was that she looked so morbid but smelled so good."

"Now I can see her spending that kind of money on perfume. She always dressed over the top and seemed to have plenty of money. She probably didn't think a thing about spending big bucks on something for herself."

"No, I imagine she didn't." Katy swatted at a lone mosquito. "I'll have to settle for some other kind, you know, like they sell at Friends Pharmacy or The Pig."

"Hey, don't be knocking the drug store perfume," Misty grinned. "That's where I get my stuff, and I smell alright."

"Girl, I think I have something in my bathroom from the Dollar Tree," Katy laughed. "And it's about five years old. Friends Pharmacy will be up-town for me. I just never put the stuff on. I do like it on other people though."

"Well, maybe Santa will treat you right this year. You never know."

"That's true." Katy raised her hand to her mouth, stifling a yawn. "Are you ready for the party tomorrow night?"

"Sure am." Misty drew in air through her nose and pursed her lips, stopping her own yawn. "I have the house clean and I bought the snacks. All I have to do is throw everything together and wait for y'all to show up. Have you thought about what you want to ask Emma?"

"Not really. I'd like to find out anything she might know about the relationship between Jessa and all the band members. I'm pretty certain there was bad blood between Jessa and Marissa. Of course, I want to see if they really did have a knockdown drag-out fight last Friday night."

"I bet she can tell us too. I'm going to try to figure out a way to bring up Jessa's love life. I'm curious about her and Coach Finch." Misty smirked, "It's going to be funny if we try to pick this girl's bones for information and she doesn't know a thing."

"I know," Katy said, stretching her tired eyes.

"Do you think she'll be able to help us find anything out?"

"Don't you worry none. I feel certain she knows a lot about what was going on with Jessa and everybody else in that band. Shoot, probably everybody else in the town. I promise you, Mike is always complaining about how she comes in with new tales to tell about everybody in Skeeterville."

"I hope you're right," Katy said. "The one thing I would like to know is how Jessa is related to the Browns. It's probably not important at all, but the Browns seem to be very careful about keeping it hush-hush."

"What about some of your connections at Dr. Roberts' office?" Misty asked. "Couldn't they tell you who Jessa was related to? Don't you have to put that information on your medical record or something?"

"Girl, you're a genius." I never even thought about that. I'll go by and talk to Trudy Mae. I bet she'll know something. She might not tell me anything because of HIPPA laws and the patient's right to privacy, but she might. Jessa's dead, and if it will help catch a killer, she might be willing to let me look at her records."

"See you tomorrow night." Misty slapped her arm as she slid into her car. "Unless these mosquitos eat me alive first."

Katy climbed in her car. Hopefully, by this time tomorrow night, she'd have an idea of who Jessa Williams really was and why somebody wanted her dead.

❧

"I hope you don't mind me stopping by," Todd said as Katy walked into her kitchen. He held up a white paper bag with grease stains on the bottom. "I brought supper."

"You know I don't mind." Katy took the bag and smiled. "It saved John from a peanut butter and jelly sandwich and me from a bowl of cornflakes. What's in the bag?"

"He got me and him hamburgers and fries." John held up a partially eaten burger. "I don't know what's in there for you."

"It's one of those salads you always order. I told them to add extra avocado too, so it should be all green and slimy just like you like it."

"Well, aren't you just the sweetest thing?" Katy peered in the bag. "To what do we owe this honor?"

"I want to go over the day we found the body with you again. I need to make sure I have all the details about Laney Finch."

"Okay." Katy walked over to the sink and

156

washed her hands then returned to the bar. "Did you find something in Jessa's car that's making you more interested in Laney?"

"Yes, ma'am, I did. There was a note in Jessa's glove compartment from Laney threatening her. Here, I took a picture of it." Todd pulled out his phone and handed it to Katy to read.

Jessa,

I know who you are and what you are doing. I could care less, but I do care about my husband and my marriage. Leave him alone or I will make you sorry. I will do whatever it takes to keep my family together. DO NOT SEE HIM AGAIN.

"It's not signed," Katy said. "How do you know it's from Laney?" She began picking off all the unwanted croutons and tomatoes from her salad.

"Well, the main reason is that her fingerprints are all over it. Then there's the fact that you saw her snooping around the car the day we found Jessa's body." Todd's lips curled down as he watched Katy take her salad apart. He shivered and looked away. "That's why I want to make sure we've got all the details straight. I think the sheriff's going to bring her in to talk to her, but he wants to make sure that he has all of his ducks in a row before we pick her up."

"I wrote down everything about that night in my notebook. Hold on a minute." Katy ran to her bedroom and grabbed her clue book and returned to the kitchen. "The part about Laney is a couple of pages over because I didn't remember seeing her there until later when Misty told me that Coach Finch had sent flowers to the funeral without a card."

"Look on the next page too." Katy slid the notebook over to Todd. "I ran into Laney this morning at the grocery store and I recognized her perfume as the same one that I smelled on Jessa's body that night."

Todd flipped through the yellow note pad scanning the information. "My word, Aunt Katy, you have more information on this case than the entire police department."

"I told you she's been very preoccupied with this," John said, looking over Todd's shoulder at the pages of notes.

"I'm not preoccupied. I'm just trying to keep an innocent guy from going to jail and trying to stop a murderer from going free. Besides, a lot of that stuff is just things I think could have happened."

She turned the notebook back towards herself and flipped to the page about Coach Finch. "See here? I jotted down that Coach Finch could have been having an affair with Jessa and that's why he sent the flowers. I don't know that for sure, but it looks like that's probably what was going on."

Todd picked up his phone and started taking pictures of each page. "I'm going to take all of this stuff to the office and upload it on the computer. Is there anything else you want to add to these notes? It looks like you've been pretty thorough with all of your details."

"I've been wondering this whole time how Jessa is kin to the Browns." Katy flipped the notebook to the last page where she had recorded her thoughts about Mrs. Tellman's conversation and Jessa's relationship to the Browns. "The Browns have been very vague about how they're related to her, and even a little secretive. I was planning on trying to talk to Trudy Mae at Dr. Roberts' office tomorrow and see if she knew who Jessa had listed as next of kin. It may not be important, but I think that may have something to do with the secret Laney is talking about."

"Do you think she was some kind of con artist or criminal or something?" Todd studied the information written on the page. "That sounds kind of farfetched."

"I don't know, but I know the Browns don't seem to be very proud of her branch of the family tree."

"Leave talking to Trudy Mae to me. I don't think she can tell you anything about Jessa's private medical files, anyway. I'll get in touch with her in the morning, but for now, I have to go through all this and see how it connects to Laney and Coach Finch."

"Do you think one of them might have killed her?"

"Who knows? But it will give Sheriff Reid another suspect to talk to besides Joe Phobs."

"I stopped by to see him again on my way home from work," John said, popping a fry in his mouth. "He seemed to be in pretty good spirits today."

"I'm so glad you're reaching out to him." Katy reached over and picked up his last fry and dipped it in her salad dressing. "He needs friends."

"He said his momma came by today and that Marissa Holmes had been back too." The corners of John's mouth turned down as he watched Katy put the fry in her mouth. He didn't like salad dressing and hated to see a fry wasted that way. "Between you and me, I think she might be a little sweet on him."

"I think so too, Uncle John," Todd answered. "I heard her talking to him and she offered her shoulder to cry on and basically everything else, if you know what I mean."

Katy finished her salad while John walked Todd to his vehicle. *What have Laney and Coach Finch gotten in to? Laney's about five foot two like me, but she probably doesn't weight one hundred ten pounds. She's not strong enough to lift the monkey wrench over her head and bring it down with enough force to kill Jessa,* Katy thought. *But even if she could, there's no way she could have moved the body from that shed to under the flatbed trailer. Coach Finch, on the other hand, could have done both without any trouble. Did he and Laney do this to-gether? Had Laney truly done whatever she needed to do to keep her family together?* She hoped and prayed she was wrong about this.

Chapter Seventeen

Katy stared at the red numbers on the alarm clock next to the bed... finally five o'clock. Flipping and flopping all night, checking the time about every hour made for a long restless night. She usually didn't get up quite this early, but staying in the bed flouncing like a beached whale certainly wasn't restful. She eased out of bed and slipped on her fuzzy robe and slippers the girls had gotten her a few years ago for her birthday. She had to admit, they were some of her favorite pieces of clothing. The slippers would have to be replaced soon, but hopefully they would hold up through one more winter.

She added way more creamer than the one teaspoon suggestion on the back of the bottle to her morning coffee. The sugar and the caffeine made a terrible combination for starting the day, but oh well. She sipped from her green Yoda mug and walked to the recliner to wait for the two poisons to kick in.

Hopefully, Todd would be able to make heads or tails from her notes. At least he was taking her seriously now. If she had to guess at a scenario based on what she knew, she would think that this murder was about some kind of love triangle thing between Jessa Williams, Coach Finch, Laney Finch and Joe Phobs.

Laney said in her note that she knew what Jessa was doing and didn't care. That sounded like Jessa had something going on other than her love life that she didn't want people to know about. She got up from her chair to retrieve her clue book from her nightstand before the caffeine rush kicked in. Reading over all her notes before turning out the light last night was probably why she didn't get any sleep.

Katy listened as John's baritone voice sang "Victory in Jesus" from the shower. *Would I do whatever I had to do to keep my family together? Thank God I've never had to ask myself that question. John's my best friend and honest as the day is long. He drives me crazy sometimes, but he would never betray my trust.* She walked back up the hall, studying her clue book. *Laney Finch has been backed into a corner by her cheating husband and she has come out fighting. I wonder if the sheriff decided to bring her in last night, or will that happen today? There's no telling how that's going to play out, but I hope Todd won't keep me in the dark.*

Katy texted Todd to find out if they had brought in Laney Finch, but he didn't answer. He was either too busy to talk, did not want to let her know what was going on, or couldn't talk because he was in a place where he could be overheard. Any of those three were possible. There were other ways to get information besides Todd. She picked up her cell phone and called Misty.

"Deep South Florist, this is Misty. How can I help you today?"

"I was just checking to see if you needed me to do anything last minute for you before the make-up thing tonight."

"Nope, not a thing. Just show up ready to get gorgeous and give ole Emma the once over. I think it's gonna be fun."

"I hope so. I need some fun. I didn't sleep worth a toot last night. I bet I looked at that clock fifteen times before I finally got up at five."

"I hate nights like that. Why don't you go take a nap? Or do you have to see a patient today?"

"No, I'm free today since I saw Mrs. Tellman yesterday."

"Well, go close your blinds and get you a little snooze," Misty said, sympathy ringing in her voice. "I know I would if I was home. I'm having to pull six days a week until Brittney returns, but she said she'd be back on Monday. I'll be getting my life back soon."

"That's good. I'm glad her little one is doing better." Katy looked down at her hardwood floors. "I can't take a nap. I'm too worked up. Besides, I mop the kitchen on Fridays, and I haven't done that yet."

"You and that cleaning schedule. Mop the kitchen on Friday, scrub the toilets on Tuesday. I could stick to that for about half a day at my house. I feel accomplished if we have supper at the same time for two days in a row. Anyway, what are you so worked up about? You are my laid-back friend. You're not supposed to be getting worked up."

"Well, I am," Katy sighed. "Have you heard anything interesting or unusual about the Finches?"

"I don't guess I would call it unusual, but when Brittney called to say she would be back at work on Monday, she told me that the daycare was short-handed today because Laney hadn't shown up for work. She said they were scrounging to get help since she was a no-show and were glad her kid would be out one more day."

"That pretty much tells me what I want to know," Katy said. "Maybe now I can focus on my own life and get a few things done."

"Why are you worried about Laney Finch's work habits? Have you found out something about her and Coach Finch and his affair?"

"I'm afraid so." Katy walked through her kitchen and looked out the backdoor at their hound dog flopped out across the grass. "Todd found a note in Jessa's car from Laney threatening Jessa because she was fooling around with her husband. It didn't say that exactly, but I'm pretty sure that's what it meant. Todd said they might bring her in for questioning, and I was just trying to find out if he had followed through on that. I guess since she didn't show up for work, she must be at the sheriff's office."

"Aww. That's so sad. Those three little boys of theirs will have to deal with all the gossip that this is going to cause."

"I know. Jessa's death seems to be affecting a lot of people who are just innocent bystanders. I'll be glad when all of this mess is over with."

"Me too, girl, me too."

Katy hung up the phone and walked to the laundry room to gather up the mopping supplies. She looked in the cabinet for the floor cleaner, but the Pine Sol bottle was empty. She didn't feel like running to the dollar store, so she just mixed up some vinegar and dishwashing liquid in the hot water. Now her kitchen would smell like Easter eggs for the rest of the day. She pulled up some mopping music on her phone and got to work. About fifteen minutes later, the phone started buzzing as she poured the dirty mob water down the drain.

"Hey Todd."

"Hey Aunt Katy. I'm sorry I didn't answer your text, but it's been crazy around here."

"I heard Laney didn't show up for work this morning. I guess y'all decided to bring her in to question her, huh?"

"No, we didn't. We planned on it, but when we got out to their house nobody was there. We checked with her mother. Laney never picked up her sick kid from her house yesterday. She said Coach Finch had dropped the other two off with her after school and was going to see if he could find Laney."

"My word." Katy tiptoed across the wet ceramic tile kitchen floor and pulled a barstool from the counter to sit on. "Did he find her?"

"Not yet. We talked to him at the school a while ago. He said they had a big fight yesterday morning, and he thought she'd just gone off somewhere to blow off steam and would be back."

"Has she ever done anything like that before? I mean, leaving her kids and all?"

"No, not according to Coach Finch, but he said they went at it yesterday morning. He didn't call the cops to report her missing because he feels like she'll be back sometime today."

"Well, ain't that something?"

"Yes, ma'am. I figure everybody in town will know since we went to the school to talk to the coach and everybody saw us. I just wanted to tell you so you can add it to your book."

"I sure will." Katy smiled. "I appreciate you letting me know."

"Well, you seem to have a better handle on what's going on than any of these guys around here. As long as you keep it on the down-low, the sheriff says I can let you know what we find out. Just keep us in your loop about anything you learn."

"You know I will, Todd. I just want to figure this thing out and get back to our boring little town."

"Same here."

Chapter Eighteen

Katy attended church with Laney's mother, Amanda Carson, and felt that she needed to do something for the woman to let her know she was thinking about her. She left the mop bucket in the middle of the kitchen floor, grabbed her purse and hopped in her car. She would do what every other good southern Christian woman did for her neighbor in need. She would take her food. At The Pig, she grabbed some ham and cheese from the deli, and then rushed around the store picking up the rest of the things for sandwiches along with snacks for the three boys. She threw in a box of ice cream sandwiches, chocolate chip cookies, and juice boxes. The kids were probably allowed to have sugar since Laney was stocking up on pop tarts yesterday. Laney sure hadn't seemed like a woman who was planning on abandoning her family.

The Carson's home was a couple of miles outside of town. Two little boys and a big yellow lab came bounding around the corner of the single-wide trailer at breakneck speed as Katy pulled into their drive. She waved to the young group as she headed to the front door. They quickly disappeared around the back and Katy could hear them calling to their grandmother that they had company. Their footsteps sounded a lot like a herd of wild buffalo coming up from the back of the trailer. A Few seconds later the same two boys opened the front door before she even had a chance to knock.

"Well, hello there, boys. Is your grandmother home?"

The older of the two, who appeared to be around eight or nine, was the spokesperson for the group. "She's changing Gunner's diaper, but she'll be right here."

The younger brother, who was probably six, interrupted. "Do you want to come in? Granny won't care. What you got in those bags?"

"You don't invite strangers into the house, Tyler," the older brother said, slapping his sibling on the back of the head. "Just be quiet."

The younger boy turned and gave his older brother a look that promised retaliation at a later date, then ran out of sight.

"My name's Katy Cross and I go to church with your granny," Katy said, sticking her hand out to the boy. "It looks like you're doing an excellent job of watching out for your younger brothers."

The boy puffed out his chest and shook Katy's hand. "Daddy said I'm supposed to help keep them out of trouble. That's why I can't invite you in."

"Oh, I understand," Katy said, smiling at the child's inner struggle between minding his father and being polite. "I have the same rules at home with my grandkids. No strangers are allowed in my house either."

The corners of the little boy's mouth turned up in relief. Before the conversation could progress any further, a heavy-set woman with bleached blond hair stepped up to the door with a fat little fellow that Katy assumed was Gunner perched on her right hip. The pale blue sweatpants splattered with bath water, and a tee-shirt with skinny Elvis on the front, spoke volumes of how the woman had spent her afternoon. The shirt had seen better days.

"Come on in, Katy," the woman said, a smile crinkling the corners of her eyes. "It's crazy around here, so just part through the toys and have a seat."

Katy stepped into the trailer that, despite Amanda's description, was extremely clean with only a pile of brightly colored mega blocks piled in front of the entertainment center which took up an entire wall. "I'm sorry to just drop in unannounced like this, but when I heard," Katy paused to look down at the young boy who was keenly listening to what the women were saying. "When I heard about what was going on, I decided to come over and see what I could do to help." She placed the three plastic bags of groceries on the couch beside her as she sat down. "I brought some stuff for sandwiches and some snacks for the boys."

"That was mighty thoughtful of you. You're just like your momma, always helping out." Amanda looked down at the little boy who was watching them intently. "Grey, take those bags to the kitchen for me, sweetie."

"Ice cream sandwiches are in one of the bags that will need to go in your freezer, Grey," Katy said, handing the two heavier bags to the older boy. She passed the third bag to the six-year-old who had reappeared quietly behind his big brother.

Both boys squealed in unison and looked at their grandmother. "You can each have one and go in the backyard to eat it." She smiled and tousled the hair of the older grandson who was standing within her reach. "Now be careful and don't let the dog take them from you."

Both boys took the bags to the kitchen and soon disappeared out the back door. Amanda set the toddler on the floor and he immediately busied himself with the mega blocks.

"I guess you heard that Laney didn't come home yesterday." Amanda sighed, sitting on the love seat across from Katy. "I'm sure it's probably all over Skeeterville by now."

"I found out just a while ago. I came over to see if you needed some help with the boys, or if I can help in any other way."

"Oh, the boys are fine. They stay over here as much as they stay home, so that isn't anything out of the ordinary for them. Laney works at that day-care through the week and then cleans houses on the weekends. I practically raise them anyway." Amanda reached across to an end table and grabbed a tissue from the half-empty box. "I'm trying not to cry in front of the boys, but Grey knows something's up. Laney's never just taken off and not told anybody where she was going."

Katy watched, trying to think of a tactful way to approach her suspicions about Laney's marriage. "Has anything unusual happened lately that might have caused her to act this way?"

"Something happened, it's not that unusual, but

it happened." Amanda blew her nose and wiped her eyes. "Her and Jake are always fighting, and I mean every blooming day. He has a roaming eye and Laney caught him stepping out on her about two years ago. She left him for a couple of months. He talked her into taking him back and that's how they ended up with little Gunner, bless his sweet little heart. Laney thought another baby would solve their problems."

Katy got up from the couch and stepped over to the love seat and sat down. "It's so hard to watch our kids go through things that hurt them." She put her arms around Amanda and gave her a hug.

"And it's even harder to watch them just keep making the same mistakes over and over again," Amanda said.

"Is Jake cheating again? Is that why you think Laney's left?"

"About three weeks ago, she came over here fit to be tied. She'd found a credit card statement with a purchase for that ridiculously expensive perfume that Jake buys her. The only problem was, he had given her a bottle a couple of months ago, on her birthday. She searched their house and couldn't find this second bottle, so she began to get suspicious."

"I've smelled her perfume. It's very nice."

"I guess it's alright, but I wish I'd never heard of it. If they'd quit trying to live above their means, Laney wouldn't have to work six and seven days a week." Amanda looked down at her hands to the tissue she had shredded to pieces. "I'm making a mess."

Katy took the tissue from the distressed woman's hands and placed it in the wastebasket by the chair. "Amanda, you don't have to talk about this if you don't want to."

"No, I need to talk to somebody over the age of eight who is basically sane." Amanda wiped a strand of hair away from her tired eyes and let out a sigh. "Anyway, when she couldn't find the perfume, she searched Jake's truck and found another cell phone. It was full of pictures and text messages from that woman that got killed last week. You know the one, she worked at the auto place."

"Yeah, I know the one."

"She confronted Jake, and he's been fooling around with that woman for over four months."

"Amanda, I'm so sorry. I know Laney must've been crushed."

"She was. She was just about crazy for the next couple of weeks and then that girl ended up dead." Amanda looked at Katy and a sob caught in her throat. "Oh Katy, I feel so guilty for even thinking this, but at first I thought that Laney might have been the one that killed that woman."

Katy patted her hand and waited while she grabbed another tissue. "But she didn't kill her, did she?"

"No, she was home with the kids. Grey told me that their daddy had been gone that night and his momma let all three of the boys sleep in the bed with her." Amanda pulled her hand through her hair and then fell back on the love seat, defeated. "I feel terrible about suspecting my own child that way, but I feel even worse because I'm glad that she doesn't have to worry about that other woman anymore. I didn't want the woman dead, but since she is, at least she can't wreck my daughter's family. I'm a terrible person."

Katy took both of Amanda's hands in hers. "You're not a terrible person. You're just trying to cope in a hard situation."

"You think so? Do you really think so?"

"Yes, I really do. You must be stressed to the hilt."

"Oh, Katy, I am. And now Laney is just gone. It's so funny. After that woman was dead she calmed down and seemed alright, but then yesterday morning she came over here all worked up again, saying that Jake was spineless and that she was going to take care of things so that she wouldn't have to deal with this again."

"What do you think she meant?"

"I thought she had finally decided to leave him for good. I still think maybe that's what she meant, but I just don't believe that she would run off and leave her children without telling anybody where she's going."

"Do you think she possibly went out of town to see a lawyer and had a wreck or something?"

"I don't know, but something just ain't right and Jake is about as useless as a tit on a bore hog."

Katy stood up from the love seat. "Let me fix you some tea, or Coke, or water, or something, Amanda. What do you want?"

"There's bottled water in the fridge. Get us both one if you don't mind."

"Now tell me, what can I do to help you?" Katy asked as she returned with the water. "Can I wash dishes, or take the boys with me for a little while and give you a break, or fix your supper? Just tell me and I'll do it."

"You're too sweet." Amanda reached down to the floor and scooped up the baby, who was drooling contentedly on a bright yellow mega block. "I need to keep the boys with me. They keep me busy and I must keep my head on straight while they're around, so I'm better off with them here. Johnnie will be in from offshore on Sunday, so if I can just hang on until then, I'll be fine."

"Well, can I pray with you?"

"Oh Katy, would you? That would help me more than anything."

Katy sat by the woman and they both bowed their heads together. Amanda hugged the child to her chest, finding comfort in his closeness as well as the words of Katy's prayer. Katy prayed for peace for Amanda and her family. She prayed for a safe and quick return of Laney, and that she could work out her problems with Jake so that their family could heal. When she was finished, she visited a while longer and listened as Amanda bragged about her only three grandsons.

Jake had left school early, after the police came by to question him, and brought the older two children over for Amanda to care for. Katy didn't know where he was now but had decided to not ask. Amanda had too much to deal with right now. She didn't need to be reminded of her wayward son-in-law.

Katy left Amanda's house around three. When she got home, she added a few more details to her clue book. Laney had an alibi and didn't kill Jessa, but what about Jake? Amanda said he had not been home with his family. Something else had stirred up Laney yesterday, causing her to leave town or at least not go home. Laney and Coach Finch were apparently in financial distress, with Laney working two jobs.

Katy wrote everything down and closed her notebook. She had a lot to do before she could get ready for the party at Misty's house, and she was running way behind.

Chapter Nineteen

Katy's worry of having a hard time getting Emma Robinson to tell what she knew about Jessa Williams and her friends had been a very ignorant assumption. She and Emma were the first two to arrive at Misty's house. Emma was quickly transforming the formal dining room into a home spa area to expound on the wonders of her beauty enhancement products. After Misty's introduction, Emma immediately dominated the conversation. Luckily, she wanted to talk about the murder herself and was more than willing to share all her facts along with a slew of theories about what had happened. Thankfully, the girl couldn't keep her thoughts to herself. All Katy had to do was act interested and Emma talked nonstop.

"Mrs. Katy, you found poor Jessa's body?" Emma's Barbie doll eyes stretched wide with animation. "I would have just died myself if that would've been me looking under that ole hay trailer and seeing a corpse and all. Did it just freak you out?"

"No," Katy said, smiling politely, "not exactly. It was unsettling, though."

"Well, I should say so. And you know, we saw her just the night before, right at that very spot." Emma waved her perfectly manicured hand in the air. "Poor little ole Todd had to come and ask Tubby for an alibi since they found those cigarettes behind the shed or somewhere around there. Thank the good Lord Tubby could clear his name, or that would have looked bad. Poor, sweet Tubby. He couldn't kill a mosquito, but we don't blame Todd for doing his job. Heaven knows somebody's got to figure out what's going on."

"So, you don't think Joe Phobs killed Jessa?" Katy asked.

"Oh, no, ma'am. He left the stage area that night before we did and when we came home, we could hear Hank Jr just a blaring from his trailer." She squatted down and grabbed a bundle of pamphlets from her tote box, then stood back up. "We have to drive right past his place to get to ours, and I feel pretty sure he was in there drinking. Every time he drinks, he plays Hank so loud that everybody around there wants to come over and throttle him. Tubby stopped by and beat on his door and told him to turn it down before somebody called the cops."

"Did you and Tubby see him in his trailer that night?"

"No," Emma said slowly, tapping her fake nail against her cheek. She glanced around the table and then reached back in her bag for more supplies. "No, not exactly. Tubby just beat on the door and yelled at him, and the music got turned down. If his neighbor hadn't still been in the nursing home, she would've done called the cops. That's what happened last time."

This woman was amazing. She had covered Misty's glossy oak dining table with a black satin cloth and placed little mirrors around for each woman, along with disposable makeup brushes and trays to use during the party. She talked about the events of the past week at lightning-fast speed, barely slowing down long enough to take a breath while simultaneously preparing Misty's dining table for her event. Katy wondered if Emma could do that thing where you pat your head while rubbing circles on your belly at the same time. She could probably talk while doing just about anything, from the looks of things.

"Did Tubby tell Todd about stopping by Joe's trailer?" Katy looked around the table, trying to sound casual. "I mean, while he was there giving his alibi."

"You know, I don't know," Emma answered. "I'll ask him and find out."

"If he didn't, he probably should, huh?" Katy looked across the table and made eye contact with Emma.

"It wouldn't hurt, I guess." Emma fiddled with the collar of her silk blouse. "Joe needs all the help he can get to establish his own alibi right now. I'll talk to Tubby tonight and find out." She blew out a deep sigh. "Poor Joe. That Jessa was just using him from the start, and he never even knew it. Some guys are just too good looking for their own good."

"Oh, really?" Katy sat down at one of the make-up stations and watched as Emma continued to set up her staging area for the presentation.

"Yes, ma'am. Everybody knows the only reason that Jessa was seeing him was to make Marissa mad. Jessa didn't care about Joe at all."

"No, I didn't know that." Katy glanced behind Emma at Misty, who was silently doing a little victory dance. She quickly cut her eyes back to Emma. "Did Marissa and Joe have a history?"

"Well, no, ma'am, not really. Marissa was sweet on Joe during high school. Then when she and her old man got that divorce a couple of years ago, she started trying to get to know Joe again. She invited him to all *The Wildcats* practices and was always looking for places to bump into him. If he would've given her even an ounce of encouragement, she would've been stuck on his arm like a seed tick. But he just never saw her as nothing but a friend."

"And you think that Jessa was seeing Joe to aggravate Marissa?" Katy kept her eyes focused on Emma as she spoke, not daring to look up at Misty again.

"Everybody thought that, not just me. You see, Mrs. Katy, before Jessa moved here Marissa started *The Wildcats* and would have these band practices every Saturday night out at her pawpaw's barn. It was kind of like a little party. We would go out and sit around and listen to them play. We would talk and just hang out and have a good ole time. But then Jessa showed up and things changed. At first, she was all sugary sweet to Marissa. She even started booking *The Wildcats* some gigs, like at the county fair and Christmas in the Park last year. Marissa thought that was great because she didn't know how to do any of that stuff. She just liked to get together and sing."

"That's how *The Moonlighters* are. We just enjoy the music."

"Exactly. That's how it used to be for us, too. Anyway, after a while, Marissa found out that Jessa was telling everybody that it was her band and how she was trying to get them rednecks whipped into decent performers and stuff like that. Marissa confronted Jessa about it, and Jessa just blew her off. But right after that, Jessa started paying attention to Joe and in about a month, she had him wrapped around her finger."

"And you think she did it to spite Marissa?"

"You bet I do." Emma's head bobbed up and down. "She was sending her a signal that she would take whatever she wanted from her, and there wasn't nothing Marissa could do about it. It worked too because Marissa just shut up and started letting Jessa do whatever she wanted with the band."

"Wow, I bet the practices weren't quite as fun after that."

"No, ma'am they weren't. Half the time Jessa was fighting with Joe or ordering everybody around and telling us not to get too loud because we were messing up their practice. All of us that just showed up to listen pretty much quit going."

Their conversation ended as the rest of the party started showing up. Hopefully, Katy could get Emma alone again to ask her about Marissa's scratches and missing fingernail. For now, though,

Emma's focus had completely turned to selling makeup and skincare.

Katy moved around the table and took a spot between Misty and her sister-in-law Pickle. She felt like a fish out of water between these two women. She had never seen either woman without their hair and make-up being perfect and their clothes looking like something from an Ann Taylor ad. The thing that Katy didn't understand was that they both acted like this was no big deal. They just seemed to naturally get up and make themselves look this way every day before they stepped out of their homes. She, on the other hand, struggled to make sure her top didn't have a grease stain across her chest and there was no bacon stuck between her teeth. It seemed she was always running for the door, desperately trying to reach her destination before she was considered rudely late.

She couldn't blame this character flaw on her upbringing. Her mother was born and bred in the south and had taken great pains to teach her the importance of proper grooming and a good appearance. For some reason, it just didn't stick. She was always clean and fairly neat, that wasn't the problem. She just never looked put together or finished. She didn't have that sixth sense that other southern ladies seemed to have about wearing discreet amounts of animal prints only and never wearing tee-shirts as dress clothes. Maybe she could start some kind of support group for women with this character flaw. She glanced around the room at the other partygoers. It didn't look like any of these ladies would qualify as a member.

Katy made it through the evening without any complaints. She started to enjoy the party when she stopped comparing herself to the other ladies at the table. As she listened to the comments being made, she soon realized that everyone there seemed to have their own set of insecurities about their looks.

They cleaned all their makeup off with the cleanser Emma provided on cotton balls, then toned, then applied a serum, then applied a moisturizer and finally a primer.

"I hate to admit this," Katy sighed as she rubbed a cotton ball over her face for what seemed like the fiftieth time, "but I never do any of this stuff. I use Dove soap and Jergens lotion on my face and that's about it."

"Now, Mrs. Katy, don't brag." Sarah laughed from across the table as she applied the eye make-up remover to her black-lined lids and lashes. "We all can't be born with natural good looks. Some of us have to help it along a little."

Katy smiled as the girl began to remove the mascara from her lashes, leaving a black ring around her eye socket that resembled a raccoon's mask. "Sarah, I'll pay you ten bucks for that sweet comment later. You know I'm not bragging. I just don't have the inner drive to fool with all this stuff every day." She looked over at Emma apologetically. "Not that I shouldn't, mind you. My skin feels great and all. I just tend to get distracted with breakfast and making the bed and stuff in the morning."

"Unfortunately, there are a lot of women like you." Emma's bright pink smile remained stretched across her pearly white teeth and her cheerleader tone never faltered. "They spend all their time on other things for their family, but very little time on themselves." She leaned across the table and handed Katy a tiny plastic pouch containing a make-up sample labeled Ivory Dream. "Lucky for you, I don't see too many signs of neglect on your skin yet, but they're coming. You can only let yourself go for so long before it catches up with you."

Katy took the make-up sample from Emma and waited for the instructions on how to apply it correctly, which she was sure would follow. "Well, good grief. I wouldn't say I'm neglecting myself. I do bathe and use lotion."

"You just don't take time to pamper and polish yourself the way a lot of women do." Misty patted

Katy's leg under the table. "I certainly don't see it as neglect. I think it's more of an evidence of your giving spirit. You do for others instead of doing for yourself."

Emma's smile never faltered, but an edge of irritation began to ease into her voice as she handed Misty a pouch labeled honey beige. "Of course, that's not a bad thing. I'm just of the mindset that when we look our best, then we feel our best, and this enables us to be a better person. Taking a few extra minutes every day to take care of your skin can take years off your appearance. Who doesn't want that?"

"You may be right, Emma." Katy glanced around the table at the other ladies who were nodding their approval. She felt like she was in some kind of political debate over foreign policy instead of a girl's night out. Emma took the skincare business seriously. "Obviously most women follow these simple guidelines to care for their appearance and I'm just out of the loop." She rubbed her cheek with her fingertips. "I have to admit that my face hasn't felt this soft in probably years."

Emma smiled, pleased that her opponent had conceded the debate. "See what I mean? And you can feel this way every day if you want to. It's just up to you."

She continued around the table with the make-up samples. Each sample was delivered with an approving compliment of how glowing the customer's skin now looked and how dewy fresh each person appeared after just one use of this wonderful line of skincare.

"Don't drink the Kool-aid just yet," Misty said, leaning over so only Katy could hear. "Wait until the price list is handed out for these little gems before you sing their praises too loudly. This is one of the most expensive brands of make-up in the independent beauty market."

Katy nodded at her friend and began to massage the make-up pouch to blend the color beads as Emma was instructing from her post at the end of the table. "I feel like I'm being interrogated for the Kennedy assassination or something. This is serious stuff."

Misty held up her little mirror and pretended to be looking at the skin around her eyes. "Just keep your mouth shut and do what you're told and if you're lucky, we may just make it out of here alive."

Katy put her hand over her mouth and tried not to laugh out loud but was not successful. She coughed a couple of times to try to cover up her rudeness.

"Are you okay, Mrs. Katy?" Emma waited for

her to quiet down. "I can get you a sip of water if you need it."

"No, that's okay. I'm fine now. You continue with what you were saying. I'm learning a lot."

Misty rolled her eyes at Katy from behind her mirror. "Kiss up."

"Hush Misty," Katy whispered, desperately trying to suppress the urge to giggle. "We're going to make her mad and she won't answer our questions later."

"Oh yeah, I forgot the mission there for a minute. Sorry, boss."

Katy smiled one more time then turned her attention back to Emma and her lecture on the importance of upward strokes when applying foundation.

Chapter Twenty

Eventually, the presentation ended, and everyone oohed and aahed at how gorgeous they'd all become. Emma shamelessly took credit for everyone's transformation and assured them that it was in their best interest to obtain this flawless look daily. No price could be placed on fabulous skincare, but unfortunately, her company did have to pay for the all-natural products and these expenses had to be passed on to the customers. She assured them that they were getting products equal to those used by the professionals who did the makeup for the stars and supermodels at a fraction of the cost.

She passed out a glossy pamphlet to each lady with pictures of women of all ages scattered throughout the pages. They each had beautifully airbrushed complexions and had given a written testimony of how using About Face make-up and skin care had turned their lives around and placed them on the path to freedom. On the back page, in small print, was the price list.

Katy put on her reading glasses and almost laid an egg. "Seventy-five dollars for a tube of eye cream that's the size of a pack of chewing gum?"

"I warned you." Misty's eyes sparkled as she pretended to study the pamphlet. "Look, you need this laser in a bottle. It takes ten years off your forehead in just ten applications and it is only one hundred seventy-five bucks."

Katy frowned at her friend, then continued down the price list. She found something called cooling spritz for thirty-five dollars. That seemed to be the cheapest thing on the list, and she quickly placed her order. She was flabbergasted as the women around her bought product after product and pulled out their cards to pay for bills reaching two and three hundred dollars. She knew for a fact that the younger girls in her band had incomes that she would not consider affluent, but they didn't seem at all concerned about the amount of money they were spending.

After the orders were placed, Emma began gathering her gear and passing out samples of some of the high-end products to everyone. Katy busied herself by helping Misty and Pickle prepare and serve the snacks.

After a lot of snacking, laughing, and talking, the party started to wind down. Misty, always the perfect hostess, was escorting everyone to the door, so Katy began picking up the dishes from the dining table, giving her a good excuse to remain in the room with Emma.

"You're very good at this, Emma. Do you make a pretty good income with these parties?"

"I do okay, but I wish I had more time to spend on it. My goal is to make enough to quit my bank job, but that's down the road a year or two."

"Wow, I didn't even know that was possible. This has been a completely new experience for me."

"You mean to tell me you've never been to a skin care party before?" Emma got a little glint in her eye that Katy could not exactly understand. "Well, Mrs. Katy, you need to book a party for sure. You probably have tons of friends who would just love the benefits of my product."

Katy seriously doubted that, but she didn't want to just shoot Emma down before she could steer her in the direction she needed the conversation to go. "I may, I'm not sure about it though. Misty took me to the nail salon for the first time a few days ago, and I have to admit that your friend Marissa really impressed me with my new nails and the eyebrow wax.”

“Yeah, Marissa knows her stuff. I’ve tried to get her to start selling About Face, but she says she doesn’t have time because of work and the band and stuff. She could make a fortune just selling to the people who come in to get their nails done.”

“I need to go back to see her again next week to get my nails touched up.” Katy glanced at her hands as she placed the few remaining homemade chocolate chunk cookies in a zip-lock bag. “I hope those scratches on her neck have healed. Things get infected so easily nowadays.” She glanced to see if Emma would take the bait.

“They’re okay. I saw her yesterday and the scabs are already peeling off. I told her to put antibiotic ointment on them. You never know what people have under their fingernails.”

“Oh, did somebody scratch her?” Katy cleared her throat with a cough. “I wasn’t sure how she got them, but you’re right. Scratches from fingernails can turn nasty quickly, even if they’re not very deep.”

“Well,” Emma glanced at Katy for just a moment with a look of indecision. “Not a lot of people know this, but Marissa got into a little tussle with Jessa last Friday night after everybody left. After Joe left and the crowd had thinned down, Marissa jumped on Jessa for being so hateful to Joe when he obviously didn't deserve it."

"Oh, really?" Katy continued to slowly cover the spinach dip with plastic. "I hadn't heard that."

"It was just me and Tubby there when it happened, and she asked us to keep it to ourselves. I shouldn't be telling you, I guess. But I've already let the cat out of the bag, so I might as well finish it. They went at it for about three seconds, but Jessa got the upper hand really quick. Marissa realized pretty fast that she had bitten off more than she could chew."

"Is that how she lost her nail?"

"You don't miss anything, Mrs. Katy. I bet you're one good nurse." She wiped a cookie crumb from the corner of the table onto the floor. "Yeah, that's when it happened. She pushed Jessa real hard. I think it surprised her when Jessa didn't fall down. Jessa stumbled back, but I don't think this was her first catfight. She jumped on Marissa and pinned her against the shed like she was a rag doll. Marissa got in one good scratch, but that was about all the fighting she did."

"Wow," Katy said, raising her eyebrows. "That night was a lot more interesting than any of us had suspected."

"Aww, it wasn't much. Jessa just told Marissa

that she was running things and... lets see, I believe her words were, 'You're becoming more trouble than you're worth. Don't make me get rough.' That might not be exactly right, but it was something like that."

"Did Marissa leave after that?"

"Yeah, she ripped and cussed all the way to her car, but she didn't get close enough to start anything again. I think she knew she was no match for Jessa. After she left, we were right behind her. Me and Tubby don't go in for all that fighting and stuff. We just want to hear good music and laugh and talk. If I was caught fighting like that, poor Tubby would just die."

Katy lifted her tray now full of leftovers and balanced it on her hip. She looked around for something else to add to it so she could continue the conversation. "I'm the same way, Emma. I hate fussing and I don't know what I would do if two grown women started fighting in front of me." She wiped a few crumbs that were on the edge of the table into a napkin. "Uh Emma, did you tell Todd any of this?"

Emma stopped stuffing the unused make-up samples into the shiny gold zipper bag. "Marissa asked me not to Mrs. Katy. I haven't told a soul. Todd didn't ask me anything about Marissa, so I didn't mention it. Do you think I could get in trouble?"

"I'm not sure. I don't know a lot about the law, but I would imagine that the sheriff would think this is important. He might think you are withholding evidence. I'm not sure about it, but I wouldn't take any chances."

"Oh, my word." Emma began to pick up her products and throw them into the tote at a much faster pace. "Tubby told me to tell Todd what happened, but I didn't because I didn't want to be involved. Oh man, I've got to go. I need to talk to Tubby and see if I can get in touch with the sheriff, or Todd, or somebody. I mean, Marissa is my friend, but I ain't going to jail for nobody."

Katy set down her tray and began helping Emma place all her different make-up articles in the tote box at her feet. Before, Emma had wrapped each little mirror in a small piece of gold felt. Now she just raked them all into the box helter-skelter. She was upset.

"Emma, just go to them and tell them what happened," Katy said, taking Emma's hand. "Tell them what you told me about not wanting to get involved. You haven't done anything wrong. I'm sure it'll be okay."

Emma stopped and suddenly reached over and hugged Katy. "I'm so glad you were here. I've been worried about this since last week, but I didn't have anybody to talk to about it except Tubby." Tears began to form in the young woman's perfectly lined eyes. "I have to try to keep up a respectable appearance so people will invite me into their homes. If this gets out and people think I was somehow involved, I won't get any more sales."

"Look, Emma, if you do the right thing and tell the police, everyone will respect you. Some people will talk, but some people are going to talk no matter what's going on. You just need to give this to God and weather the storm."

Emma sniffed and began to wipe the bleeding mascara from the corners of her eyes with a tissue. "This stuff is supposed to be waterproof. I'm gonna have to quit telling people its tear-proof." She looked at Katy and smiled. "Thank you, Mrs. Katy. I'm going home and calling Todd. You and Tubby are right."

"I'll pray for you tonight, Emma." Katy patted her hand one more time. "God will take care of you if you'll let him, you know."

"Yes, ma'am, I know." Emma put the lid on the tote box. "Me and Tubby were both raised in church, and we plan on starting back one day before we have kids and all. We just haven't made time for it lately."

"Aren't you glad that God hasn't put off watching after you until you have kids?"

"You're right. I need to do better. Maybe God has been kicking me in the pants. I might just call my momma when I get home too. She will roll over and die when I tell her me and Tubby might go to church Sunday."

Katy finished cleaning the table off and helped Misty with the dishes before she left. She checked her phone once she got in her car and noticed she had two missed calls. One from Magnolia Home Health and one from Trudy Mae, the nurse at Dr. Roberts' office. She would return their calls when she got home.

Chapter Twenty-One

John was waiting when Katy got home, a glass of iced tea for her, and a cup of coffee for him. His eyes crinkled with amusement as he reached for another chocolate chunk cookie, "You're telling me that you paid thirty-five dollars for a bottle of water to spray on your face?"

"It sounds pretty ridiculous when you say it like that." Katy took a sip of her tea. "But yeah, I guess I did." She raised one eyebrow and stared at her husband. "You go ahead and laugh, but the party was a success. Emma Robinson was just a well of information. At first, I didn't care for her. She seemed kind of pushy and superficial, but I think she's just trying to look professional or something so she can sell that high-dollar make-up."

"Honey, don't be dogging on the woman's make-up. You're looking more and more like a combination of Dolly Parton and Reba McIntire every day."

"Oh please, give me a break," she said, rolling her eyes. "If I bought everything she put on my face tonight, I would have spent around three hundred dollars. I wouldn't have bought the spritz stuff if I hadn't been trying to get some information from the poor girl." She stood and took his empty coffee cup. "Don't get me wrong, it's good stuff, but I just don't have that kind of money to invest in my face."

"Three hundred dollars does sound a bit pricey to me," John said, following her into the kitchen eating the last bite of his cookie. "I guess if you think you need it, I can sell the four-wheeler or the riding lawnmower. We can probably get enough for one of them to set you up in beauty stuff for a few years."

Katy laughed as she put their dishes in the dishwasher. "Well, if you think it's absolutely necessary, I'll give her a call. I'm sure she'll fix me up." She paused, looking over her shoulder and batting her eyelashes. "I'm happy with the old me, but I'll do anything for you, dear."

"Don't do it on my account." John draped his arm around her shoulders as they walked down the hall to the bedroom. "You know I don't go in for all that make-up stuff. Some people like their cake with a lot of frosting. Not me, I'm a sponge cake and an angel food cake kind of guy."

"So, what are you saying, I have a face like a sponge?"

John laughed and pulled his wife into a comfortable hug. "No, dear wife of mine, I'm saying you have the face of an angel. Now go wash all of that junk off so we can get into bed."

Chapter Twenty-Two

When Katy returned her phone calls after leaving the skin care party, she learned that Trudy Mae's mother was out of the nursing home and would be admitted the next morning. She ran by the office that morning to pick up the paperwork and was surprised to hear from the office clerk that her new admission was Joe Phobs' next-door neighbor. That explained why no one was home to hear him blaring Hank Jr. the night of the murder. Mrs. Simmons, Trudy Mae's mother, was still at the nursing home that night having rehab. *If the old lady had just been home, she probably could have cleared Joe of the murder charge,* Katy thought. *Oh well. No need to ponder what could have been.*

At five after eight, a black Tahoe pulled up in the trailer park next to Katy's civic with Trudy Mae behind the wheel. Trudy Mae always came across as larger than life, and today was no exception. Her broad shoulders and full figure were covered in a hot pink scrub top with turquoise kittens plastered from front to back. Luckily, the scrub pants were just plain turquoise without any further felines for distraction. Dr. Roberts' dress code wasn't strict. Of course, Trudy Mae had been working there so long that Dr. Roberts probably could have cared less what she wore. She ran his office like a naval base, even if she did dress like a psychedelic battleship.

Trudy Mae hopped out of her vehicle and waved at Katy to come on over. She disappeared around the other side of the SUV to help her elderly mother out of the car. Katy wasn't sure what she expected Trudy Mae's mother to look like, but it was not the petite, well-groomed woman she saw slowly stepping from the passenger's side of the Tahoe. While Trudy Mae was around five foot ten and what people politely called pleasingly plump, her mother was about five foot two and looked like she could use a biscuit or two.

"Yes, girl, this is my mother, and no, I'm not adopted," Trudy Mae laughed.

Katy quickly closed her mouth and tried to put

on a polite smile. "Uh, I'm sorry, Trudy Mae. I guess I was expecting you two to uh, favor a little more."

"Honey, don't worry about it," she said, waving her hand in the air swatting away Katy's apology. She grabbed her mother's walker from the back seat and placed it in front of the elderly lady to support her as she guided her to the front steps. "I look like my daddy's people. I passed Momma up when I was twelve years old."

"Now honey don't you let Tru mess with you none," Mrs. Simmons said, looking over her shoulder at Katy. "She might have gotten taller and a little plumper than me, but I spanked that young' uns behind until she was eighteen." She looked at her daughter and grinned. "I guess I could still give her a lick or two if she needed it."

Trudy Mae smiled down lovingly at her petite little mother. "You sure could, Momma, if I was a mind to show out."

Katy watched from behind as Trudy Mae slowly helped her mother up each of the three steps leading to the covered deck connected to the front of her trailer. They made it as far as one of the four rocking chairs that were lined up across the front before Mrs. Simmons refused to go any further.

"I think I want to just sit out here a while. I

haven't been able to sit outside in over a month and it'll be too hot in a couple of hours to stand it out here, even in the shade." She eased herself into the rocker and waited for the other two ladies to follow suit.

"Will it be okay if we do her signing up out here?" Trudy Mae looked at Katy apologetically. "She's been cooped up in that nursing home for quite a while."

"Of course it's okay." Katy smiled and sat in the chair next to her patient. "I have everything I need with me to assess you. I'll have to look at your bathroom and stuff before I leave, but I have at least an hour's worth of paperwork that we can go over right here to get us started."

Trudy Mae sat down on the other side of her mother and patted her hand. "See Momma, I told you Katy was easy to deal with." She leaned over in front of her mother toward Katy. "She's been worried sick that she was going to get some hard-nosed nurse that would give her a rough time in her own home. I promised her I would make sure that she liked you before she signed any papers."

"Well, did I pass inspection?" Katy laughed. She watched as the little woman tried without success to place a hand over her daughter's mouth as she was speaking.

"Yes, honey," Mrs. Simmons answered sheepishly, "you passed." She quickly placed her hands back in her lap. "I'm fixin' to find a belt just as soon as you're gone though and tear that girl's tail up. I ain't had a secret to myself since she was four years old."

Trudy Mae leaned in and bear-hugged her mother and kissed her on the cheek. "Aww Momma, you know you love me too much for all that child abuse."

"You might as well get started, honey," Mrs. Simmons smiled. "This one will keep you talking nonsense all day long."

About an hour later, Katy wrote down the ninth and final medication Trudy Mae retrieved from the suitcase. "It's so nice when a family member is a medical person who is familiar with home health," she said, smiling. "It keeps me from worrying whether my patient is being taken care of between visits when I know her caregiver is competent and reliable."

Mrs. Simmons reached her softly wrinkled hand up and patted her daughter's cheek. "She may dress like somebody that ain't got good sense, but she knows how to take care of her momma."

"Gee, thanks, Mom. I love you too." Trudy Mae stood up and reached under her mother's elbow to help her stand. "Alright, young lady. It's getting close to ninety degrees in the shade. I believe it's time we take this party inside."

"Tru," Mrs. Simmons said, refusing to budge, "you take Katy and go on in. Y'all look at my bathroom and all that stuff, then come back and get me. I just want a few more minutes before I go in. I know once I get inside, I won't be able to come back out until you get off this evening."

"Is that okay with you, Katy? I should be able to answer any questions you have."

"That should be fine. I watched her walk and climb the stairs, but if I need to ask her anything about the living quarters, I can just run back out here."

"Everything should be spruced up and ready to go." Trudy Mae began unlocking the front door. "I had Laney come over a couple of days ago and change the sheets and clean out the fridge so it would be ready for her."

"Is Laney Finch the person who cleans your mother's trailer?" Katy asked, her tone suddenly serious.

"Yeah, that's right." Trudy Mae turned to look at Katy. "She's been cleaning Momma's house for about six months. She always does a nice job. Why, is something wrong?"

"Trudy Mae, Laney Finch has been missing for two days. When did you talk to her?"

"Well, I called her Tuesday night to let her know that I needed her to come to check out Momma's trailer on Wednesday when she got off her day job. I left the key at the front desk at work and she picked it up early that morning." She stuck the key in the door lock and shook her head. "I sure didn't know the woman was missing."

"My word, Momma," Trudy Mae said, opening the front door of the trailer, "your light bill's gonna be three hundred dollars if the air has been running this cold the whole time you've been gone. What's it set on, fifty?"

"Tru, you know I'm cold natured." Mrs. Simmons gawked from her rocker a few feet away. "I keep the air on about eighty. The only one who turns it down is you when you come over for a visit. The first thing I do after you leave is go turn my air back up. You know good and well I haven't turned that thermostat down."

"Well, you could hang meat in here. Must have been Laney. Come on in Katy and have a look around." As Katy walked past, Trudy Mae whispered, "and tell me about Laney Finch missing. What in the world is going on in this town? People getting killed and other folks missing. My word."

"Momma's room is at the end of the hall there, Katy," Trudy Mae said in a normal tone, as she flipped on the light switch. "You go on to her room and start looking around while I find that thermostat. We're gonna have to leave the doors open and let it warm up about twenty degrees before I'll be able to coax Momma in. Ain't nobody got time for all this nonsense today. I got to get to work after lunch."

Trudy Mae continued to grumble to herself as she went to the left through the living room and kitchen while Katy went the opposite direction down the hall to Mrs. Simmons' bedroom and connecting bathroom. The hall and doors seemed to be wide enough for the patient to get her walker through without increasing her risk of falling, so that was good.

She opened the door to the bedroom and received another blast of cold air while feeling along the inside wall for the light switch. A mini blind and a pale-yellow curtain covered a lone window. The scant amount of sunlight coming through the window drew her eye as she flipped the switch, causing a sudden flood of bright, white light. Katy's eyes took a couple of seconds to adjust to the sudden change from the dark hallway. The room looked clean and orderly until she turned her gaze to the floor. Short beige carpet went from one wall to the other and a small green throw rug lay beside the bed. Laney Finch's body was sprawled out across the floor with her head and shoulders on the rug.

Chapter Twenty-Three

Laney's face was turned away from view. "Laney," Katy shouted. She did not get an answer and immediately dropped to her knees and rolled the woman on her back to check for a pulse. There was none.

"Trudy Mae, call nine-one-one!" She removed her face shield from her bag and gave a couple of rescue breaths. "Trudy Mae, get in here!" Katy was positive the woman had been dead a while. She felt stiff. She tilted her head back with a lot of difficulty to give rescue breathing. "Trudy Mae!"

"I'm coming girl, what the..." Trudy Mae stopped in the doorway and put her hand over her mouth. She had dialed nine-one-one while running down the hall. When she reached the doorway and saw why Katy was screaming, she immediately requested an ambulance and the police.

"Look, lady, I got to get off the phone and help with this CPR. Yes, ma'am, I'll just lay the phone down, but I gotta go." She dropped to her knees beside Katy and began to assist with two-man CPR. "Lord, girl, this is Laney." She gave two rescue breaths as Katy pumped on the young woman's chest. "Look at that girl's eyes. They're fixed. She's either with Jesus or the devil, but we ain't gonna bring her back. She's been gone a while."

Katy kept pumping. "I know, but I didn't know what else to do. I'm sure she's a full code, and we're nurses. I had to do something."

Trudy Mae gave more rescue breaths. "I know, I know. Well, keep pumping one more round, and then we'll switch. That ambulance will be here in a minute."

They continued working on the ice-cold body for what seemed like hours but was only a few minutes. They traded positions, and Trudy Mae was doing compressions when the ambulance finally arrived.

The younger paramedic placed leads on Laney's chest while the older man asked questions and examined her pupils. The defibrillator showed no rhythm and they immediately called the code.

"Have the police and coroner been notified?" he asked.

Katy looked at Trudy Mae, who remembered she still had nine-one-one on her cell phone. "Oh yeah, I asked them to send the police when I told them I needed an ambulance. I guess they're on their way." She picked up her phone and talked to the dispatcher, then continued. "They should be here any second."

The paramedics disconnected the leads from the electrodes on Laney's chest and began gathering up their equipment. "Ladies, if you don't mind, the older paramedic said, taking out his clipboard, "we're going to step into the other room to write all this down. There's nothing more we can do here except turn this over to the coroner."

"I hate to leave you in here by yourself," Trudy Mae said, looking at Katy, "but I need to check on Momma. I've got to call Helen and have her come take her to my house. Thank you, Lord, that she decided to stay on the front porch. God was sure looking out for her this morning."

When Trudy Mae left, Katy decided to look around. If things worked the same way they did with Jenna, she would be asked to leave as soon as the sheriff and the coroner arrived. Of course, they had rolled Laney's body over for CPR and probably messed up some evidence, but that couldn't be helped.

She stood directly over Laney's body and began assessing her just as she would a patient. Laney was wearing make-up, and nothing was smeared. She didn't see any bruises on her head or face. She leaned in and looked closer at her neck. When she had tilted her chin into position to initiate CPR, she noticed that Laney's neck was swollen and discolored. There was dark purple bruising on either side of her trachea, and the very front of her neck was black with bruises. She'd never seen a strangulation victim before. She placed her hands in the air as if grabbing someone around the neck. Yep, the thumbs would crush the windpipe if the person had adequate hand strength and grabbed you from the front. Katy dropped her hands to her side as she thought about what a horrible thing had probably happened to the young woman lying in front of her.

She continued the assessment, moving to the arms and chest. They had cracked ribs while attempting to perform life-sustaining measures, so there was no way to tell whether the woman had received any injuries from her attacker in this area. There was no bruising or discoloration on her chest. The CPR had been hard to do, but Katy thought that was probably because rigor mortis was already setting up. It was possible that Laney had been laying on Mrs. Simmons's bedroom floor for two days. How awful.

She continued downward, examining one hand and then the other, not finding anything unusual. The only other thing she could see that was the least bit odd was that Laney was barefoot. She looked under the bed and around the room and bathroom but didn't see any shoes that would fit her. Mrs. Simmons had a closet full of size fives, but Laney looked to be at least a seven. Where were her shoes?

She stepped into the hall and let the paramedics know that she was stepping outside. The sweltering heat of the front porch was a welcomed reminder of how a normal Mississippi day was supposed to feel. Trudy Mae's elderly mother was still sitting in her rocker, patiently waiting for more details about what was going on inside her home. Katy walked over and sat back in the rocking chair she had occupied just a few minutes before. Mrs. Simmons placed a frail arm around Katy's shoulder and gave her a much-needed hug.

"Honey, you're as pale as a ghost and cold as a frog."

"Oh, I'm alright Mrs. Simmons," Katy said, smiling weakly, embarrassed that the shock of what she had just witnessed was so obvious to her supposedly feeble patient. "I just need to sit a minute to collect my thoughts."

"Tru said that sweet young girl is dead in my bedroom. Is that so?"

"Yes, ma'am," Katy sighed, trying to hold back the tears. "I'm afraid so. It's Laney Finch."

Mrs. Simmons leaned back in the rocker and stared at the pine trees in the field across the road from the trailer park. "Dear Lord, I hope nothing in my home caused her accident. If she tripped and fell over something I left on the floor and hit her head, I just wouldn't be able to stand it."

Poor lady. Trudy Mae must have decided not to tell her mother that Laney had been strangled, if she had even noticed this herself. Well, Katy wasn't going to let that cat out of the bag. Trudy Mae would tell her mother what she wanted her to know.

"I don't know exactly what went on in your bedroom," Katy said, as she leaned over and squeezed her shoulder, "but I'm positive that you are not to blame in any way."

"I guess you would be able to tell," Mrs. Simmons said, her voice dripping with sadness, "being a nurse and all."

"Yes, ma'am, I can. I promise you that her death was not caused by anything in your home." Both ladies turned their heads toward the road in unison as the distant sound of sirens grew louder and louder.

"Mama, I called Helen," Trudy Mae said, stepping into view from around the corner of her SUV. "She's coming to get you and take you out to the house. You're going to stay with me and Hank for a while."

"Alright Tru. If you think that's best."

Trudy Mae looked back at her mother with surprise. "What, no argument? This is a first."

Mrs. Simmons drew her boney shoulders back and narrowed her eyes. "Tru, I know you're trying to use that smart mouth of yours to get my mind off what happened. You know I love you for that too. You also know good and well that your momma ain't sleeping in the same room where you just found a dead body. I don't care how sweet the person was while she was alive and breathing, I ain't staying there tonight. I ain't completely senile."

"Now that's the momma I know and love." Trudy Mae chuckled. "Not that woman who said whatever you think best. I don't know who that woman is."

Two police cars with sirens blaring turned into the trailer park's gravel drive. The ladies cringed as the car in the rear nearly clipped the corner of the fancy metal sign that the park owner was so proud of. They all coughed and began waving their arms around, trying to clear the dust as the vehicles descended upon the previously peaceful scene.

Mrs. Simmons coughed again and shouted over the siren that the rear car's driver had failed to silence. "Well, if anybody wasn't wondering what was going on before, I bet they're about to bust a seam to find out now."

Katy and Trudy Mae both tried to keep from grinning at Mrs. Simmons' logic. She was completely right, of course, but Katy doubted the sheriff or Todd would appreciate that observation.

Trudy Mae took Todd and the sheriff into the trailer where the EMS workers were waiting with Laney Finch's body. Katy decided to sit with Mrs. Simmons and wait for Helen, one of Trudy Mae's younger sisters.

"I sure have missed sitting on this porch every morning talking to the good Lord about all my business," Mrs. Simmons said, as Katy sat down beside her. "Now don't get me wrong. Those folks at the nursing home were good to me, but you know what Dorothy said."

Katy thought for a second. She knew Trudy Mae didn't have a sister named Dorothy, but they were a big family. Dorothy could be a niece. "No, ma'am, I don't guess I've ever met Dorothy."

"Well," Mrs. Simmons turned her head slowly

from the tree line and winked at Katy. "Dorothy says there's no place like home."

"Oh, that Dorothy." Katy laughed and rolled her eyes. "Well, I guess I might have figured that out if I only had a brain."

"This has been a rough morning for you and my Tru." Mrs. Simmons leaned her head back against her chair and closed her eyes. "I imagine you both need a little time to just sit and take everything in."

Katy followed Mrs. Simmons's example and leaned back against her rocking chair, relaxing as a small bead of sweat trickled between her shoulder blades and ran down her spine. "You're a very wise woman. I know you're laughing and joking to try to ease the tension, just like your daughter. You're sharp as a tack."

Katy smiled as the elderly woman began to make soft snoring sounds through her thinly pursed lips. She had dozed off just that quickly.

Chapter Twenty-Four

Helen arrived a few minutes later, and Katy helped load Mrs. Simmons into the cream-colored Cadillac. Trudy Mae assured Sheriff Reid that she could answer any questions he might want to ask her mother. Mrs. Simmons had not set foot in her trailer since she broke her hip about six weeks ago and had not seen the body or had any contact with Laney Finch in about six weeks either. He was satisfied and gave permission for the old lady to leave. While Trudy Mae and Helen transferred their mother's necessities from the tall black SUV to the long cream-colored Cadillac, Katy decided to sit in the back seat with Mrs. Simmons to make sure the shock of what happened hadn't been too much for her. Plus,

Helen's car was running with the air conditioner blowing so her mother would be comfortable while she waited.

She climbed into the back seat of the luxury vehicle and admired the black leather interior. The cool touch of the leather seeped through her thin nursing uniform and felt like a little piece of heaven to her sweltering hot skin. The back of her scrub top was damp with perspiration. Hopefully, her salty sweat wouldn't leave a stain on the expensive leather seat. She had no idea if saltwater affected leather in a bad way. She had never heard of cows swimming in the ocean, so it probably wasn't a good thing for this natural material to be drenched with her sweat, but oh well. She was here now.

Her patient seemed to be taking the whole 'dead girl in my bedroom' thing extremely well. Since the sheriff's arrival, Mrs. Simmons had not asked any more questions about Laney Finch's death. Katy assumed the old lady was a little forgetful and probably more concerned about where she would sleep tonight and getting her medications on time than she was with this unusual situation she had come home to today. Katy was wrong.

"Katy, honey, what time did you get here this morning?"

"Around seven-forty-five. You and Trudy Mae

drove up about five minutes after eight. I remember because we were scheduled to meet at eight. I glanced at my dash clock before getting out of the car so I could document my time for the admission. Did you miss a medication or something? Trudy Mae said you got all of your morning meds before leaving the nursing home."

"She's right, I did." Mrs. Simmons turned and looked out of the back-car window. Her two daughters were still at the SUV digging through a tote box full of her things. "I hope they didn't lose my false teeth glue. There is nothing worse than floppy teeth." She slowly turned her gaze to Katy. "I'm just wondering about a couple of things. I don't expect you to tell me anything, and that's okay. I still want to have my say."

"Go ahead, I'm listening." Katy closed the admissions folder and glanced at her watch.

"Well, first of all, I know Laney didn't just have some kind of accident in my trailer."

"She didn't?"

"No, she didn't," Mrs. Simmons said. Her eyes sparked with insight as she spoke. "The police wouldn't come flying out here with sirens blaring loud enough to wake the dead if that girl had just tripped over a mop handle or fell in my shower and broken her neck."

Katy puckered her lips absently as she slowly

nodded her head. "That makes sense." She had been looking past Mrs. Simmons through the back-passenger side window, but now she moved her gaze to the woman's face. Mrs. Simmons was studying her carefully, like a cat watching goldfish in a bowl. "I mean, I guess that makes sense. I don't know much about these sorts of situations."

"I don't either." Her eyes never left Katy's face. "As a matter of fact, I don't think anybody in this town is an expert on these sorts of things. That's why it's like a three-ring circus in my front yard right now. But never mind that. There's something else I find odd. What happened to Laney's truck?" She paused, waiting for Katy to respond.

"Her truck?" Katy looked at her patient with newfound respect.

"That girl's been coming to my house to clean every week since last March," she continued. "She always parks that big ole red truck in the same place on the left side of my porch, away from the gravel drive. I asked her why she parked there since it made her have to walk a little further around the back of her vehicle to get to my front steps. She said she didn't mind if it kept her baby from getting hit by a rock from the gravel drive when some idiot kid came flying down that road."

"She called her truck her baby?"

"Oh, she loved that truck. She was so proud of

it. Said she was paying every note without any help from her husband. She offered to take me for a ride right after she started doing my cleaning, but I told her I couldn't lift my legs that high to get in the thing."

"So, her husband never brought her to work?"

"No, never met him. She always drove her baby, and she always parked on the left side of my porch."

Katy was impressed. She had not even thought about how Laney had gotten to the trailer. Mrs. Simmons had laughed and joked with her daughter this morning. She had allowed Katy to treat her like a forgetful old woman during her admission. She had sat quietly while all kinds of strangers entered her home to handle a situation that was scary and tense, to say the least. Yet all this time she had been working out the details of the event in her mind and asking questions that Katy had overlooked. She had underestimated her. Did Trudy Mae know how sharp her mother was? She probably did. Trudy Mae acted like a clown most of the time, but she soaked up what was going on around her like a sponge. Katy jumped as Trudy Mae slammed the trunk lid.

Helen opened the driver's door and slid behind the wheel of the Caddie. "I guess we've got everything you need for a night or two, Momma," she said as she adjusted the rear-view mirror. "We'll come back and get anything we missed once the law lets you back in your house. You ready to go?"

"I sure am, baby doll. My stomach is gonna go to growling if I don't feed it soon." She cut her eyes back to Katy, who opened her door to get out. "Now, Katy, you think on what we were discussing, and we'll have to revisit this conversation next time I see you."

"Yes ma'am, I will. Considering the circumstances, why don't we plan on a follow-up visit tomorrow?"

"You gonna see me on a Sunday? That's the Lord's day child. I ain't sick, I'm just old."

"Yes, ma'am, I don't mind coming by after church."

"Now there ain't no need in that. I'll be staying with one of the finest nurses in this county. I guarantee you that she'll call you if I hiccup one too many times." She leaned over and patted Katy on the cheek. "Now you do what the Lord intended for us to do on Sunday. You rest."

Katy smiled. She didn't think rest would be coming very easy for her tonight. Not at all. It was going to be a rough day.

After Helen took Mrs. Simmons to Trudy Mae's house, Katy hung around waiting for Sheriff Reid to give her permission to leave. She sat on the porch for three hours while he talked to Trudy Mae and did a lot of walking in and out of the trailer making phone calls, talking with the coroner and giving orders. She completed Mrs. Simmons' paperwork during the first hour and a half. After that, she sat twiddling her thumbs. That was not her most favorite pastime.

They brought Laney's body out on a stretcher covered with sheets, so Katy couldn't get another look at her neck. She felt certain that Laney had been strangled. Sheriff Reid followed behind the emergency workers and sat down in the rocker beside her. "Here, Katy. He handed her one of two little six-ounce bottles from Mrs. Simmons' fridge. "Drink a Coke with me before we get down to business. I need to take a breather."

Katy gratefully took the ice-cold bottle from the sheriff's hand as she leaned back in the rocker. She sipped the drink, enjoying the burning fizzle it made going down her throat. She watched a Robinson log truck pull out from a dirt road in the field of pine trees across the highway.

The sheriff followed her gaze as the truck made its way into the busy traffic of the five-eighty-seven. "I need to send Todd over and make sure they have flags and signs up for them trucks. The last thing I need today is a wreck on that highway."

Katy watched the orange flag whip in the wind

that was tied to the end of a log sticking off the tail of the long dirty truck. It disappeared from sight as the truck shifted gears and gathered speed, heading toward town. She didn't answer the sheriff. He seemed to be talking to himself, anyway.

"Okay, Katy," the sheriff said, slapping his knee. "I guess I better get down to business. Mrs. Hawkins said you met her here this morning to sign her mother up for home health."

"Yes, sir. Dr. Roberts set it up through my company yesterday, and my office called me last night telling me to start her services today."

"Alright. Is that the way it normally works?"

"Yes, sir."

"Now when you went into the bedroom you found the Finch woman's body on the floor?"

"Yes, sir. I turned on the light and saw her. I started CPR, but after a few seconds I was sure she was dead. We continued until the ambulance team came in and took over."

"That's the same thing Mrs. Hawkins said. Did you move anything or remove anything from her body?"

"Well, she was facing away from me, toward the window. I had to roll her onto her back to check her pulse and begin the rescue breathing and chest compressions. We rumpled up her shirt doing all of that, and the EMTs did the same thing when they stuck the leads to her chest."

"All that is expected and couldn't be helped," Sheriff Reid nodded. "Y'all were just doing your jobs and trying to help the woman."

Katy watched as the sheriff flipped through the pages of his pad, making little notes. After a minute or two, he closed the book and looked at her while running his hand through his thinning grey hair. "You know Todd showed me your notes about the Williams girl."

"Yes, sir."

"First of all, I want to tell you that there have been two murders in the town in less than two weeks and you are smack dab in the middle of both of them."

Katy clutched the little glass bottle between both hands. If it had been an aluminum can, like she always bought, she would have just crushed the container and spilled the last swallow of her favorite vice on the front of her scrub shirt. "You know that's just some kind of weird coincidence, don't you, sir?" She felt sweat forming on her upper lip. It had never occurred to her that somebody would think she was connected to these deaths.

"Calm down, Katy," Sheriff Reid said, noticing the white knuckles of her death grip on the Coke bottle and the deer in the headlights look on her face. "I don't think you're involved in any of these killings."

Katy started breathing again. When had she started holding her breath, and why was she so nervous? She had done nothing wrong. Neither had Joe Phobs, but he had been stuck in a jail cell for a week. She pulled a tissue from her scrubs pocket and wiped the perspiration from her face along with the last few traces of her morning make up.

The sheriff casually watched her fidgeting. "The thing is, I know these two murders are connected. I'm not exactly sure how, but they are. We have that little note Laney Finch left for Jessa Williams for one thing."

Katy sucked the last drop of Coke from the glass bottle and set it at her feet on the porch. "So, what do you need from me, sheriff?" She wiped her damp hands on the legs of her pants.

"I read all of your notes about both women wearing the same perfume and how you think there is some kind of love triangle going on."

"Yes, sir, I'm sure of it. I spoke with Laney's mother yesterday, and Jake Finch really was having an affair with Jessa Williams."

"Hmmm," the sheriff raised his thick grey unibrow, "sounds like you might be a little ahead of me again. What else have you found out since your last uh, report?"

Katy desperately wanted to smile, but she quickly ducked her head down to recover her serious face. The sheriff didn't think she was a suspect. He just wanted to find out what she knew. She quickly filled him in on the discussion she had with Laney's mother, confirming her love triangle theory. She told him about Laney's alibi, then moved on to what she had found out from Emma Robinson.

"They heard Joe Phobs in his trailer the night of Jessa's murder, even if they didn't see him," she said.

"I guess Phobs could have been in his trailer," he said, scribbling in his notebook. "I think I might just need to go door to door around here and see what the good folks of Piney Acres know about last Friday night. I need to see if anybody has seen anything going on at Mrs. Simmons' place since she's been gone too. We'll just kill two birds with one stone."

"Sheriff, I know that Laney had an alibi, but what about Jake?" She paused as he glanced up from his notes. "Do you think he was involved in all of this?"

"You know he was involved up to his ears. Now did he kill his girlfriend or his wife? That I don't know, but I plan on finding out." He snapped his notepad shut one last time and shoved it in his shirt pocket. "Alright, ma'am, I'm done." He stood up from the wooden rocker and walked to the steps of the front porch and started to descend. He paused and turned back to Katy. "I know you're a smart lady, but I just want to warn you to be careful."

Katy stood from her rocker and squatted down to retrieve their empty Coke bottles. She stood back up slowly, eyeing the sheriff.

"Whoever killed these women does not want to be caught," Sheriff Reid said, his voice flat. "If he finds out that you're starting to put all the pieces together, he'll have no problem with killing you too. Make no mistake about that."

"Yes, sir. I've already thought about that," she said, trying to swallow, but suddenly her mouth was drier than a cotton patch. "That's why I'm making sure that nobody but Todd and my husband see my clue... I mean my notebook."

The sheriff took the empty bottles from Katy's hands and followed her to her car. "Good, that's good. But be careful. Jake Finch might be the killer, but he might just be a cheating husband who is being set up."

"Do you think Joe Phobs is innocent?"

"Well, we know for a fact he didn't kill the

Finch girl, and I would bet my best coon dog that whoever killed the first woman killed the second woman too."

"Do you think there's a serial killer here?" The thought entered Katy's mind for the first time. At this point, she just didn't feel like anything could be ruled out completely.

"Oh no, I wouldn't go that far. And whatever you do, don't talk like that in front of anybody else." The sheriff looked over her shoulder toward their small town. "Folks were already shaken up about the first murder. Most people considered the Williams woman an out of towner, even though she'd lived here for over a year, but Laney Finch grew up here. When word gets out that she's dead and that it doesn't look like an accident, people are going to start acting stupid. Whatever you do, don't add fuel to the fire with the words serial killer. Besides, that's highly unlikely."

She assured him that she would keep her mouth shut and continue to be careful. She left Piney Acres completely exhausted and drove home on autopilot as her mind played through the events of the last twenty four hours. They would be bringing Jake Finch in for questioning. If he didn't have an alibi for the time of either of the murders, they would lock him up in the cell next to Joe. She needed to talk to Trudy Mae about Jessa Williams and try to figure out her relationship to the Browns. Todd probably wouldn't have time to fool with that now that he had two murders to deal with.

That would just have to wait. Trudy Mae was probably home with her momma, anyway. All Katy wanted to do was go home, take a shower, and take a nap.

Chapter Twenty-Five

When Katy got home, she found a note from John saying he'd gone fishing with Mike and would be home sometime later in the afternoon. After a hot shower, she slipped her tired body into a pair of pajamas and climbed into bed to try to sleep away the fatigue brought on by the stress of the morning. Unfortunately, her brain just wouldn't cooperate. Every time she dozed off, she would think of something she wanted to ask Todd, or find out from Trudy Mae, or talk to Mrs. Simmons or Mrs. Brown about. Her mind just would not shut down to sleep. She finally got up and made a cup of coffee. If she couldn't sleep, maybe the caffeine would give her a little kick in the pants.

She attempted going over the Sunday school lesson, but decided it was a waste of time. Her thoughts kept coming back to Laney Finch's murder. Amanda Carson said her daughter was all riled up when she saw her on Tuesday. Why had she said she was going to fix all her problems? What had worked her up like that? She already knew about Jake's affair and Jessa had been dead several days. Where was her truck? The way Mrs. Simmons talked, the truck should have been at her trailer since Laney was always in 'her baby.'

Now that she was awake and not feeling like something the cat had drug in, she decided to get out of the house. Sitting at home thinking about other peoples' messes would drive her crazy. She had planned on running a few errands this morning after the admission, but those plans had changed for obvious reasons.

She looked in the mirror and sighed at the comfortable pair of jeans, flip-flops, and an old tee-shirt she had changed into. The half-way stylish Katy with nice make-up, hair, and decent clothes who had made an appearance earlier that week was nowhere to be seen in this reflection today. Old habits do die hard. She grabbed her purse and headed out the door.

She went by the cleaners to get John's suit and then by the bakery to buy some iced tea cakes for her class. She had written on her list to try and find a new top to wear tomorrow, but she was not in the mood to shop. That left the pharmacy. She needed to pick up a refill of John's blood pressure medicine and, her errands would be done. Hopefully, John would be home by the time she got back. He was not going to like that she had been the one to find Laney Finch's body, but she didn't like it either. It had happened that way, and fussing wouldn't change it.

The cool air and smell of freshly mopped floors hit her in the face as she walked into Friend's Pharmacy. The prescription area in the back of the small mom and pop establishment had four people in line at the counter. Mr. Friend's business thrived because of his personal interest in the customers. His staff knew everybody in town and made sure they got their medications on time.

Katy stood quietly in line behind a young man talking on his phone. He looked vaguely familiar, and when he turned his head to the side, she realized it was Tripp Brown. His loud and forceful tone made his conversation impossible to ignore.

"I told you I'll be right back. I've just got to pick up this medicine. Undoubtedly you can take care of things long enough for me to do that." He raised his empty hand in the air as if the person on the other end of the phone could see him. "Look,

Momma, just tell him to wait ten minutes or come back later when I'm there. Well, if he won't wait, let him go somewhere else. We ain't gonna starve if we lose one customer. Just do what I said, okay?" He mumbled a curse and shoved the phone in his back pocket.

Katy's eyes shot daggers at the back of his head. His grandmother had said that she didn't really care for her spoiled grandson. She had thought the elderly woman was exaggerating, but not anymore. It sounded like she had a good reason to think less of the man.

Tripp stepped up to the counter next, and Katy eased up in line as well. "Mr. Brown, do you want the teaching on the Xanax and Wellbutrin?"

"Kid," Tripp smirked as he glared at the young clerk. "If I did, I would be talking to old man Friend and not to you."

"Well," the girl said, keeping her stiff smile in place, "please sign the refusal line on the screen."

He paid for his meds and hurried out of the store. Katy stepped up to the counter and smiled at the young redhead. "Susan, do you have John's medicine ready?"

"Yes, ma'am, I pulled it from the bin when I saw you in line."

"Thank you, dear. You do such a good job for

your pawpaw. I know he's proud to have you working for him."

"I try, Mrs. Katy. He wants me to go to pharmacy school and take over the business one day, but I don't know if I'm going to yet." She slipped the white bag of medications across the counter and leaned in toward Katy. "Have you heard about Laney Finch?"

"I'm afraid I have. I feel so sorry for her poor family."

"Me too, me too. Especially those three little boys. Pawpaw heard that they have Coach Finch at the sheriff's station questioning him." She looked from side to side, then back to Katy. "Do you think he did something to Mrs. Finch? It seems weird that she would just fall over dead while cleaning somebody's house."

"I imagine they just have him there because he is her next of kin." Katy took the bag from the girl and pulled out her debit card. "We sure wouldn't want to start a damaging rumor about Coach Finch when he's trying to handle this tragedy."

"Oh, no, ma'am," Susan gasped, stretching her big china blue eyes even bigger. "We don't want that. I guess somebody will tell us what happened when the sheriff figures it all out."

"I'm sure someone will, dear. Don't you worry."

She left the pharmacy and got in her car. The

Finches lived just a few blocks from the pharmacy. Maybe she could just drive by their house and see if the red truck was in their driveway. That couldn't hurt anything. She turned left at the stop sign and headed toward the subdivision. Their house was always getting toilet papered during the football season since Jake Finch was the coach. She slowed the car as she neared their house. There were bicycles, toy trucks, and a T-ball stand in the small front yard. A sporty, newer model jeep was parked in the driveway, but there was no sign of Laney's baby. She turned at the next stop sign and headed back through town towards her home. That was enough nosiness for one day.

❦

Katy pulled her Civic under the carport beside John's truck. Good, she didn't want to come home to an empty house.

"Hello, Columbo." John smiled, stepping onto the carport. "I hear you had an unusual day."

"Yeah, that's one way to describe it." She stepped into his embrace and felt some of the tension leave her neck as she laid her head against his shoulder. "It wasn't as bad as Laney Finch's."

"This is true. How are you holding up?" He

eased her back and looked into her face. "You need ice cream?"

"Of course I need ice cream. I need ice cream when I lose my car keys, much less find a dead body." The corner of Katy's lips turned up just the smallest amount as they walked into the kitchen. "I wish we hadn't finished off that Rocky Road."

John reached over her head and opened the freezer above the refrigerator. "I didn't get Rocky Road, but I did get Death by Chocolate and some chocolate brownies. I didn't think about how tasteless the name would be on a day like today until I'd gotten home and put it in the fridge."

"Yeah, I guess Moose Tracks or Fudge Ripple would've been a better choice, but I'm going to eat it, anyway."

John warmed the brownies in the microwave, then topped them with the ice cream while Katy poured two tall glasses of sweet iced tea. They both took their treasures and went to relax in the recliners in the living room.

"How did you find out I was at Laney Finch's murder scene?"

"Todd called to make sure you were okay. He said the sheriff quizzed you down before he let you go. By the way, check your phone. It must be on silent or dead or something. I've been blowing it up for a couple of hours trying to get in touch with you."

"Oh, I forgot to turn the ringer back on after the admit. Sorry."

"I was getting kind of worried," he said, scooping a spoonful of ice cream from his bowl. "I was about to send the army out to track you down."

"What stopped you?"

"Misty saw your car at the drugstore and happened to tell Mike. After that, I figured you had just lost your phone or something."

"I don't see how anybody can keep a secret in this town," she said, pointing her spoon at John.

"Well, with the flower shop being across the street from Friends, it wasn't that hard for Misty to notice your car."

"I know, I know. I don't have any secrets, anyway." Katy took another bite of her ice cream and brownie. "It's after five. What do you want for supper?"

John scraped his spoon across the bottom of his bowl to get the last few crumbs of his sweet snack. "Probably nothing. What about you?"

"I'm good. I feel like I'm going to pop now. You fixed me a huge bowl."

"Well, let me just eat those last couple of bites for you."

"Aww, ain't you just the sweetest thing," Katy said, handing him the bowl. "Here, help yourself."

While he finished off the rest of their chocolate supper, she told him about her day. She described the marks on Laney Finch's neck and shared her theory that the girl had been strangled by someone standing in front of her. John listened without any comments.

"So how did the fishing trip go?" She looked at him and sighed. "Anything unusual happen?"

"Nope, pretty boring stuff. We didn't catch a thing. Since we don't have church tomorrow evening, we're going over to his dad's big pond off the five-eighty-seven."

"Well, good luck. I think I'm going to find a book to read. Maybe some Jane Austin."

"That sounds safe enough. I sure don't want you stumbling across any crime scenes in our backyard."

"Okay, Mr. Smart Mouth." Katy grabbed a throw pillow from her chair and threw it at his head. "I'll try not to. I guess I could go fishing with you and Mike. Maybe y'all could kill a few fish if I'm in the boat with you."

John caught the pillow and stuck it behind him. "Maybe so, but you better bring that book to keep you company. We don't talk much while we fish."

"Nah, I think I'll pass. I would be as red as a

beet if I sat out in the sun in that dinky little aluminum boat all afternoon."

"Suit yourself." He dropped the spoon into the glass bowl with a clink. "I'm full as a tick. Why did you let me eat so much?"

"Better you than me, honey."

While John went to the kitchen with their dishes, Katy pulled out her phone and checked her missed calls: twelve from John, two from Misty, and one from Todd. Good grief. John's had started with a simple, "Call me," but had worked their way into longer, slightly panic-driven sentences about needing to hear her voice. The final one was after Misty had seen her at the pharmacy.

"Hey you. You scared me half to death. Anyway, Misty saw you at the drug store, so I guess you're alright. I'll see you when we get home. I love you. Oh, and learn how to turn on your phone before you make me have a stroke or something. Bye."

Katy wiped the mist from her eyes. Sweet talk and chocolate ice cream all in one afternoon. She loved that man.

Chapter Twenty-Six

Sunday was a sad day for the church. Even though Laney hadn't attended since she married nine years ago, her three boys were there most Sundays with their grandparents. None of the family were at church that morning. Misty said Laney's body would be at the funeral home Monday evening and buried Tuesday at two. Katy would have to go to The Pig to get some canned peaches for her cobbler.

As expected, her Sunday school class was more interested in talking about their football coach being locked up in jail than about the stoning of Stephen. She allowed this to continue for a few extra minutes, then passed out the iced cookies while she told them the Bible story. After she finished the lesson, they had prayer for the Finch family, and asked for a special blessing on the three little boys.

"You know," Victory said, reaching for the last cookie, "I never have loved Coach Finch, but I didn't think he was a woman killer." Most of the girls nodded their heads up and down.

"We don't know what happened to Mrs. Finch," Katy said, looking across the table at Victory, "and we sure don't know who's to blame in all this."

Victory took a small bite of the soft cookie and let the crumbs fall onto the front of her hot pink tee-shirt. The pale pink icing from the cookie smeared her bubble gum lip gloss. "I guess not, but I heard that they picked him up for questioning and he's at the jail."

"I know, but the sheriff's just doing his job trying to gather information," Katy said. "That doesn't mean your coach has done anything wrong. Besides, where did you hear all of this from?"

"On the radio, of course." Victory looked at Katy with one eyebrow raised. "Rob Clay said the police are wondering if this killing is connected to that other one and if Coach Finch is some kind of woman killer." She looked around to her class-mates for support. "They couldn't be saying all of that stuff if they didn't know something was going on."

All the girls' heads turned in unison toward Katy. Why couldn't they be this interested in something useful, like their lesson? "First of all, wondering about something and knowing something are two entirely different things. If that radio person had really known what was going on, he would have said it plain and simple. It sounds like he's just trying to get a story people will listen to without actually telling a bald-faced lie." Katy paused and held up two fingers. "Second of all, when we start gossiping about all of this, we're going to make things worse. Just a few minutes ago we prayed for that family, and now we're sitting here talking trash about one of them. How do you think that makes God feel? We ask him to help them while we mow them over. Think about poor Mrs. Amanda and Mr. Johnnie. Do we want to be saying such awful things about their son-in-law, especially when they're grieving over the death of their only child?"

"No, I love Mrs. Amanda," Victory whispered, eyes downcast. "When I have to sell stuff for Beta Club, she always buys a lot. She says she remembers when Laney was selling that stuff and how hard it was to raise money to go on the trip, so she buys two boxes of the Countries' Best Chocolate right by herself. I wouldn't want to do anything to hurt her."

"Well, try to remember that, Victory, and help keep the gossiping to a minimum."

"I'll try, but it sure ain't gonna be easy when we go to school tomorrow."

"I know." Katy looked around the table at each face. "But all of you girls just try to stay out of all this, okay? I'll be praying for you, and y'all pray for each other too."

They agreed to try, although a couple agreed half-heartedly. Unfortunately, gossip was something that started at an early age in most people, and if they didn't learn to at least attempt to control their mouths, they could do just as much damage at the age of thirteen as they could the age of thirty-three.

John stepped into the aisle of the church sanctuary to let Katy into the back pew beside him just as the music began to play. "You skipping the choir?" he whispered.

"Yeah. I just need to listen today." The extra talking in her class had made her get out a little late, so she didn't have time to speak to anyone before church started. That was just as well. She was sure she already knew what everybody was talking about.

"Scoot over, honey," John whispered, poking her in the ribs. "Somebody wants to sit by us."

Katy moved down a few feet. She leaned over to see who the person was and almost squealed out loud. Joe Phobs stood on the other side of her husband, shaking his hand and grinning like a schoolboy. She smiled so big she was sure her back molars were showing. She leaned around her husband and hugged her welcomed guest, then turned back to sing. The goofy-looking smile remained on her face for the rest of the service.

At the end of the sermon, the pastor announced that there would be no service tonight. He informed the people about the arrangements for Laney's funeral and encouraged everyone to reach out to this family as they were having to deal with such a hard thing. He also reminded everyone to please support the family in other ways, such as not speaking ill of things and people when it was not our place to do so. Katy wondered if all the classes this morning had to try to curb the gossip the way she had with the young girls.

After this, he did as he always did, and asked if anyone else had anything to share before everyone was dismissed. To Katy's utter shock, Joe Phobs raised his hand and stepped out of their back row.

The pastor shook his hand when he reached the front, and Joe whispered in his ear. The pastor nodded in agreement to whatever Joe had said, then stepped aside to allow Joe to address everyone.

"A lot of you know me, but for the ones that don't, my name is Joe Phobs. I used to come here every summer as a kid for VBS on the church bus. That's about the extent of my churchgoing. My momma tried to teach us about God at home, but, well, y'all probably know how young' uns are." Joe looked around at the crowd of people who were listening. Most had an encouraging smile on their faces, which made it easier to continue. "I want y'all to know that me coming up here to talk to y'all ain't easy. Anyway, what I want to say is this, I got picked up and thrown in jail for the murder of my girlfriend Jessa Williams week before last. I told the authorities I didn't do it, but they were sure I did. I ain't gonna go into the details about it. Being in the Lord's house doesn't seem to be the place to talk about all of that. At the time, I thought I was done in. I didn't think a soul in this town was on my side. But then some people from your church started showing up. At first, it was just one of your ladies, then her husband." He looked to the back of the church and nodded at John and Katy. "Then I told Mr. John how lonesome I was and how I wasn't getting any visitors, and the man started coming by almost every evening and bringing by y'all's preacher. Next thing I knew, I had different ones of y'all visiting me off and on every day. Most of y'all prayed with me and just talked to me and let me talk to you. Momma said a couple of you older ladies have even come by to see her this week." He paused again and smiled, showing perfect white teeth. "I have about talked myself out. I just wanted to let all of y'all know how much I appreciated it. The preacher here said that this is just the church doing what it is supposed to do. I don't know about all of that, but I do know that me and my family are grateful for what you did to get me through that rough spot, and I don't want to forget it."

Joe turned to look at the preacher, who stepped up and placed his arm around his shoulders. He whispered something in Joe's ear, and he nodded his head in agreement. The preacher had everyone bow their heads as he prayed a prayer of thanksgiving for getting Joe back home. They walked to the back of the building and stood together as everyone passed out of the back doors.

Katy picked up her Bible and started to ease from the pew into the congested aisle. So, her husband had been doing a little more visiting than she had known about. She had been so wrapped up in her own world with these two murders that she hadn't even bothered to find out what he had been up to. He was like that, though. He often went out of his way to help people and never told a soul. If anyone tried to give him recognition for anything he had done, he got uncomfortable and would change the subject. She was so proud of him.

She had been discouraged when she came out of her class this morning. Everyone seemed to be focused on the wrong thing and wanting to talk about the Finch's marriage problems and speculate if Coach had killed his wife. She had heard several little clusters of conversations going on as she had made her way from the classroom building to the sanctuary and had intentionally ducked her head and kept walking so she wouldn't be drawn in.

After hearing Joe, though, her faith in her church family was restored. She knew they were like her. They could easily get caught up in the talk going on all over town about who did what to whom.But in the end, they would try to do the right thing. Joe was proof of that.

She nudged her husband in the shoulder as they walked toward the car. "Did you know he was going to do that?"

"Yeah. He called me this morning and told me that they had let him out last night. He asked if it would be okay if he thanked everybody for supporting him. I told him that it was a great idea. I was going to tell you, but you were late getting out, so I didn't have a chance."

"I didn't know you had been going by to see him so much."

"I just dropped by and saw him on my way home from work every day. I didn't stay long, just had prayer with him. I got Pastor Scott to go with me last Wednesday, and I guess he got everybody else involved."

Katy climbed into the truck seat beside her husband and used her Sheriff Andy Taylor voice. "Well, it was a good thing you did, Mr. Cross, a mighty good thing."

"Aww shucks, ma'am. It weren't nothing."

Katy had a roast in the crock pot, and the aroma of slow-cooked onions filled their nostrils as they entered the kitchen. She had her Bible in one hand and her shoes in the other as she padded across the kitchen toward the bedroom to get into her usual Sunday afternoon get up of old sweatpants and a faded tee-shirt. They had stopped by The Pig on the way home so she wouldn't have to leave the house again today. She was looking forward to sitting on her back patio in the shade and losing herself in the troubles of Jane and Elizabeth Bennett.

Chapter Twenty-Seven

Katy's eyes shot open as a small scream escaped her lips. Something was crawling up her leg. The corners of her mouth turned up as she felt it again. Her cell phone, still on vibrate from church, lay in the recliner beside her where she had sat down with her book earlier. While asleep, the vibrating had felt like a bug or maybe a mouse wiggling against her thigh. At least she hadn't wet her pants. She fished around in the side of the chair for the phone and turned on the screen.

John called about an hour ago. He had left on his fishing trip four hours earlier and was probably calling to let her know what time he would get back. She sat the recliner up and slid her feet into her slippers. He would call back in a minute. In the meantime, she would start making the peach cobbler to take to the grieving Carson family. The buzzing started again before she could put her phone in her pocket.

"Hello."

"Hey, did I wake you?" John asked.

"No, well, not this time anyway."

"You ain't going to believe what's going on over here."

"What happened?" Katy walked into the kitchen and grabbed the cookbook from the drawer under the microwave. "Did you sink your boat trying to haul in the big one?"

"You're almost right." The background noise overtook the line as Katy waited for him to continue. "Hey, hold on a minute," he finally said.

She could hear machinery noise and what sounded like a crowd of people talking. "Where are you?"

John waited a second or two for all the noise to die down. "I'm still at the pond. It's a little crazy out here."

"It sure sounds like it. What's going on?"

"Me and Mike got to the pond and put our boat in the water, just like we always do. You know this pond's a lot bigger than the one we've been going to over by the preacher's house."

"I've never been to either one of them, but if you say so, I believe you."

"It is. Anyway, we got in the boat and after about an hour of not catching anything, decided to paddle over to the far side to see if we'd have better luck there. You won't guess what happened."

"Mike fell out of the boat," Katy said. She flipped through her cookbook. Most of the pages were shiny white from lack of use.

"No, nothing like that. We paddled a little way over and all of a sudden the boat started dragging like it was hung up on something."

"What was it?"

"Wait," he said, cutting her off, "don't mess up my story. Mike started poking his paddle down in the water and sure enough, there was something hard that the boat was hung on."

"Okay, Mark Twain." Katy turned toward the back of the book to the dessert section. She could probably make the peach cobbler from memory, but she was too chicken to try. "Get on with your story. What snagged the boat, a tree, a dead moose?"

"No, but something just as weird. A truck."

"A what?"

"A truck. There's a vehicle in that pond. Like I said, it's a big pond, and fairly deep in places, but off the east bank, just barely under the water, is a truck."

"What kind of truck? Is it an old truck? Does it look like it's been there a while?"

"Hold on, Columbo. I'm afraid I don't have any answers to your questions. The water's pretty muddy, so you can't see much. We could just make out the top of the cab where our boat was dragging across it."

"What did y'all do?" She looked up from the cookbook, cobbler forgotten for the moment. "It sounds like a three-ring circus out there."

"Oh, it is. We used our paddles to push the boat off the top of the cab, then sat there for a little while trying to decide if this was important."

"Well, of course it's important. You found a truck in a pond."

"Now don't get your britches in a wad. What if that truck had been in the pond for ten years? Just because we found it today doesn't mean it hasn't been there a while."

"Oh," Katy said, closing the cookbook and returning it to the drawer. "I see what you mean. Well, what did you do?"

"First, Mike called his daddy and asked him if he knew there was a truck in his pond."

"That makes sense," she said.

"He said that was the first he'd heard of it. He

seined the pond last spring before restocking it, and there wasn't a truck in it then."

"So, it is important." Katy slammed the kitchen drawer. "I knew it."

"We figured it might be," John agreed. "I called Todd and now half of the county seems to be out here."

"Really?"

"Well, no, not really. Mike's daddy and uncle came over, and then Todd and the sheriff pulled up. Tubby saw the sheriff turning into the logging road with lights a blazing and sirens squealing, so he came over with Joe Phobs."

"Wait, are you in the woods across from Piney Acres?"

"Yeah. Mike's dad owns that track of pine trees Tubby's daddy is cutting. The pond's in a clearing right behind where those logging trucks are working."

"You probably have half of Piney Acres over there seeing what's going on," Katy grinned.

"There's about three or four more trucks here now, and I don't even know who some of these people are."

"I told you nobody can keep a secret in this town."

"I believe you're right. Plus, anything that goes

over the police scanner has half the county listening in."

Katy pulled a bag of flour from the cabinet. "What're you and Mike doing now?"

"Just sitting here watching the show," John said, laughter in his voice. "The sheriff's taping off the area and trying to keep everybody from going near that side of the pond. He even let Todd use the bull horn a couple of times when some guys in waders tried to walk into the edge of the water."

"Why don't you just come home? I don't imagine you're going to get anymore fishing in today."

"We would, but the sheriff said he needed us to hang around until he can talk to us. I think he's forgotten about us though, with all these people showing up meddling in his stuff. They got him running around like a chicken with his head cut off."

"Nah. He'll get to you, eventually."

John sighed. "I've had two days of fishing, and the only thing I've caught is a flip-flop and a turtle."

"A flip-flop?" Katy stopped measuring out the sugar. "Where did you hook a flip-flop?"

"In this pond." John's voice dripped with disgust. "That's why we decided to row to a different spot. We sat on the other side for an hour and

Mike caught one tiny little catfish and I caught a turtle and then a flip-flop."

"It just isn't your weekend for fishing."

"I guess not. If I'd caught two shoes, at least it wouldn't have been a total loss. I could have given them to one of the girls."

"I hope you're joking," Katy said. "Who in their right mind would want slimy pond shoes? That's pretty nasty, even for you."

"I'm joking," John laughed. "But Mike said that this is an expensive shoe. He said Misty has a pair just like them and they cost over fifty dollars."

"Fifty bucks for flip-flops?" Katy dumped the flour into the mixing bowl a little harder than necessary. "Are they gold plated or something?"

"No, but they do have a lot of fake diamonds and rubies and stuff on them. Kind of fancy-looking to be worn fishing."

"John," Katy said slowly, "I bet you a plate of fried pickles that I know what color that truck is."

"And just how do you know that? Nobody here knows what color that truck is."

"By what you just told me. I know who owns that truck too. I just don't know how it got in that pond."

"Slow down, Sherlock. You've lost me. What did I say?"

"You said the flip-flop is too fancy to wear fishing. That's because the flip-flop came out of that truck y'all found in the pond. Laney's truck is missing, and remember, I told you she was barefoot when we found her." Katy paused to take a breath as the words tumbled out. "Mrs. Simmons said that Laney always took her shoes off when she cleaned, so she could feel if there was any dirt on the floor that she missed with her broom."

"Well, I guess that's possible, but you can't know for sure. This place is just strewed from can to can't with beer bottles and Coke cans. I think teenagers come here to park. If things got a little rowdy, a flip-flop might have just ended up in the pond."

"I don't think so. I bet you money that those are Laney Finch's flip flops and the other one is in the cab of her truck stuck in that pond."

"You may be right, but I ain't sold yet. I'll let you know when they find out something. It shouldn't be too much longer because the sheriff is getting Tubby to pull the truck out with his skitter."

"What are you gonna do while you wait?" Katy asked.

"Mike found a deck of cards in the glove box. I think we're going to play a little rummy."

"Try to find a shady spot to play in," Katy said. "The last thing you need is to get a bad blister."

Katy's phone rang again about an hour later. She answered it and put John on speaker so she could continue with the laundry. "Am I right? Is it her truck?"

"I don't know yet," John said. "Todd got our statements, and I told him what you said about this being Laney Finch's truck. He didn't think the flip-flop was that great of a clue for you to base your assumption on."

"I'm not giving up on that idea yet," she said, pulling warm towels from the dryer into the laundry basket. "I'll wait until he can take a look in that truck. I bet the other shoe is there and that the truck is hers."

"He said you may be right," John conceded. "He seems to think that you know more about what's going on with these murders than most of the police department. He just wasn't ready to agree completely. I told him not to tell you that because you already think you're Mrs. Marple."

"Ha-ha," Katy said sarcastically. "Right now, the only thing I'm trying to figure out is how in the world two people go through so many towels and washcloths in just two days." She lifted the lint trap and raked it clean. "This is ridiculous."

"I may have used a few extra washcloths yesterday when I got home," John said. "I had to give Belinda a bath."

"You used my good washcloths and towels to give that bloodhound a bath?" Katy held a washcloth to her nose and sniffed. "You know that I keep rags for that."

"I know, but I couldn't find them." John paused as the loud sound of the skitter drowned out his voice. "Look, I'm going to be a little bit longer," he shouted. "This looks like it might get pretty entertaining."

"It sounds like you're at a monster truck pull," Katy said, lifting the clothes basket to her hip.

"But this is even better," John said with a grin, "this is free."

Chapter Twenty-Eight

Katy took the cobbler out of the oven and frowned. She pulled the recipe book back out of the drawer and read it again. Talking to John while mixing everything together had been a little distracting. The ingredients were strewn all over the counter, but everything seemed to be accounted for.

"Oh, shoot." She looked at the two cans of peaches, opened but never poured into the bowl with all the other stuff. *Can I make the cobbler again without going back to The Pig? No,* she thought, *not enough sugar. Should I change from my holey orange sweatpants and paint-stained tee-shirt for the trip? Yeah, probably.*

She put on some jeans and another tee-shirt in

slightly better condition and headed out the door. She decided to order pizza to pick up on the way home. There was leftover roast, but they could eat that tomorrow night. She wanted to call John to see what was going on, but had promised to wait and let him call her.

The Pig was not crowded this afternoon, so getting in and out of there was easy. The pizza place was a different story. It seemed that everybody in town was having takeout pizza tonight. She pulled into the packed parking lot and went inside to stand in line with the rest of the town.

"Hey, Mrs. Katy. You having pizza too?" Katy turned around to see Emma Robinson smiling at her with a perfect set of lined and glossed lips. She sent up a thank you prayer that she had changed out of her holy sweatpants.

"Hello, Emma. Yeah, we're having pizza too. Probably shouldn't, but I do love thick crust pizza."

"Me too, and of course, Tubby loves it all." Emma moved her hands rapidly as she talked, and several silver bangles slid from wrist to elbow with every other word. "Did you hear about Joe getting out of jail?"

"Yes, I did. He was at church this morning."

"Wow, did the roof cave in?" She laughed at her own joke. "I'm just kidding. That's probably what people will say when me and Tubby start back to church."

Katy smiled as Emma continued with her flow of words. The young woman reminded her of a wiener dog puppy waiting for a pat on the head. She seemed to have energy seeping from her pores.

"Tubby called me a while ago and said he is doing something for the sheriff." Emma continued at a rapid-fire pace. "I can't imagine what that could be, but I figured it would be better to be on the sheriff's good side than on his suspect list like poor ole Coach Finch."

Katy started to comment while Emma caught her breath but wasn't quick enough.

"I guess you know they have him in jail now. He said he was out driving around looking for Laney the night she was killed and then came home to an empty house. Do you think he will be in jail long?"

"I'm not sure," Katy shrugged, "since I don't know what all they are holding him for."

That was all the encouragement Emma needed to continue with her news. "I heard, and I'm afraid I can't say where I heard it, but I heard they're thinking he might have killed both women. There was a pair of gloves in the back of his jeep that the sheriff thinks was worn while he strangled his wife."

"Gloves," Katy said, looking at Emma intently. "What kind of gloves?"

"Oh, you know, them ole nasty work gloves you buy at the hardware store. Tubby buys packs of them to keep in his truck, so he won't get blisters or splinters from the logs. They're made from some kind of stiff cloth like canvas. Tubby buys the white kind with the little black rubber dots on them. He says they keep your sweaty hands from slipping off when you're holding stuff."

Emma happened to notice that she knew the person who had walked up behind her and turned to start another conversation. Katy was thankful. Emma talked so fast and spewed out so much information at once that it kind of put her teeth on edge.

So, gloves connected to Laney's murder were found in her husband's jeep. The type of gloves Emma described were fairly common. John had a couple of pairs in the toolbox of his truck. There must have been some other way to link them to Laney's murder. She hadn't been bleeding, so there shouldn't have been bloodstains on the gloves. Maybe Laney's saliva was on them. Since the victim and the suspect lived in the same house, saliva could have gotten there some other way. It seemed unlikely, but possible.

Katy was brought out of her mystery-solving

thoughts by the tall, skinny, pimple-faced teenager behind the counter asking her name and order. She paid for her pizza and returned to her car. If John didn't call soon, she was going to forget her promise and call him, anyway. The waiting was driving her nuts.

When she got home, she mixed up the cobbler one more time and put it in the oven. As she was setting the oven timer, her phone finally rang with Conway Twitty's familiar 'Hello Darlin'. Katy grabbed the phone from her purse. "Well?"

"Well, hello to you too."

"Oh, John, I'm sorry. I've just about gone stir crazy waiting for you to call."

"Kind of like you did when we were teenagers, huh?" John laughed.

"Not exactly," Katy smiled. "That was a few pounds ago for me and a lot of hair ago for you." She tapped her fingers on the bar. He was going to drag this out. "Are you going to tell me if I was right?"

"Yes."

"Yes, you are going to tell me, or yes I was right?"

"I guess yes to both, and yes, I owe you some fried pickles."

This time Katy slapped her hand on the counter, and a puff of white smoke went up in the air from the spilled flour that she had not cleaned up. "I knew it, I just knew it. I've got to write some stuff down in my clue book."

"I'm on my way home, half-starved and completely filthy. I got a little too close to the action while Tubby was pulling the truck out and got slimy pond mud slung all over me."

"I bet you smell just fabulous."

"You know it. What's for supper? I can stop and get a thing of fried chicken from the gas station if you want me to."

"I'm one step ahead of you. I've got pizza waiting and I'm gonna make some fresh tea."

"Sounds good. I'll see you in about twenty minutes."

Katy slipped her phone in her purse. She decided she should probably wipe off the counters before getting out her clue book. If that sugary peach syrup and pasty flour dried together on her counter, she would never get it off.

She began wiping the counter in slow motion as she thought about everything she knew. If she took all the information she'd gathered at face value, Jake Finch had killed his girlfriend, then put the monkey wrench in the back of Joe Phobs' truck to frame him. After that, he had followed his wife to Mrs. Simmons' trailer, strangled her, and left her there. Then he took her truck and drove it off in a pond across the highway. He somehow got back home to be at school the next morning, but left the gloves he used to strangle his wife in the back of his jeep. Either this guy was as dumb as a rock, or there was something else going on.

By the time she finished the counters and fetched her clue book from her nightstand, she heard John driving under the carport. She laughed as he stepped through the kitchen door. His bright blue eyes and white teeth were about the only parts of him that didn't have a muddy brown coating.

"Kiss me, baby, I'm yours," he said, holding his arms out toward her like Frankenstein.

"You weren't kidding when you said he slung mud all over you."

"And just between you and me, I may have slipped down a couple of times too." John stripped down in the kitchen doorway and streaked to the bathroom to shower.

Katy gathered the filthy clothes and put them on the carport with his equally nasty rubber boots. They would have to be hosed off before she put them in the washer.

After John's shower, they had pizza and tea at the kitchen bar. Katy told John what she learned from Emma Robinson. He agreed that things didn't add up. Why would Coach Finch wait to kill his wife at some stranger's house, then dump the truck in the pond?

John leaned back and rubbed his stomach. "I don't think I can eat another piece."

"You ate seven pieces," Katie said as she counted the crusts on his plate. "My word, John. I don't know why you don't weigh three hundred pounds."

John stood up and took his paper plate to the trash can. "I know why. None of the Cross men are fat. Uncle Gater got a little plump when he hit his eighties, but that was those steroids the doctors put him on to help him breathe."

"Yeah, I guess you're right." Katy looked at her clue book then up at John. "Hey, did they find the other flip-flop?"

"It was in the cab of the truck, just like you said. I had to give back the one I caught too."

Katy jotted down the last few details of today's discoveries and closed her book. "Oh well. Maybe you'll catch something just as nice on your next fishing trip."

"Yeah, maybe so."

Chapter Twenty-Nine

Trudy Mae's house was outside of town at the end of a narrow gravel road. A big yellow lab flopped across the bottom steps lazily watching Katy as she walked up the concrete stepping stones to the house which was kept in perpetual shade by the sprawling branches of two enormous oak trees.

She leaned over and patted the dog's head. "Hello, big fella. You guarding the castle?"

The front door opened while she straightened up and Helen invited her in. Katy had known Trudy Mae for probably fifteen years and considered her a good friend, but they had never been to each other's homes or socialized outside of work, or bumping into each other around town. She was just more than a little curious to see if her over the top personality was reflected as much in her home as it was in her wardrobe.

The ranch-style home was decorated in a south-western style. Well, a south westerner who had one too many margaritas would be more accurate. The living room walls were painted a deep sunset orange, and a huge white longhorn cattle skull was mounted above the rough-cut stone fireplace. The couch and love seat were covered in canary yellow leather, and bright blue Indian blankets were draped across the back of each. An orange and white cowhide rug lay on the floor in front of the fireplace, and an enormous painting of a desert scene painted in bright primary colors complete with lizards, vultures and coyotes was the centerpiece of one of the adjoining walls.

Katy took a seat and waited while Helen went to fetch her mother. The hearth in front of the fireplace had several pairs of well-worn cowboy boots in various sizes sitting on either side of the grate. She wondered if these had belonged to Trudy Mae's family over the years.

"Well, is it what you expected?" Mrs. Simmons asked, walking into the living room pushing her walker with Helen close behind.

Katy looked at her patient questioningly. "Is what what I expected?"

"Tru's house. Is it what you expected?"

Katy smiled as the elderly lady took a seat across from her on the matching yellow couch. "Oh yes, ma'am, and maybe a little more."

"That's my Tru. Her light has to shine through wherever she's at."

"Yes, ma'am, I believe it does."

Katy checked Mrs. Simmons' vital signs and asked her all the questions from her nursing assessment. Her patient seemed to be doing well and not suffering any ill effects from the drama at her home on Saturday.

Mrs. Simmons answered the health-related questions and waited until Katy replaced her computer in its carrying case before addressing what was on her mind. "I guess we know what happened to poor little Laney's truck baby now."

"Yes, ma'am, I guess we do."

"That's such a shame. She was a good girl, a little too nosey for her own good, but a good girl."

"Yes, ma'am. I didn't know her very well, but I know her mamma," Katy said. "She's going to have a rough time ahead."

"No mamma should have to bury her child. It just ain't natural." Mrs. Simmons was quiet for a long moment, then deliberately smiled as she leaned back onto the blue Indian blanket. "So how did I check out? Everything still ticking like it should?"

"Yes, ma'am, you won't be needing home health long. A little physical therapy, and we'll be cutting you loose in about a month."

Helen walked into the room with a T.V. tray loaded with grits, eggs, bacon, a biscuit, and a steaming mug of black coffee. "Momma, you ready for breakfast?"

"Bout to starve slap to death, honey." The petite woman dug into the enormous plate of food with the gusto of a high school football player.

Katy laughed as she watched her shovel in the buttery grits. "There's nothing wrong with your appetite."

"Oh no, never has been." Mrs. Simmons smiled as she slurped down the runny grits. "I love my food."

"Well, that's a good thing. I figured you would be a picky eater since you're so tiny."

"Not me. I eat like a horse. Being skinny's just in my blood. Poor Laney used to laugh and say I must have a sugar daddy tucked away somewhere because I spent a small fortune on groceries."

"That's not hard to do nowadays," Katy said as she stood to leave.

"I felt so sorry for that young girl. She would come in and show me her new pair of two-hundred-dollar shoes, then ten minutes later tell me she couldn't buy groceries till payday. She always talked about how other folks just had it way easy while she had to work so hard to make ends meet." Mrs. Simmons reached out and grabbed Katy's hand and patted it. A sad expression glinted in her eyes. "She didn't know how to count the blessings the good Lord gave her."

"I'm afraid there's a lot of people in that same boat." She eased back onto the couch.

Mrs. Simmons bit off an enormous bite of bacon and nodded her head in agreement. "You're right, I'm sure. Poor ole Laney would go in these rich folks' houses to clean, then get it in her head that she had to have what they had."

"I believe she cleaned the Browns' house, didn't she?"

"Oh yeah. That was one of her favorite topics. She was always going on about Mrs. Brown's newest purse or shoes and how she wondered what the woman did with her stuff once she was done with it."

"Really?"

"Yeah. She said one day that she had seen Mr. Brown's bank statement while she was cleaning his desk. She was busting a gut to tell me how much money he had, but I wouldn't let her."

Katy looked at Mrs. Simmons as she took the last bite of her biscuit. "Didn't she realize how unethical it was to snoop in their private affairs like that?"

"I don't think she thought about it much. She kind of felt like rich people owed her something I think."

"Wow. If people found out that she was snooping in their personal business, then telling, they would get real mad."

"Now you're following me, child," Mrs. Simmons said, nodding her head. "I know if she was telling me things, she was probably telling other folks as well. Some of that telling probably got her killed."

❧

Katy pulled up in front of the Browns' paved circle drive and parked her car. The daylilies looked as beautiful as ever, standing tall in the morning sun. An old green pickup truck was parked in the drive. Jack's Lawn Care could barely be made out from the faded logo painted on the side. She presumed that was Jack on the riding lawn mower making leisurely loops around the expansive front lawn. She grabbed her gear and headed to the front door, determined to get the second visit of the day finished before noon.

Nelda answered the door, as usual, wearing a white scrub suit and the ever-silent tennis shoes. "Good morning, Mrs. Katy. Mrs. Tellman is waiting for you in her room."

Katy followed the sitter through the house. Mrs. Tellman was sitting in her blue recliner with her feet elevated.

"Perfect timing," she smiled. "The Price Is Right just went off, and my soap doesn't come on until this afternoon."

Katy set her bag in the chair by the recliner and began pulling out her BP cuff and thermometer. "Good, that way I can have your undivided attention." She placed the cuff on the frail little arm covered in the pink satin sleeve of a house robe. "How're you feeling? Have you been taking the antibiotics?"

Mrs. Tellman winced as Katy pumped up the cuff and waited until she pulled the stethoscope from her ears before she answered. "I'm finished with those horse pills. I don't think they did me any good, but I choked down every last one of them."

Katy stuck the thermometer under her patient's tongue and finished her head to toe assessment. She looked at the wound on Mrs. Tellman's leg and was very pleased with how it was healing. "Your family's taking very good care of you. The place on your leg will be completely well by next week."

"Well, it should be. I ain't ever seen so much fuss given to a little ole scratch." Mrs. Tellman looked over Katy's shoulder toward the door. Nelda had stepped out of the room, leaving them alone. She leaned in toward Katy and whispered, "I guess you heard about that Finch woman dying."

"Yes, ma'am, I did."

"You know she cleaned this house every week."

"Did she?" Katy answered vaguely.

"Oh yes," Mrs. Tellman continued in a conspirator's whisper. "I went a round or two with Evelyn a while back because I found that girl snooping through my dresser drawers and run her out of my territory. Evelyn said I was being paranoid, and the girl was just cleaning, but I know snooping when I see it."

"Did the girl try to explain what she was doing?"

"She just laughed and acted like she thought I kept my socks in too many drawers and she was trying to organize them for me. I run her out of here and dared Evelyn to let her back in."

"Well, she won't be snooping anymore, that's for sure."

Mrs. Tellman nodded in agreement and glanced again toward the door. "You know, Evelyn had decided to let her go, anyway. She was planning on giving her the sack this week."

"You don't say?"

"I do say. I'm not sure what it was about, but I heard Evelyn and my son-in-law Miles arguing over where some papers had gotten left. It had something to do with Wild Thang."

"Wild Thang?" Katy asked, her forehead creasing in confusion.

"You know. The other one that lived here."

"Tripp?"

"No, not Tripp," Mrs. Tellman snapped. "The one that died first... the Williams woman."

"Oh, Jessa Williams."

"Yes, that one. Apparently Snoopy had gotten into some of Wild Thang's papers or something cleaning up her room and now they're missing."

Katy couldn't help but smile at Mrs. Tellman's habit of labeling people with colorful nicknames. She wondered what she called her in her absence. "Do you think that girl possibly moved the papers when she was cleaning?"

Mrs. Tellman gave Katy a 'don't be stupid,' look. "No, I think she took them."

"Oh, I see." Katy hoped the old lady was wrong. Laney Finch's reputation was slipping more and more as the day went along. She didn't want to believe the young woman was a thief. "Why do you think she would take Jessa Williams' papers?" Katy had her own ideas, but had no intention of sharing them with her patient.

"I'm sure it was something seedy. Wild Thang was no angel, believe me. Evelyn should have taken a stand a long time ago and kicked that one out. I don't care what that son-in-law of mine said."

Their conversation was cut short by the sound of feet coming down the hall to the bedroom. Mrs. Tellman sat back in her chair hurriedly, like she had been doing something illegal.

Katy turned toward the sound just in time to see Tripp Brown step through the bedroom doorway. "Nanna," he said, not acknowledging Katy at all, "has Mom been around this morning? She's not answering her phone."

"She was going to the beauty parlor. Maybe she's under the dryer and didn't hear it ring."

Tripp placed his hands on his hips and glared at his grandmother. "And maybe she's ignoring my calls, so she won't have to help with the work."

"And maybe she wants a minute's peace from

her spoiled rotten son." Mrs. Tellman's glare was just as strong as her grandson's.

Tripp started to make another comment but seemed to notice Katy's presence for the first time. "Well, when you hear from her, tell her I'm looking for her."

Mrs. Tellman's sugary sweet smile dripped with sarcasm. "Oh, you know I will."

"Where's Nelda?" he asked, throwing both hands up in the air. He didn't wait for an answer but walked out of the room, calling the sitter's name at the top of his lungs.

Mrs. Tellman watched him leave and looked back at Katy. "If I could, I would get a switch and turn that one over my knee."

"I think he's a little too big for that," Katy said.

"I think you're right," Mrs. Tellman chuckled, "but I have threatened to give him a whack or two with my cane."

"Where is your cane?" Katy looked on either side of the baby blue recliner. "You must have left it somewhere."

Mrs. Tellman scanned her massive bedroom, trying to remember where she had last used it. "Go look in my bathroom. I bet it's by the sink. I know I had it in there this morning."

Katy went to the connecting bathroom to search. Sure enough, there it was, propped against the sink. She picked it up and started back to her patient, but paused behind the doorway, just out of sight. Tripp had returned to Mrs. Tellman's room and continued with his verbal escapades even more strongly now that he thought his grandmother was alone.

"Look, Nanna, you ain't got any business talking to that Cross woman about this family. Did you know that she was the one that found Jessa under that hay trailer? And there you go, just spilling your guts to her about the family."

"Hush boy," Mrs. Tellman hissed. "I ain't spilling nothing. Jessa Williams ain't none of my family and don't you forget it."

Tripp placed one hand on either side of the recliner's arms and leaned over his grandmother. "Well, you just remember one thing. Our business is our business and nobody else's. If you can't remember that, there's a room down at the old folk's home just waiting for you to move into."

Mrs. Tellman leaned into her grandson's face, meeting him nose to nose. She didn't seem the least bit intimidated by his bullying technique. "And you remember one thing. I still sign all my own legal papers. I ain't going nowhere unless I want to. And when I do go... my money goes with me."

Katy held her breath, waiting for Tripp to respond. *Dear Lord, keep that little woman safe,* Katy silently prayed. *She doesn't seem to know when to keep her mouth shut.*

Tripp's face was beet red and his posture rigid as he stared at his grandmother. But reason finally won out. He let go of the chair arms and stormed out of the room without another comment.

Katy walked into the room and propped the cane next to Mrs. Tellman's chair. "I found it. It was right where you said it would be."

"I leave it in there about half the time." She waited until Katy sat back down before finishing. "I know you heard us a few seconds ago."

"Yes, ma'am, I did."

"I apologize for the rudeness of that boy. He's always been a hothead, but when he quit smoking, it got a lot worse."

"I've heard that people can get real edgy when they try to quit."

"He's turned into a plumb bully," Mrs. Tellman said. She rubbed her wrinkled hands together as she spoke. "I guess he quit about six months ago, so I would think all the nicotine would be out of his system."

"Yes, ma'am, I would think so too."

"He's got some pills he takes. Says they take the edge off. I can't tell that they are working."

Katy nodded again. That must have been the

Xanax and Wellbutrin she saw him picking up at the pharmacy. She glanced down at her watch. "I'm afraid it's time for me to go."

"Alright, dear. Will I see you next week?"

"Yes, ma'am and call me if you need me sooner."

Chapter Thirty

Katy peeked under the foil covering the metal throw away pan. The peach cobbler looked okay. She had taken extra pains trying to pay attention as she stirred it together for the second time last night, but still, looks could be deceiving. She got a teaspoon out of the silverware drawer and dipped a tiny taste out of the corner of the pan. She smiled, dropping the teaspoon in the sink. Thank goodness, sugary sweet and peachy keen, just the way it always tasted. If she lost her touch making peach cobbler, she would have to resort to a store-bought cake from The Pig every time she needed to give someone a sympathy dish. She knew it didn't matter, but good grief. Undoubtedly, she could still master the only edible dish she managed to make consistently for a few more years before the dementia kicked in.

She crimped the foil back around the edges of the pan and scooped it up. She had texted Todd when she got home an hour ago asking him to call her when he got a chance. The only response she had received was the letter k. She had taken her time changing, but if she didn't get the dish over to Amanda Carson's house soon, she wouldn't be back in time to make it to the funeral home with John tonight. She made sure her phone wasn't on silent before dropping it in her purse and heading out the kitchen door.

She knocked on the front door of the Carson's trailer. As with her last visit, she heard little feet running from a distant area of the home. This time the door was thrown open immediately by the six-year-old grandson to give Katy entrance. "Mawmaw heard you drive up, and we peaked out the mini blinds and watched you get out of your car."

"You did?" Katy's eyes crinkled with a smile.

The little boy smiled back at Katy. "Uh-huh. We were looking from Mawmaw's bedroom. She still has Gunner in the tub and said I could come and let you in." He stepped to the side of the doorway and swept his hand forward toward the inside, urging her to the living room.

Katy stepped inside the room and the little boy slammed the door shut behind her, making the nearby photos on the wall rattle in place.

She turned and looked as he slapped his hands together as if wiping away some imaginary dust. He was wearing a white button-up dress shirt, black slacks, and black loafers. His wet brown hair was slicked over to the side, and his smile of accomplishment at answering the door beamed, showing the hole where his two front teeth had once been.

"You sure do look nice in your dress-up clothes," she said.

He looked down at his shirt then back up at Katy. "Mawmaw says we all got to stay clean and not fight tonight at the funeral home."

"I'm sure you'll make your Mawmaw very proud," Katy said softly, eyes damp with heartbreak.

He nodded his head in agreement and the smile left his face as he thought about the plans for the upcoming evening. "We have to go tell Momma bye tonight. She had to go to heaven to be with Rex. He needed her. He was our dog, but he got hit by a car and he's already in heaven."

Katy squatted down and hugged the boy to her chest with her one empty arm. The other arm balanced the pan of peach cobbler.

Tyler allowed himself to be hugged for a few seconds before pulling away. "You can put your food on the table with the other stuff. I'll see if Mawmaw has Gunner out of the tub yet." He ran through the living room, down the hall, out of sight.

Katy set the cobbler on the dining table then stepped back into the living room. She took a closer look at the family portrait of the Finches that had rattled when Tyler slammed the door. It must have been just a few weeks old because all the children looked the same. Laney was sitting in a rocking chair holding the toddler, with Grey, the oldest boy, standing to one side of the chair. Tyler was in his father's arms on the other side. They all looked so happy. Katy blotted more tears that were forming in her eyes. The youngest boy would never even remember his mother.

She heard Amanda coming up the hall and turned to greet her. Amanda appeared to be holding up remarkably well. She had the youngest of her grandsons riding on her hip, and the other two followed close behind. All three were dressed in identical outfits and looked to have just gotten out of the bathtub.

Amanda leaned in and hugged Katy with her free arm. "Thank you for stopping by. It means a lot to us." She sat on the couch and patted the spot beside her. "Can you stay for a minute?"

"Of course I can," Katy said, sitting down beside her friend. "I can stay as long as you need me to."

"Grey, why don't you and Tyler go back to the toy room and turn on some cartoons for a little while," Amanda said, turning to the two older boys who had snuggled up beside her. "Mawmaw wants to talk to Mrs. Katy for a second."

The boys stood and Grey took his little brother's hand and led him down the hall obediently. The toddler squirmed for a second, attempting to get out of his grandmother's arms and follow his brothers. Amanda leaned over and set the child on the floor at her feet. She reached under the couch and pulled out a shallow plastic box containing several brightly colored plastic blocks for him to play with. He immediately started digging through this new treasure and lost all interest in his brothers.

Amanda sat up and turned to Katy. She glanced back over her shoulder to make sure the children had indeed left the room. "I guess you heard who is in jail."

"I'm afraid so."

"He wasn't much of an h-u-s-b-a-n-d," Amanda spelled out in a whisper, "but he's always been a good d-a-d-d-y. I just can't believe that he would do what they're saying. He would never hurt his kids by risking leaving them without either parent like that."

Katy reached out and squeezed Amanda's hand.

"Don't get me wrong." Amanda looked into Katy's eyes, needing her to understand what she was saying. "He was a cheating jerk to Laney, but he didn't k-i-l-l her. He knew she was the reliable parent that the boys leaned on. He just wouldn't hurt his kids this way."

"I believe you, Amanda," Katy said, nodding slowly. "I'm just so sorry that he can't be here with his kids right now to help them get through this."

"Me too, although I don't know how much good he would be." Amanda leaned over and rubbed Gunner on the top of his head. "Johnny talked to him on the phone earlier and he said that the man is a basket case."

Katy didn't know what to say. She squeezed her hand again. "Is there anything I can do for you or your family?"

"Not today. Johnny's down at the funeral home now, tying up all of Laney's arrangements. Me and the boys are leaving in a little while to go there. Jake's parents are taking the boys with them tonight and keep them for a couple of days."

"That's good that they're helping you."

"They're good people, even if their son is a

lousy husband." Amanda reached for a tissue from the box on the end table. "They're almost as torn up about this as me and Johnny. They'll do whatever they need to do for the grand-babies."

"It sounds like you're holding up pretty good, but are you sure there's nothing that I can help you with?" Katy leaned over and hugged the grieving mother. "I cannot even begin to imagine how you're feeling right now."

Amanda's shoulders shook lightly in a silent sob as she allowed herself to have a few moments of relief from her sorrow. This only lasted for a brief minute. She lifted her head and smiled at Katy, wiping away the tears. "I have to be strong for my boys. They're trying so hard to be little men, especially Grey. I can't let them see me break down."

"Well, just remember that if I can do anything to lighten your load, or make things easier, I'm available," Katy said, wiping the tears from her own eyes.

"As a matter of fact," Amanda swallowed hard and looked at Katy. "There is something I need help with."

"Of course, what do you need me to do?"

Again, Amanda looked over her shoulder toward the toy room down the hall to make sure they were still alone. Satisfied that she was not being overheard, she turned back to Katy. "Laney comes... I mean, Laney came to the house just about every day. In the toy room under the bed is a box of her stuff. I'm not sure what it is, but she was always going back there and putting things in and taking things out."

"What kind of stuff are you talking about," Katy asked, tilting her head to the side.

"I don't rightly know. Papers and stuff she would take out of her purse. I asked her what it was a couple of times and she always said it was just things she needed to keep and not to worry about it. I figured she was gathering stuff about Jake in case she decided to leave him."

"Is it still there?" Katy asked, looking past Amanda and down the hall.

"Yes, it is," Amanda said. "I haven't touched it, and that's why I need a favor. I hate to ask you, but would you mind being here when I go through it? I just need somebody with me when I open it, so I won't fall apart if I don't like what I find."

As Katy listened, the wheels in her mind began to turn. Had the woman truly been taking things from the people that she cleaned for? Is this what had happened to the missing papers Mrs. Tellman was talking about earlier? She blinked her eyes as she realized Amanda was waiting for a response. "I'll help you, Amanda, of course, I will. You just let me know when you want me to come over and I'll be here."

"Thank you so much," Amanda said, her voice shaky. "I would ask Jake's momma to help me, but I'm afraid what we find is going to just confirm what I already think about him. There's no need to share his dirty laundry with his momma. I don't want Johnny to do it either because if he hears any more bad news about Jake, he's liable to go down to the jail and beat him within an inch of his life."

"I don't mind, but don't you think you should give the stuff to the sheriff?"

"I will if it's anything he needs to know, but well, if it just turns out to be a bunch of nonsense then I don't want to drag my girl's name through the mud any more than it already is." Again, Amanda looked at Katy, willing her to understand. "I don't know why somebody would want to kill my daughter, but if I can preserve her good name, even a little bit, I'm going to try."

"Of course you are. Any mother would do that for her child and don't you worry. I'll be here for you and whatever is in that box will be sorted out."

"You just don't know how I appreciate this." Amanda let out a long, haggard sigh and reached down to scoop Gunner into her arms. "I think I'll make it through this with prayers, my friends, and Johnny."

"John and I are praying for you and your family," Katy said, as both women stood. "I'll be waiting for a call from you to take care of the box, but if you need any help with anything else, you just call. I'll be right over."

Amanda walked Katy the few steps to the front door and hugged her one more time before saying goodbye. The woman's world would be upside down for the next several days. She would love to know what Laney had been stashing in the box, but she would have to wait.

❧

She was planning on waiting until she talked to Todd before she looked at her clue book, but since he hadn't returned her call, she decided to pull it out when she got home to jot some things down before she forgot.

The last thing recorded was that Coach Finch was in jail, possibly for both murders. This was followed by a question mark. She walked back to the living room and sat down in her recliner. Emma Robinson said that the police had found gloves used in the murder in the back of Jake Finch's jeep. She wrote this down, but also added 'need more info, need to talk to Todd.'

Mrs. Simmons said Laney Finch needed money

and didn't mind looking at peoples' private papers. She also didn't mind telling others about her discoveries. Mrs. Tellman said Laney was fixing to be fired for stealing some papers that belonged to Jessa Williams. And last, Amanda Carson had a box of 'stuff' that Laney had been secretly collecting.

Katy looked at her notes and sighed. She needed to get a list of everybody that Laney worked for. She was pretty sure the woman had stuck her nose into something that had gotten her killed. She got up and went to the kitchen and pulled her phone from her purse to check her messages. Todd still had not tried to call. He must be very busy with something.

She walked back to the bedroom to put up the clue book and pick out something to wear to the funeral home. A pair of loose-fitting black linen pants and a white peasant blouse with little black polka dots caught her attention. She quickly changed and got ready. She needed to get supper together, so when John got home they could eat before going to the funeral home. She listened as his truck pulled under the carport as she was walking back into the kitchen. Oh well, so much for plan A.

He showered and changed while Katy made them grilled cheese sandwiches. This was not the supper she had planned, but at least they wouldn't have growling stomachs in a couple of hours. They wolfed down the melted cheese on the toasted bread and headed out the door.

There were quite a few more cars in the parking lot of the funeral home tonight than there had been when Jessa Williams was there. As John and Katy were walking to the front entrance, they saw Jake Finch's parents leaving with the three boys. They were several feet away, but the two older boys waved vigorously to Katy as she passed by. Katy teared up again as she thought about how the past couple of days had changed the children's lives forever.

John placed his arm around her shoulders and gave her a squeeze. "We need to do some serious praying for that family, Katy. I need to drop by and talk to Johnny too and see if we can do anything to lighten their load."

"I just can't imagine having to face everything they're dealing with," Katy said, laying her head on John's shoulder.

Laney's casket was closed with a large framed portrait of her and the boys sitting on top. A spray of white roses surrounded the picture, which looked like it was taken at the same time as the one Katy saw in Amanda's house earlier that day. They made their way through the crowd, speaking to all the different people from the small town. Daycare workers and parents of the children Laney cared for, kids from the school where Jake coached, and, of course, all the people that Laney had grown up with in the town, were crowded into the building paying their respects, along with the extended members of the Carson family.

There were flower arrangements and plants all along the walls that had been sent by loved ones. Poor Misty, she had probably been working her fingers to the bone for the last couple of days. Katy didn't see her in the room with the casket. She excused herself from the group she and John were talking to and stepped into the foyer to see if she was there. She thought she had seen her car in the parking lot when they came in, but it may have just been someone else's that looked similar.

She scanned the crowd of people who were grouped together in little bunches of three or four all around the massive room with wanderers roaming from group to group. Most were talking quietly, some smiling, some crying. There were comfortable chairs all around the walls, and most of these were taken as well.

She began working her way through the room, speaking to people as she went. A few people asked her if it was true that she had been at Mrs. Simmons' house when the body was found. She knew that people would soon find that out, even if the sheriff was trying to keep it quiet. Too many folks had seen her there, and people just liked to talk. She had answered them with a brief yes, but she couldn't talk about it. She would let them draw their own conclusions as to why.

Misty was nowhere in the foyer. She was about to give up her search and go back to her husband when she happened to glance out of one of the enormous floor-to-ceiling windows on the front wall. There was Misty, sitting on the steps of the entryway with her back propped against a massive brick column.

Katy stepped outside and walked over to where she was sitting. "Hello, friend. You need some company?"

"Well sure," Misty said, her voice slow with fatigue, "as long as you don't ask me to move or arrange a flower." She patted the step beside her. "Grab a seat. They're hard to find around here tonight."

Katy sat down next to her and gave her a brief hug. "All the flowers are gorgeous. You and your mom always do such splendid work."

"Thank you," she said softly. "This has been a very, very hectic couple of days."

"I believe you. This place is packed with people and flowers."

Misty nodded. "I had to help with deliveries today. You probably already know this, but they let Coach Finch come up here earlier to see his kids and be with them when they arrived."

"No, I didn't know that," Katy said, "but I'm so glad they did. Were you here when they were together?"

"Yeah, I was arranging the roses on the casket. The poor fellow was just completely torn up."

"I imagine he was. His world has fallen apart. Please tell me they didn't make him wear that ugly orange jumpsuit and handcuffs to his wife's funeral."

"No, they didn't. How tacky would that have been? He had on a suit. Todd was in the room with him, but he stayed at the door while the family visited."

"Well, thank heaven for small favors." She reached up and pushed a stray hair out of her eyes. "Those little guys didn't need to see their daddy in a prison get up."

"I hadn't thought about that. That would've been bad for them."

They watched as people continued in and out. Katy guessed that Todd had been busy getting Coach Finch ready for his visit with his kids and that was why he hadn't called. Poor kid. His job was probably just a little more crazy than usual here lately.

Eventually, Mike came out looking for Misty. Katy told her friends goodbye and returned inside to search for John. She was ready to get home and call Todd.

Chapter Thirty-One

Katy checked her phone as they got in the truck. Todd had texted about an hour earlier saying he was home and could talk. She punched in his number.

"Hey, Aunt Katy." He picked up on the first ring. "I've been waiting for your call."

"We've been at the funeral home," she answered. "I heard you were there earlier with Coach Finch."

"Yeah, that was just sad. I've never really cared for that guy. He was kind of rough on the ones of us that didn't play football. Back then, he was just out of college, and I guess he had something to prove. But man, he's just falling to pieces. Phobs handled all this way better than this guy is."

"Well," Katy sighed, "he's being accused of killing the mother of his children. I don't know how I would handle something like that either."

"Wait," Todd sputtered, "who thinks he killed Laney Finch?"

"I guess the sheriff does." Katy paused for a second, reviewing all her notes in her mind. "He did arrest him, didn't he?"

"I just figured you already knew everything," Todd said. "You're always one step ahead of us, but today I know more than you."

"I don't understand," Katy said. "You're not making sense."

"Look," he said, "I'm in my truck just a few minutes from your house. Can I just drop by and catch you up?"

"Of course you can. I'll dip us up some ice cream and be waiting on you."

Katy and John arrived home just a couple of minutes before Todd pulled in behind them. They decided to skip the ice cream and have tea.

"Alright, I'm confused," Katy said. "I heard that y'all arrested Coach Finch because you found some work gloves in his jeep with evidence on them that linked him to the murder."

"Actually, that's only about half true." Todd paused, sipping his tea. He was enjoying this brief moment of being the most informed person in the room. "When we talked to Coach Finch about his wife's death, he said he had been driving around town somewhere trying to clear his head and figure out where she had gone, so he didn't have an alibi. We brought him to the station to try to help him retrace his steps and see if maybe he had stopped at a gas station or gone through a drive-through during the evening. That way he would have a witness for his whereabouts during the time of her death."

"How in the world did Emma Robinson get the tale she told me about the gloves and murder and stuff from that?" Katy looked from Todd to John in exasperation.

"Well, honey," John said, "you can't expect accurate facts from the town gossip while standing in line at the takeout pizza place."

John was right. She should have tried to verify that information before just swallowing Emma's tale hook, line, and sinker.

"Now wait a minute. There's more to this story." Todd leaned forward and set his empty glass on the coffee table. "Emma wasn't too far off base. While the sheriff was inside the station talking to Coach Finch, I decided to go snoop around in his jeep. I had driven it from the school over to the station behind him and the sheriff when we brought him in. He said to look all I wanted, that there wasn't anything to find. So, I did."

John set his glass down beside his nephews. "Let me guess. You found something like maybe... a pair of gloves."

"Sure did," Todd grinned. "A pair of work gloves were in the glove box with what looked like dried blood all over them."

"Now wait a minute," Katy threw her hand up in the air. "I know I can't be wrong about this part. I was there when we found Laney's body, and I know there wasn't any blood on her. She was strangled."

"Okay, Aunt Katy. Don't get your feathers ruffled." Todd sat back on the couch and looked at his aunt and uncle, like the cat that had swallowed the canary.

Katy could see that he wanted to gloat just a little bit, but she couldn't wait. "Come on, Todd, spill it."

"The blood wasn't his wife's. We think that the blood was Jessa Williams.'"

"What?" Katy was speechless for a whole five seconds. "That makes absolutely no sense. Why would he put the monkey wrench in Joe Phobs' truck to frame him, then leave the gloves in the jeep for anybody to find? It's got to be a setup."

Todd bobbed his head up and down. "I know

Aunt Katy, I know, but you still don't know the whole story. The sheriff decided that he had enough to arrest Coach Finch for Jessa's murder. I don't think he believes that Coach Finch was dumb enough to leave them gloves in his Jeep where they could be found, but he ain't taking any chances. Plus, that ain't all."

"There's more? Please don't tell me he confessed to Jessa Williams' murder because I don't believe it."

"No, no, nothing like that," Todd said. "You know I took Coach to the funeral home this evening?"

"Yeah."

"The sheriff talked to Mr. Johnny, Laney's dad, and set all that up. Mr. Johnny said he didn't want anybody to talk to his grandkids about their dad being in jail. The sheriff thought that was a good idea, so he talked to Coach Finch, and they decided to tell the kids that he was staying in town just to help the sheriff with some work. The sheriff sent me over to his house to get his suit, so the boys wouldn't think anything was strange. You know, like they would if he showed up in the jumpsuit. Then we brought them all in together before the place got crowded."

"Misty told me she saw him there in his suit with his kids."

"Yeah, she did. But what I want to tell you about is what happened when I went to get his suit."

This time it was John that interrupted. "It didn't have anything to do with high dollar flip-flops, did it?" John was enjoying teasing his wife. This had been a tense week for her, and he usually helped to defuse her stress with humor.

Todd grinned. "No, nothing like that."

"Hush John." Katy shot John a look from her recliner. "Let the boy tell his story."

"Okay Todd, quit dangling the bait. What happened?" John said.

"I don't know if you have ever been by the Finch house, but there's always a lot of toys and stuff scattered in the yard, sort of junky. Well, today was the same way, but when I stepped onto the carport, I noticed that the door leading into the house was open. I grabbed my Taser and went on in. The place looked like a bomb had exploded in there."

"A bomb! How could a bomb go off on that quiet little street and nobody know?" Katy looked from one to the other but couldn't believe what she was hearing.

"No, wait," Todd said, holding up his hand. "I said it just looked like a bomb went off, that's all. The furniture was all turned over and ripped up.

Junk was strewed from one end of that house to the other. Pictures were ripped off the walls, the beds were torn up. It was a mess."

"Was anyone there?" John asked, all humor gone from his voice.

"No." Todd shook his head. "The house was empty. I don't know what went on there, but somebody demolished the place."

Katy had an idea what had happened at the Finch home but was not ready to share her theory with her nephew or her husband. "So, what did you do?"

"I called the sheriff, and he came over and taped the place off. We spent the rest of the day talking to the neighbors to see if anybody saw anything, but most of the people around there are at work in the day, so we didn't get any leads."

"This is just getting plumb scary." Katy rubbed the back of her neck to try to ease some of the knots she felt accumulating in her muscles. "What do you think happened?"

"I don't rightly know. The sheriff got Coach Finch's suit, and when we finally got back to the station, he quizzed him down, but he wasn't much help either."

John stepped into the kitchen to grab the tea pitcher and began to refill their glasses. "How long has the house been empty?"

"Since early yesterday morning when Coach Finch left for school."

Katy looked at her glass. She needed more ice but didn't want to leave the conversation long enough to go to the kitchen to get it. She sipped the tepid tea and frowned. "Was anything stolen?"

"We aren't sure. It's such a wreck that we can't tell, and Coach Finch is at the jail, so he doesn't know anything."

"Were any of the door locks broken?"

"That's the funny thing." Todd rubbed the tan stubble across his chin. "The carport door was open, but the lock wasn't broken. None of the locks or windows were broken. We asked Coach Finch if he left his house unlocked and he said of course he didn't, there's a killer loose in town."

John sat back down in his recliner and sipped from his tea glass. "So, the guy didn't break in through the door, but the door was open?"

"Yep, and the front door was still locked up tight."

Todd gulped down the last of the second glass of tea and stood to go. "If you think of anything that might help us figure this out, give me a call. I'm ready for this mess to be over."

"You know we will." John stood and slapped his nephew on the back. "In the meantime, you be careful."

"Oh, I am." Todd stopped at the living room door and turned back to Katy, who was still in her recliner, deep in thought. "The old ladies from the church have almost scrounged up enough money to get me that vest."

"At first I laughed," Katy said, looking up with a weak smile, "but now I think they might have the right idea."

Chapter Thirty-Two

Katy left her house at eight the next morning to see a new patient and start wound care. The patient's home ended up being little more than a shack and definitely didn't have the luxury of air conditioning. The 8x8 bedroom with low ceilings and one single forty-watt bulb to illuminate the darkly paneled interior had one tiny box fan in a single screen-less window. She did the wound care to the poor lady's backside with sweat dripping from the tip of her nose.

The little couple had lived in the tiny shack their entire married lives. The husband had worked as a janitor for the hospital in a nearby town until he retired, and his wife had been a cashier at The Pig when Katy was young. They had raised five kids in that dark little house and proudly displayed all five 8x10 glossy college graduation photos on their living room walls.

"Three schoolteachers, one lawyer, and one pharmacist," Mr. Byrd boasted. "Two went on football scholarships, two on band scholarships, and one on blood, sweat, and tears."

Now the couple were both in their eighties. The husband explained that all their kids were trying to get them to move closer to this one or that one, but they loved their little home place and would stay there as long as they had sense enough to make their own decisions.

"If we move in with any of the kids, they'll be trying to take care of our banking and make us go to their church. And I just can't listen to that new-fangled church music. I want my hymns played on the piano like I grew up on." Mr. Byrd grinned a toothless grin. "Now don't get me wrong, I think their church is just fine for my kids and their families, but I've been teaching my Sunday school class for almost thirty years, and my men depend on me."

"Now, honey, don't be talking bad about the boys' church music. I kind of like it as long as they don't put it up too terribly loud."

"I know, honey." Mr. Byrd quickly agreed with his wife. "It's alright for them, and I'm sure the

Lord thinks its mighty fine, but, well, I guess I'm just happy where I am."

After the paperwork was completed outside under the shade tree, Katy led the couple into the tiny bedroom adjoining the living room for the wound care. Her patient, Mrs. Jemima Byrd, had developed a boil on her hip which Dr. Roberts had lanced and cleaned in his office. Katy's job was to teach Mr. Byrd how to clean the wound and pack it daily until it healed. She would check the wound weekly and again any time Mr. Byrd called with problems. Mr. Byrd was an apt pupil.

"I've helped pull many a baby calf in my life and seen a ton of puppies being born. I even lanced a place on our old dog when the kids were little and put a poultice on it every day 'til it finally healed. This seems to be about the same thing."

"Yes, sir, it's the same principle. I'm sure you won't have any trouble with this." She instructed him on all the steps for the aseptic technique and then watched as the little old man gently cared for his wife.

"Now honey, you tell me if I hurt you," he said as he put on the rubber gloves.

Mrs. Byrd lay on the old bed facing the dingy paneled wall with her eyes calmly closed. "I'm sure you'll do just fine, Calvin. It's a little sore when you push that packing in."

When they were finished, she sat with the elderly couple in their dusty front yard under the shade of their massive oak tree and drank a glass of sweet tea. The little man still seemed pretty spry. He probably weighed one hundred and twenty pounds, tops, but he was only about five foot eight. He described himself as small and wiry.

Mrs. Byrd was the complete opposite of her husband. She was around five foot seven when she stood up straight, but for several years now she tended to stoop forward at about a twenty-degree angle which made her a couple of inches shorter than her spouse. She weighed two hundred and seven pounds on Katy's scales and moved at the pace of a turtle.

"Mrs. Cross, I hope you're being careful running up and down these roads," Mrs. Byrd said, repositioning herself in the lawn chair very slowly to ease the pain in her hip. "Until they catch the killer, I ain't sure you should be just going in strangers' houses like you do."

"I'm trying to be very careful, Mrs. Byrd," Katy said, smiling at her concern. "Ain't it a shame that we have to feel so unsafe in our own little community?" Mrs. Byrd never considered that even though Katy recognized the lady from a childhood memory, she had been a stranger to her only two hours before.

"We don't even have locks on our doors," Mr. Byrd said, wiping a bead of sweat from his upper lip with the back of his hand. "Never needed them before. Ain't got nothing worth stealing, so we ain't ever worried about it. But these two women getting killed, and for who knows what reason, has spooked us."

"Do you think you might need to purchase a couple of locks, just to play it safe?" Katy asked.

"Naa." The old grey-haired man chuckled and shook his head. "Wouldn't do any good. Anybody with a lick of sense could get in through those windows. We have to sleep with them up in this heat or we'd melt."

"I guess you have a point, but it's a scary time we're living in right now."

"And you know these things always happen in threes." Mrs. Byrd patted her sweaty brow with a damp paper towel. "My momma always said when two folks die, just go ahead and keep the black dress out because somebody else will be passing shortly."

Katy drank the final swallow of tea from the ancient metal Tupperware tumbler. "Mrs. Byrd, I hope you're wrong. I'm praying that the police catch this person before anyone else is hurt."

"Well, honey, so am I, but you should know, being a nurse and all, that people always pass in threes. I've seen it myself too many times to doubt."

Katy had heard the old wives' tale often and knew several people, including some nurses who believed it to be true. She immediately thought of Jessa's unborn child as being victim number three, but didn't say anything more on the subject. "I hate to rush off," she said, standing up and handing the glass to Mrs. Byrd's waiting hand, "but I have to get back to the office and do some paperwork. Another nurse will be out tomorrow to watch Mr. Byrd do the wound care one more time, then our visits will be weekly."

The elderly couple watched her from their lawn chairs as she walked across their grassless front yard to her car parked in the boiling hot sun near the highway. They waved goodbye as she headed back toward town. They probably spent most of their days right there under that hundred-year-old oak tree, watching the cars pass up and down the busy road. She wondered if they'd be looking for her car on the road now that they knew her.

After the paperwork was completed, she decided to drive by the Finch's house. The yellow police tape looked eerie draped across the front door with the bright blue and red little Mickey Mouse riding toy just two feet away on the lawn. The fact that someone had been in the Finch's home and looked through all their personal belongings gave her the creeps. Had the intruder been looking for whatever Laney had hidden under the bed at her mother's house? If he had, then the Carson family could be in danger by keeping that box. Katy tried to call Amanda Carson from her cell but didn't get an answer. She turned her car back toward her house and tried to decide what to do. Amanda thought that only she and Katy knew about Laney's box, but what if Laney had told someone else? Mrs. Simmons said Laney liked to talk. Maybe she was wrong. Maybe Laney could keep the important secrets. Katy sure hoped she had kept this one.

She pulled into her carport, deep in thought. She slipped off her dusty tennis shoes and sweaty socks and stepped barefoot across the kitchen to the chest freezer, opened the door, and leaned over to find something to cook for supper. The jarring ringing of the house phone abruptly broke the silence. She jumped straight up from the coolness of the freezer, throwing her hands in the air, and dropping the slippery frozen yellow brick of corn on her left foot. The top of her foot was a perfect target for the pointy corner of the square block of frozen vegetables. It jabbed like an arrow into the soft flesh, right between the base of her big toe and second toe. The pain was immense and instantaneous. Katy decided to ignore the blaring phone and pay attention to the blood spurting from the puncture wound now on her foot. She picked up the bloody block of corn and threw it toward the trash can then limped to the bathroom to attend to her war wound, leaving a small trail of blood and footprints to dry on the cool, pale ceramic tile kitchen floor.

She perched on the side of the tub in her bathroom and turned the cold water on full force. The water splashing into the empty tub echoed loudly as she turned her back to the closed bathroom door and eased her injured foot under the water to wash away the blood that had now slowed to a small red trickle. The throbbing began to ease. Now that the bleeding was getting under control, she could see that the wound was not too deep. She leaned her body to the side and rested her head on the wall next to the faucet and closed her eyes. Her pulse was pounding in her ears, and her blood pressure was probably sky high. She would sit still for just a second before getting up to clean the mess she'd left in the kitchen.

The cracking of the bathroom door as it ripped

off its hinges and slammed into the toilet jolted Katy into a new instant state of panic. She grabbed for the shower curtain as she lurched forward to dodge the falling door, but lost her balance. Her behind instantly slid into the tub of ice-cold water. She sucked in a deep breath as she sat completely clothed in the tub. The clingy white shower liner and the lovely country blue ruffled curtain complete with metal rod crashed down on her head.

"What the..."

Katy struggled to untangle herself from under the shower curtain as she listened to her husband behind her, who, for some crazy reason only known to him, had just kicked down their bathroom door.

"John?" Katy's head finally emerged triumphant above the slick plastic and stiff ruffles. "Are you okay?"

"Just a minute." John stood frozen in the now empty door frame with their nine-inch black cast iron frying pan raised above his head. The look on his face was a mixture of panic, confusion, and a sprinkle of 'uh-oh' all rolled into one. "Let me get this broken door out of the way."

John set the skillet on the closed toilet lid and picked up the splintered door and propped it against their bed in the next room. Katy turned off the cold water that continued to splash down onto her scrub pants and proceeded to climb from the tub. He returned to the bathroom and handed her a towel as she stripped off her soppy wet nursing uniform. Her toe was throbbing again as she pulled on a bathrobe and then limped into their bedroom.

"Are you okay?" John asked, trailing behind her like a guilty police dog with his tail tucked between his legs.

"I'll be fine," she said, grinning at her husband's look of total dejection. "I need some gauze and tape from my nursing bag to doctor my toe."

"I'll get it." He bolted to the bedroom door like greased lightning. "Be right back."

Katy started to call him back, but decided to just wait until he returned to find out what had just happened. She gathered the rest of the supplies needed to doctor her foot and limped to the living room. The bleeding had stopped, but the area from about mid-foot to the end of her big toe was starting to swell and turn a stormy shade of blue. John walked into the living room just as she was easing herself into her recliner.

"Do you want to let me in on why you needed to kick in the bathroom door?" she asked, wincing as she eased the chair back.

"I sure do, but I also want to know what happened in the kitchen." He handed her the gauze and tape while he sat on the edge of the couch to watch her bandage her foot.

"Well." Katy winced as she dabbed the raw flesh with alcohol.

"You want me to grab the hydrogen peroxide for you?" John's wince was a little more pronounced than hers. "It won't burn."

"I'm almost through cleaning it." She smiled at his sympathy pains. "I'll just tough it out."

"Well, okay, but I know that's got to hurt like the dickens." He waited until she pulled the blood-tinged gauze from the wound to continue. "You know all everybody is talking about are these two murders."

"Yeah," Katy nodded. She gently blew on her foot to relieve the stinging.

"All I've heard today is how people better be protecting themselves from the Skeeterville serial killer." John ran his hands through his hair, glancing from Katy's face to her foot. "Folks are dead bolting their doors even when they're home inside, and sleeping with their guns by their beds. It's crazy."

She listened while she applied the antibiotic ointment and gauze dressing. "Uh-huh."

"Well, I guess I just got a little edgy. I drove up and saw your car home, but when I turned the knob, the door was unlocked."

"That's because I just walked through the door."

"Yeah, well, seeing as how we talked just last night about locking the doors, I was kind of surprised." He stood up and started to pace, something he only did when he was very excited. "But then, when I came on in, the trash can was knocked over with garbage scattered everywhere. And to top it all off, there's blood on the floor with footprints going toward the bedroom." He paused to glance at Katy to see how she was reacting. "You have to admit that this is not the usual scene I come home to in the afternoons. Anyway, I just imagined the worse, so I grabbed something heavy and went to see what was going on."

"Aww, you were coming to rescue me with the iron skillet," Katy said, grinning from ear to ear.

"It seems absurd now, but I was fit to be tied a few minutes ago." John slowed his pacing and started to chuckle. "I was fixing to lay somebody low or die trying. What in the world happened in the kitchen?"

"Nothing, really. I was getting a bag of that sweet corn we put up earlier in the summer from the freezer when the phone rang. The bag was slippery, and I dropped it on my foot. The corner jabbed into me, making my foot bleed. I threw the block of bloody corn at the trash can, but I guess I knocked the can over without realizing it."

"Well, at least you're okay, or mostly okay."

"This ain't too bad." She winced as she tried to wiggle her toes. "I may have to wear a slipper for a few days until the swelling goes down, but it should heal pretty quickly."

John held out his hands and gently pulled her up from the chair. "Want to ride with me to the hardware store to buy a new door?"

"Sure, why not?"

Chapter Thirty-Three

Katy and John spent the rest of the day installing a new door for the bathroom. It had to be taken down a couple of times and redone before it finally hung correctly. John refused to call anybody to come help, so Katy limped around and assisted as best as she could.

"I'm not in the mood to explain why I kicked down my own bathroom door while my wife was sitting in the tub with all of her clothes on. We'll just keep at this until we get it right." So, after several hours and quite a few tries, they finally had a new door up.

"Hey, there's a message on the machine," John called from the living room the next morning.

"I wonder if it's who was calling when I hurt my foot. The ringing phone is what started all that mess," Katy said, lifting the fourth and final slice of crisp bacon from the pan of piping hot grease. "Do you recognize the number?"

"Nope, probably work-related." He walked into the kitchen. "Let me fry our eggs while you check it."

"Alright, and it's time to get the biscuits out of the oven too." She passed the egg turner over and went to the living room to see who had called. Evelyn Brown's smooth southern drawl floated from the machine.

"Katy, dear, I'm sorry to call you at home. I hope it's okay. Mother has been acting a little wobbly and confused today. I was wondering if you could drop by tomorrow and check on her. I would try to get her in to see Chris, I mean Dr. Roberts, but she's not being very cooperative. Call me back when you get this, dear. Goodbye."

It was just seven-fifteen. Katy would eat, get dressed, and then call Mrs. Brown. She had planned to call Amanda Carson this morning to try to get her to take Laney's mysterious box in to the sheriff, but that would wait until after she checked on Mrs. Tellman.

"You were right," she said as she limped back into the kitchen. "It was about work." She poured two cups of coffee, and they sat down to breakfast. John reminded her again to lock the door behind him as he was leaving. Katy reminded John not to kick down any doors when he came home.

It took her a little longer than usual to shower and get dressed. She took the strings out of her left tennis shoe, but her foot was still too swollen to fit. It was more swollen today than it had been last night. She put back on the leopard print house slipper she had worn the day before and would just make the best of it.

She was supposed to be off today, but after calling Evelyn, decided to run by and check on Mrs. Tellman around ten. She made sure there was a specimen cup in the trunk of her car to check for a urinary tract infection. She slid behind the steering wheel then checked the voicemail on her cell.

"Hey, Mrs. Katy, this is Emma Robinson. I got your number from the skincare form you filled out at the party. I was just calling to let you know that your refreshing facial mist is in. Call me back so I can deliver it or meet you with it. Bye now."

She started her car and turned on the air conditioner to cool off the interior. She had forgotten about her bottle of thirty-dollar water. She punched in Emma's number. "Hey Emma, can I drop by the bank at eleven-thirty and pick up my stuff?"

"Sure, Mrs. Katy. You will never guess what happened."

"Well, why don't you just tell me," Katy said, easing her sore foot out of the way. She put her car in reverse and glanced in the rearview mirror.

"You know Joe Phobs missed his hitch to work offshore, and they let him go."

"Aww, that's so sad. I hate to hear that."

"It turned out okay. Mr. Robinson hired him to drive a skitter with Tubby's crew. He's not making the kind of money he was, but at least he's gainfully employed again."

"Oh, great. That's good to hear." Katy glanced at her watch. She needed to get on the road.

"Wait, Mrs. Katy. That's not what I wanted to tell you. Joe invited us to church Sunday, and Tubby said we're going."

"That's even better news, Emma. We'll save a spot on the back row for you."

"I knew you would be happy about that. I've gotta go, so I won't be late for work. Bye, see you at eleven-thirty."

Katy backed out of her driveway and headed toward the garden district. Hopefully, this wouldn't take too long, and she could squeeze in a visit with Amanda Carson today. She tried her number again, but no one answered. A tiny burning sensation began to gnaw in the pit of her stomach.

"She just finished breakfast and is in the bathroom sprucing up a bit," Nelda said, leading Katy to Mrs. Tellman's room. "I need to warn you that she's not too happy that Evelyn called you."

"Thank you, Nelda. Hopefully, nothing serious is going on." Katy looked at Mrs. Tellman's blood sugars for the past several days and was satisfied that her diabetes was being well controlled. She sat in a chair just as her patient opened the bathroom door. As usual, she was in a pink satin gown and matching duster, not a hair was out of place.

"I don't know why you're here," Mrs. Tellman snapped, hastily walking across the bedroom. "I feel fine. Evelyn is just jumping the gun about this. I know you ain't going to find anything wrong."

"Well, it's better to be safe than sorry." Katy smiled as the little spitfire sat in her recliner and placed the cane at her side.

"Let's get this nonsense over with," she said, flopping her arm out in front of her to have her blood pressure checked.

"So far, so good." Katy removed the cuff from the thin little arm and pulled the stethoscope from her ears. "Everything's checking out well. Let's look at your wound."

"It's almost gone. I'm telling you that this is a waste of your time and mine." Mrs. Tellman watched Katy remove the dressing on her leg. "I know how I feel."

After Katy cleaned the wound and redressed it, Mrs. Brown came in to check on her. She leaned over and attempted to kiss her mother's cheek, but Mrs. Tellman turned her face away. "So, how is our patient doing?" She sighed and turned to Katy.

"The wound looks great, and her vital signs are good. We need to get a urine specimen to rule out a bladder infection, but so far everything looks normal." She pulled the specimen cup from her bag and tried to hand it to Mrs. Tellman. "Can you give me a urine sample? It doesn't have to be much."

Mrs. Tellman crossed her hands over her chest and glared first at Katy and then her daughter. "No, I cannot. I just went and won't go again for at least two hours. If you would have talked to me about this instead of my daughter, I would have saved you a specimen from this morning. But since y'all are determined to talk about me like I'm not here, you will just have to wait."

"Okay, Mrs. Tellman, I'm sorry." Katy set the cup on the table by the blue recliner. The woman didn't seem confused, just mad as a wet hen. "You're right. You're the patient, and I should be talking to you about what's going on."

"You bet your britches you should." She turned to her daughter and wagged a long, boney finger in her direction. "And I don't know what you think is wrong with me, but if I need your help, don't worry, I'll ask for it."

Mrs. Brown ignored her mother's outburst and looked at Katy with a 'see what I mean,' look. "We'll get the specimen and run it by the doctor's office today."

Katy stood and picked up her gear. The throbbing in her foot started to increase. "That'll be fine. I'll let his office know about the assessment and to expect the specimen." She looked down at Mrs. Tellman, still sulking in her recliner. "I hope you won't stay mad at me long."

"I'm not mad, I'm aggravated. There's a difference."

"Yes, ma'am." Katy said, grinning at the woman's spunk. Mrs. Tellman dismissed them both with a glare, grabbing the TV remote and turning on a morning talk show.

Evelyn followed Katy to her front yard and watched as she climbed behind the wheel and cranked her car, waiting for the air to cool the sweltering interior. Evelyn stood outside of the car like she had something more to say. Katy had assured her on the way out that her mother was doing fine and that she didn't see any need for worry, but she let the window down so Evelyn could tell her whatever was on her mind.

"Dear, I appreciate you coming out so much. You understand that I just worry about Momma."

"There's no need to thank me," Katy said. "I'm happy to come to see her. It's part of my job."

"I know this is going to sound rude, but I'm just dying to ask you," Evelyn said, fidgeting with the collar of her shirt. "What in the world happened to your foot? That slipper, and the way you're limping just makes me feel terrible about having you drive all of the way over here."

"It's not nearly as bad as it looks," Katy assured her, giving her a description of what happened the day before. She did not tell her that it was her phone call that had started the whole mess.

Evelyn said her goodbyes, and Katy finally got underway after about ten minutes. At least the AC worked well in her little car. She was cool and comfortable except for her throbbing left foot.

She stopped at the end of the driveway to answer a call from the office. Since she was already out, they needed her to run by the Byrd's and follow up with their wound care since the scheduled nurse had called in sick. Instead of turning back toward downtown, she changed directions and started toward the highway. She would not be able to drop by Amanda's house before lunch. The woman still wasn't answering her phone.

She passed by Piney Acres Trailer Park almost to the Byrd's driveway. The car lurched forward and then slowed of its own accord. The check engine light started to flash bright red on the dashboard at the same time pillows of thick white smoke began spewing from the hood.

"Ain't this just a hot mess," she said, pulling to the side of the highway and exiting the dying little car as quickly as her throbbing foot would allow. "Well, don't this just beat all."

She quickly limped away to what felt like a safe distance. In her hurry to get out, she left her phone on the passenger's seat where she had tossed it after the last call. It looked too unsafe to try and retrieve it now. She could hobble the short distance to the Byrd's house and call John, but she didn't want to leave her purse and computer unattended in the back seat. If the smoke died down before she got back, somebody could just reach in and take all her stuff.

She would just stand and wait. Even though it was mid-morning, this road still had a lot of traffic. A Good Samaritan would be along any minute now for sure. If not, she would wait until the smoke cleared, and the car cooled down, then retrieve her phone and call for help.

The ominous smoke continued to rise from the hood. It was slowing some, but heat devils danced on the silver metal. She would need a tow truck. A mental list of things she would not get done today started to form in her head. *Lord, keep my attitude right. This could have been a lot worse.*

She watched a few cars fly by, some toward town, some toward the country, but none bothering to stop. She didn't blame any of them. After all, a killer was running around loose in their little town. John would skin her alive if she stopped to help a stranger on the side of the road.

The smoke from the hood was now rising in soft, slow, fluffy clouds, but she knew the temp of the metal would burn her hand if she touched it. Not that it mattered. Even if she could lift the hood, she wouldn't know how to fix the problem. She began limping back toward the car. The danger of it flaming up or exploding like they did on television seemed to have passed. Time to retrieve her phone and call John.

As she opened the passenger door, a wave of heat hit her in the face. She hastily grabbed her phone and computer bag before slamming the door and retreating. As she backed away once more, a shiny SUV passed by and hit its brake lights. She watched warily as it eased over onto the side of the road and stopped just a few yards from her poor little sick car. The windows were tinted so dark that she couldn't even see a shadow of the person or people in the vehicle. Her mind immediately returned to the two bodies she'd found in the past few weeks and the conversation she had with the sheriff about the killer feeling threatened by what she'd seen. The gnawing feeling in her stomach returned. Unconsciously, she began taking slow steps toward the back of her car and away from the black mystery wagon. The sweat puddled on the back of her neck and ran down her spine as she waited for the driver to step out.

"Katy, I thought that was your little car."

Katy let out a long haggard breath as Evelyn Brown, cool and perfectly coiffured, as usual, walked around the large SUV and into sight.

"Yes, it's me. I don't know what happened to my car, but I'm sure glad you were coming this way. Thank you so much for stopping."

"Of course I stopped, dear. Come on, I'll give you a ride back to town."

Katy hobbled to the SUV and stumbled into the vehicle, trying not to bump her injured foot. She must have cracked a bone yesterday. The swelling and pain were getting worse with each step, even though she was trying very hard not to put any weight on it. She dropped her computer bag on the floorboard beside her legs, careful not to touch her foot. "This sure is a nice ride," she said. "I have to admit, I was a little nervous until I saw you get out, you know, with all that's been going on lately."

Evelyn pulled the enormous vehicle around and started back toward town. Katy watched Mr. Byrd walking down his driveway toward her dead car. She waved at him through the side window but realized he couldn't see her through the tinted glass. She'd call his house in a few minutes and explain what happened.

"You can drop me by the office, or the flower shop, or anywhere in town, Mrs. Brown," she said, thinking about who she would get to help her retrieve her car. "I'm going to call John and have him come pick me up. I think my car is gonna need a tow truck."

"Just call me Evelyn, honey." She slowed the vehicle and began to turn down the logging road across from the trailer park, about a mile up from Katy's broken-down car.

Katy watched as the SUV bounced heavily down the dark, dirty logging road, hitting every mud hole and tree branch along the way. The vibration and bouncing were doing a number on her foot. Where were they going? "Evelyn, are you sure you meant to turn here? This is just a dead-end logging road."

Evelyn brought the SUV to a halt under an enormous pine at the end of the road and turned to face Katy. "I'm afraid so, dear. These desperate times are calling for desperate measures."

Katy glanced down at Evelyn's hand and felt the blood draining from her face. A small, silver pistol was casually pointed right at Katy's gut. She felt her phone by her side in her right hand and tried to unlock the screen without drawing Evelyn's attention to what she was doing.

"Okay, Katy. Don't make me use this little gun in the Suburban. I don't want to get any blood on these new leather seats. This is a company car, and Miles might start asking questions if that happens." She reached out her hand and Katy reluctantly passed her the cell phone.

She could feel her heart pounding in her chest and hear it pounding in her ears. If she stroked out right here, it would solve Evelyn's problem of where to spill her blood. She took a deep breath and tried to think. "You killed Jessa and Laney, didn't you?"

"Well, I had a little help." Evelyn smiled as she answered in her quaint southern drawl. "Once that money-grabbing hussy, was dead, I needed some manpower to get her gaudy body out of that shed."

"You hit Jessa with the monkey wrench the night of the Peanut Patch festival?" Katy turned her body toward Evelyn as she slid her hand behind her back for support. If she could keep the crazy woman distracted, maybe she could get the door open and dive out before Evelyn could get off a shot.

"Is that what you call that big ole thing? I wasn't sure." Evelyn moved her hands through the air, gesturing as she answered Katy's question, seemingly unconcerned that she was holding a loaded pistol. "That was just a stroke of luck seeing it in the toolbox of that white-trash Phobs boy's truck. I had planned on using one of Mile's fishing knives, but when I saw that, what did you call it? A monkey wrench? Well, I knew that would be better."

This woman was nuts. She was sitting here in her designer clothes, waving a pistol around with her manicured nails, talking about how she killed a woman as if it was no big deal. Katy had to keep her distracted. "So, you had planned to stab Jessa?"

"Yes, that was my original plan, but the monkey wrench thing worked out so much better. The night of that idiot Peanut Patch festival, I waited until Mother had turned off her TV and Miles was asleep." She glanced down at her French manicure. "I slipped out of the house and was never missed. That was easy, of course, since Miles and I have slept in separate rooms for years. I parked at the edge of the field and just mixed in with the crowd. Then all I had to do was wait until Jessa was by herself."

"But when did you get Joe's monkey wrench?" Katy asked, momentarily forgetting her escape plan. "And how did you get her to go in the shed? "

"You think I'm an idiot has-been beauty queen, just like everybody else in this town," Evelyn smirked, rubbing her lips together smearing her lipstick that was beginning to bleed out from the corners of her mouth. "Well, that's okay. That's working in my favor. Let everybody believe I'm too dumb to pull this off." She reached up and wiped her mouth with her free hand, effectively smearing the rest of her lipstick off her lips. "I'll just sit back and laugh while that Podunk sheriff drags the Phobs boy and that hypocrite coach to the slammer. She looked down and studied the back of her hand, now stained with bright pink lipstick, keeping the pistol haphazardly pointed in Katy's direction. "You see, everybody, and I mean everybody, brings their cars and trucks to our dealership for tune-ups, oil changes, car washes, and all that other stuff. So, when Joe Phobs left his truck at our shop at the beginning of the week to get his tires rotated, I just grabbed the heaviest thing there was out of his toolbox. The keys to the box were on the key ring when he turned it in to me." She laughed again. "I still don't think it's ever dawned on him to tell our great lawman that his truck was at our shop. I just unlocked the toolbox, took what I wanted and locked it back. Then, that night I put on an old tee-shirt of Miles' with some jeans and a baseball cap and waited in the shed until Jessa was by herself."

Katy had to admit that this woman was clever. She had underestimated her. "But how did you get her in the shed to, uh, hit her? And how did you get her from the shed to under the trailer?"

"Getting her in the shed was easy," Evelyn said, fluttering her hands around again. Katy scooted back toward the passenger door a little more, awaiting her opportunity to jump out.

"It was after midnight," Evelyn continued, "and that bunch that she hangs around with finally cleared out. I just bumped around inside the shed door when she walked by. She had done had one catfight with that blue-haired woman earlier. I knew she would have to make sure that girl wasn't in there making out with ole Phobs right there under her nose. Sure enough, soon as she heard the noise, she came charging in there yelling and cursing and acting just as red-necked as she looked in that ridiculous leopard print mini skirt."

Chapter Thirty-Four

Katy placed her hand on the door handle. If Evelyn would just look away for a second, she would make her move.

"I just stood in the dark and waited until her back was to me," Evelyn continued, her voice calm and pleasant. "Then smack. One good whack with the monkey wrench and it was over." She paused and touched a bead of perspiration forming on her upper lip. "Whew, it's getting warm in here. I don't have time to redo my make-up. I have a meeting at the country club for lunch. I wasn't planning on chatting in the truck all day."

She switched the pistol to her left hand and leaned toward the steering wheel to crank the SUV. It was now or never. Katy turned the handle behind her and jerked open the door while she pushed herself out backwards with her one good foot. She landed like a sack of potatoes on the cool, hard ground. Thank the Lord there weren't any big rocks or tree limbs where she hit, just very hard ground.

Evelyn immediately went to cursing and ripping, but Katy didn't waste time listening. She slammed the door shut and pulled herself up. If she headed up the logging road, Evelyn would have a clear shot at her. She quickly limped around to the back of the SUV out of site just as Evelyn came running around the front to the passenger's side.

"Now, Katy, I ain't got time for all of this. If you make me get these new sandals muddy chasing you through the woods, I'm gonna pitch a hissy-fit."

She paused, waiting for an answer. Katy peaked around the edge of the SUV and watched as Evelyn stood there. The pistol hand was on her hip, and the other hand holding the keys was rubbing the back of her neck. She tapped the toe of her two-inch wedge-heeled espadrilles for just a second before heading up the logging path toward the main road. Katy eased around the edge of the vehicle to remain out of sight. She was hopeful for just an instant that Evelyn would forget to lock the SUV, but that hope was dashed. She heard all the doors click as her back disappeared up the wooded logging road.

Hot sparks shot up her left leg every time the injured foot touched the ground, but stopping was not an option. She decided to head east, the opposite direction of Evelyn. The Byrds lived on the other side of the narrow strip of timberland. If she could just keep going and stay out of sight, maybe she could get to their house and get help.

The trees were so thick she had to weave back and forth between them. The vines and briers reached up from the earth and grabbed at her legs as she crept along. There wasn't a drop of wind blowing, but the heavy pine needles and thick branches kept the sun from beating down on her sweat-drenched head. She looked back over her shoulder. The monstrous SUV was no longer visible. Good. She was making a little progress.

The rough bark of the pine tree scratched through the thin nursing top as she leaned back against the tree trunk. She would only stop a minute to catch her breath. What time was it? It seemed like hours since her car caught fire, but it probably had been less than one. Would Mr. Byrd try to figure out where she had gone? Maybe he would call her office and get them to look for her, or maybe he would just go back to his house and forget about her. She had no idea. The familiar sound coming through the woods sent a chill across the back of her neck. Evelyn was calling her name.

The trees were getting thicker as she pushed deeper into the woods. The faint sunlight fighting its way through the limbs was not directly overhead. It wasn't noon. She limped on, following the direction given by the sunlight, but progress was slow. Every muscle ached. Every step pulled more energy than she had to give. Every breath was a struggle.

"I'm going to get out of this mess, and when I do, no more ice cream after supper. If I don't die from a gunshot or heart attack today, I'm joining a gym tomorrow," she whispered as she panted.

The voice was getting louder... closer. "Katy, you know I'm going to catch you. Come on out." Evelyn didn't even sound out of breath. She just sounded crazy. Evelyn must have figured out which way she was going.

Katy pushed onward, trying desperately to ignore the stabbing pain in her foot and the pounding in her chest. The trees were beginning to thin a little. She must be coming out on the other side. *Faster, you have got to move faster,* her inner voice begged.

The sun began to break through the treetops, bringing more light and heat to the edge of the woods. She reached up and pushed back a low-hanging branch. The Byrd's little cinder block house could just be made out on the other side of the open field. She could hear footfalls coming her way at a slow run. Evelyn was moving in behind her. She gulped in a lung full of air and took off in a pitiful, lopsided run. She had to make it through the wide-open field to the old couples' house before Evelyn broke through the trees and saw her.

She didn't look back, only forward. The house was growing larger with every step. Halfway there. Katy hit the ground like a stone as a bullet whizzed over her head and the thunderous explosion blasted in her ears. The dry dirt clods forced their way into her mouth and nose as she connected with the earth. She turned her head to the side and sucked in another breath of air. No new horrendous pains, just the same lightning bolt in her foot. Evelyn had missed.

"Hold still, Katy, I'm coming," Evelyn called as she trotted across the field.

Katy raised her head high enough to look toward the little house still several yards in front of her. The screen door was halfway open, and Mr. Byrd's grey head was peaking outside. Katy's mind raced. She could not let Evelyn harm the Byrd's, and she was leading her right to them.

She rolled over, trying to be ever mindful of her

injury, and pushed herself up to face Evelyn. "You win. I'll go back with you. Just don't hurt anybody else."

Evelyn held her gun free hand up to shade her eyes against the bright sun and gazed across the field to the Byrd's home. Mr. Byrd was no longer in the doorway. The screen door was shut tight. Evelyn didn't seem to notice that they were being watched. "Now you're talking with some sense." The pistol waved in front of Katy's face, motioning for her to move back toward the trees. "Come on. We've wasted this whole morning, and I'm a mess. You're about to get on my last nerve."

Katy began to limp slowly back to the cover of the trees and in the opposite direction of safety. She looked over her right shoulder toward the highway where her car was still sitting. Would anybody figure out what was going on before Evelyn had time to finish her off? She felt the pistol push into her ribs.

"You know you brought all of this on yourself," Evelyn exclaimed. "When you found Jessa, I figured that was just dumb luck."

Katy needed to stay in the open field as long as she could. She slowed her steps, trying to slow their progression, but the pistol nudged her forward. She looked over her shoulder at Evelyn.

"You're right. It was a pure accident that I found her body that night."

"I believed that at first. I was even willing to think that when you found Laney in that old woman's trailer."

Katy felt her bad foot roll over a mound of dirt. Her knees went to the ground, stumbling forward over a rut in the field. The pain in her foot was almost more than she could bear.

Evelyn grabbed the sweaty wet hair on the back of Katy's head. "Get up." Her voice was no longer pleasant, but cold and flat. "The games are over. Either get up or we'll do this right here."

Tears and sweat run down her face, blurring her vision as she pushed herself back up. How could she buy some more time? "I'm moving. Look. I know you're going to kill me. At least tell me how you managed to pull all of this off."

Now that Katy was following directions again, Evelyn's voice changed back to the sweet sing-song southern tone. "Let's see. I've already told you how I took care of Jessa."

The tree line was fast approaching. She had to keep her talking until she could figure something out. "But how did you move her body from the shed to under the flatbed?"

"I didn't move her dear," Evelyn said, slowing

their pace as they came upon the cover of the trees. "I had some help."

"But who was it?" Katy paused and turned to face her captor. "Your husband?"

Evelyn stopped, forgetting for the moment that she wanted to hurry. "Miles... actually do some physical work?" She threw her head back and cackled. "Don't be ridiculous. Besides, he wouldn't have done anything to harm his precious Jessa, anyway."

"Is that why you killed her?" Katy winced as she lifted her swollen foot, trying to ease the throb that continued to pulse upwards from her toes "She was having an affair with Mr. Brown?"

"Don't play stupid." Evelyn tilted her head to the side and glared at Katy. "I know you know that piece of trash was his daughter."

"His daughter? No, I had no idea."

Evelyn continued to stare, looking for any sign that Katy was lying. "Well, maybe you didn't. Maybe you're not that smart after all." She wiped the sweat rolling in big droplets down her forehead and landing in her lashes with the back of her hand. The thick mascara left a black scar across her nose and cheek where it landed. "Yes, his daughter. I wouldn't have cared. Heaven knows I don't love him, haven't for years, but Jessa just wouldn't stop pushing for more money."

Katy stared at the black streak across Evelyn's

face for only a second as her words soaked in. "She was blackmailing you?"

"Of course. At first, I refused to give her a penny. Then she showed me a marriage certificate for Miles and her piece-of-trash momma that was dated before ours."

"I don't understand." Katy looked Evelyn in the eye. "Why would you care if people knew your husband had been married before? Half the population is divorced. It's a normal thing."

"Don't be slow, woman." Evelyn waved the gun in the air impatiently. "He was not divorced and on his second marriage. He wasn't married to her before. He was still married to her. The jerk had managed to marry me while he was still married to her and keep it a secret."

Katy's attention shifted from the firearm waving in front of her face to the woman speaking. The dawning of understanding showed across her features as what had pushed this woman over the edge began to come clear in her mind. "Bigamy," she whispered, more to herself than to her listener.

"Don't say that word," Evelyn spat back. "Don't you dare speak that filthy word to me or anyone else. Laney thought she could threaten me with that same word. I hope you're smarter than her." She ran her fingers through her silver hair, causing it to stick up like shards of glass. "Neither one of those women were going to come into my world and steal everything I had created for my son." Evelyn's voice grew louder as she spoke, louder and more shrill. "So what if he married her first? Miles Brown was nothing until he married me. He didn't have two dimes to rub together, and my money made him what he is today. I would kill before I would give it all to some low-life Alabama nobody."

Her voice lowered to a softer, more normal pitch as she brought her emotions back under control. "I did what I had to do. I did what any mother would do." She pushed the gun into Katy's chest, giving her a shove. The conversation was over. "Now get moving. I need to get out of these woods before I get eat up with ticks and red bugs."

Dear God, please deliver me from this insane woman. The silent prayer went up as they moved forward into the thick line of trees. The sound of Evelyn's voice gnawed away in the background as the bile and vomit struggled to come up. Every effort of concentration was needed to keep both at bay.

"Making your car break down was the easy part."

The last sentence penetrated Katy's armor, and she began to focus on the words coming from Evelyn's mouth. "You did something to my car?"

"Well, yes, aren't you listening? I thought you wanted to know all of this. I did it when I got you to come over and check on Mother. At first, I was worried Mother was going to give it away, but nope. You didn't catch on at all. While you were in the house, I just took a long screwdriver and shoved it through your grill." She giggled as she looked at Katy's astonished face. "I put a hole in your radiator. That was easy. Then I just kept you there, running your mouth until the fluid had time to drain out. Pretty smart, huh?"

The smug look of pride on Evelyn's face made Katy want to slap her. "Yeah, pretty smart." She turned and stumbled along through the woods, unable to look at the woman a moment longer. Evelyn had been playing her all along.

"Finally," Evelyn said, noticing the slump of Katy's shoulders and hanging low of her head. She had won the battle of wills. "Now, Katy, let's get this over with. The pond is just a little way through the woods there." She pointed in the opposite direction of where Katy had run earlier. "I need you to cooperate and get on over there."

The gun nudged into Katy's back. Her legs felt like noodles, and her arms like lead. She was no match for Evelyn. She dragged herself on toward the pond. Her watery grave.

Chapter Thirty-Five

The sound of a diesel engine reached both women at the same time. Someone was coming up the logging road at breakneck speed. Evelyn grabbed Katy's arm and jerked them both behind the nearest pine tree. Katy couldn't stop the moan that came from her mouth as the pain jolted through her foot.

"Shut-up," Evelyn hissed as she shoved the barrel of the pistol in her throat. "I'll shoot your nosey little head clean off if you make another peep."

The sound of brakes and truck doors slamming had both women's complete attention, but for totally different reasons. "That's it. That's the SUV that picked her up." Katy recognized Mr. Byrd's voice. Bless his heart. He'd come to save her after all. She listened and silently prayed that he had brought along somebody besides his slow-moving wife.

"You sure it was a gunshot you heard, Mr. Byrd?" Katy knew she'd heard this man's voice before, but she couldn't quite remember who it belonged to.

"Yeah, boy," Mr. Byrd answered, clearly aggravated. "I'm sure. Katy came out of these here woods toward our house, but somebody fired a shot at her. Lord help her. At first, I thought she'd been hit, but then she got back up, like I done said, and headed into these woods."

"Okay, Mr. Byrd, you stay here and wait for the sheriff." Katy recognized the third voice as Joe Phobs. "We'll start looking for her and whoever owns that big black tank."

She turned her head slightly toward her captor. Evelyn was staring in the direction of the voices, fear creeping into her eyes. Katy slammed her elbow into Evelyn's ribs as hard as she could with one arm and pushed the pistol away from her neck with the opposite hand.

The gunfire was deafening. Evelyn and Katy both hit the ground, and this time the pain in Katy's foot was more than she could stand. The trees above her began to spin. The world went black.

❧

I'm going to throw up. The words popped into her mind before she could open her eyes. Rolling to her side, she heaved and lost her breakfast on a crunchy brown pile of pine straw near her head. She lay back and waited for the world to refocus. The hot coals and piercing arrows from the injured foot continued coursing up her leg, but she refused to give in to it again. Pulling in a deep breath, she turned her head to the right where Evelyn had been. She was gone. So was her gun.

The ringing in her ears from the exploding gunshot made it difficult to sit up, but not impossible. Sucking in as much air as possible while sitting hunched over on the ground, she let out a scream that would rival a banshee. Had anyone heard? She couldn't tell. "Help me, I'm over here!" she yelled out. "Somebody help me!"

An old-school telephone ringing, but as loud as a fire alarm, that's all she could hear. Only there was no telephone, just her ears. She tried to push up and stand with her good leg, but the slight movement was just too much. The bad foot refused to cooperate, and the throbbing refused to let her move. She forced down the bile that was creeping up her throat and shifted her upper body to face the direction of the logging road. If anyone was coming to her rescue, it would probably be from there. She leaned forward and eased the muddy house shoe off the hurting foot. Even doing that raised the pain back to blackout level. Her foot looked like one giant black grape with five little black grapes lined across the end. Yep, something was broken.

A movement through the woods caught her eye. Relief flooded her being as Tubby Robinson came crashing through the trees like a flannel-clad football player with just a touch of asthma. That must have been the voice she didn't recognize earlier. She waved both arms frantically above her head to make sure he saw her. He lumbered over to her side, leaned over, and put both hands on his knees in an attempt to bring more air into his lungs. His face was candy apple red, and his massive 300 plus pound frame was drenched with sweat from the brief excursion.

"You okay?" He managed to ask between gulps of air.

"I'm okay. Are you okay?" Katy responded, thankful her hearing was returning.

Tubby nodded his head. "This body wasn't built for running." He straightened back up as his breathing became more controlled. "I heard a shot and hot-footed it in this direction." He squatted down beside Katy and noticed her ugly, bulbous purple foot. "What in the world's going on? Me and Joe stopped at your car and Mr. Calvin came running up with a wild tale about gunshots in the field by his house." He stopped again to catch his breath. "I didn't believe the old guy until I heard one for myself a few minutes ago." He helped Katy get up, and they began making their way back to the SUV at a snail's pace.

"Tubby, Joe, y'all out there?" Mr. Byrd's voice called, shakily.

"We're coming, Mr. Calvin," Tubby yelled, scooping Katy up and jogging toward the logging road. "Hang on."

Mr. Byrd was sitting on the ground, propped against Tubby's work truck. Joe Phobs pressed an old tee-shirt to the back of the old man's head. "She got the best of me, Tubby," Mr. Byrd said gravely. "I was looking back up the road yonder for the sheriff, and she snuck up behind me and hit me with something."

Joe took his make-shift compression bandage away and peaked at Mr. Byrd's bloody grey-haired scalp. "It ain't too bad. I don't think you'll need stitches." He reached under the older man's arms and lifted him up. All four climbed into the double cab work truck.

"She lured me to her house today, then messed up my car," Katy said as she leaned across the seat and patted Mr. Byrd's wrinkled hand. "You were an answer to prayer. If you hadn't come out looking for me, I'd be dead right now."

"I ask the good Lord to use me every day." The corners of the old man's lips turned up slightly into a soft smile. "This is the first time he's ever used me like this."

Chapter Thirty-Six

The nurse stuck one last piece of white silky tape over the IV line, securing it to Katy's arm. "We'll have you rehydrated and feeling better in no time," she said. She checked the flow rate on the IV. "Make sure you push that call button if you need anything. I won't have you falling on my watch. The pain medication I put through your line may make you a little groggy, but your foot should start feeling better soon."

"How's Mr. Byrd? Did he need stitches?" Katy asked, looking around the exam room.

"Nah, just a little clean-up and an x-ray," the nurse said. She picked up her supplies from the bedside table and stuffed them in her scrub pocket. "I think his son is checking him out now. He'll be home in time for supper."

Katy said a silent prayer of thanks. The emergency room cot was narrow and lumpy. The safety of the bustling medical staff and security of the sheriff standing in the corner whispering with John gave Katy a peace that brought comfort beyond the slightly inadequate bedding.

A cloud of sleep began dropping over her like a warm blanket. Evelyn was out there somewhere. The sheriff had tracked her back to the car dealership, but Miles, Tripp, nor any of their staff had admitted to seeing her. Miles was supposedly going through all his inventory to see if a vehicle was missing. He swore to Todd that he would get him this information as soon as possible, but Katy felt sure that he was just blowing smoke.

The sleep pushed in all around her, but the rapid-fire thoughts fought to push it back. Where was Amanda Carson? Had Evelyn already killed her before going after Katy? The black fog of sleep muscled in, shoving her eyes down. John was here. She was safe.

"Katy," A hand pressed against her shoulder. "Katy. Wake up, for just a second, baby."

The bright blue florescent light over the emergency room cot glared into her face as she tried to focus on John's words. "Baby, I need to step out for just a second. Kelly Ann is out front." John faded from view as the warm blackness returned. "Katy, are you hearing me? Kelly Ann wants to come in, but I have to go verify that it's her before the desk lady will let her in here."

The warm, calloused hand touching her cheek was John's. She would recognize his touch even if she were in a coma. She pushed against the lead weights holding her eyelids down. The harsh, cold light exploded in her vision for just a second before she closed her eyes back to the darkness. "Okay. I'll be okay. I'll just nap until y'all get back."

The sound of the exam room door swinging shut swished softly as John exited, causing a faint gust of cool air to sweep across her arms. Goose flesh instantly popped up. She needed another blanket. The distant burning sensation from her injured foot pounded in the background through the morphine haze. The medication was wearing off. Good. She needed to wake up. She needed to think.

The cool air washed over her again as the soft swooshing noise registered in her foggy brain. Lifting her eyelids was like lifting dumbbells. She pushed them open and a sliver of the brightness crept in through the crack. "Kelly Ann, John... that you?"

"You're an idiot, and so is your husband."

Katy's eyes popped open with no trouble as Evelyn's voice triggered a rush of adrenalin. The perfect make-up and flawless hair passed through her line of vision for only an instant but was blocked by the hospital pillow descending on her face. Strange how the object that felt so good behind her head was quickly causing panic when applied to her throat and face. The soft cotton fluffiness pressed down, molding over her mouth and nose, effectively sealing off the air.

Blackness, no longer comforting, engulfed Katy as she attempted to lift her limbs and fight against her airless prison. The weight and heat of Evelyn's body pushed down against her shoulders, face, and neck through the pillow. Evelyn's hand squeezed through the softness and tightened around her windpipe. Bright bursts of light, and sharp bursts of pain began to fight for room inside her skull. Her lungs struggled to be released from the airless trap. Evelyn's laughter floated through the pain as Katy's consciousness slipped away.

"And you are sure she's going to be okay?"

"She'll be good as new in no time at all. You got back to her just in time."

John's voice, strong, manly, sincere... she loved that voice. That's what had attracted her to him in the first place all those years ago. Her tongue refused to move. Sand and glue covered the roof of her mouth, or that's what it felt like. She peeled her tongue off and tried to lick her lips. Not good. Too dry.

"Look Doc, she's waking up." The voice she loved. She fought with her eyelids to get them open. She wanted to find his face. Two Johns, both distant and hazy, gradually merged into one as her eyes found their focus. "Woman, you scared the life out of me." John leaned down and planted a soft kiss on her forehead as he spoke.

"Wha..." The sound of a croaking toad rose from Katy's throat as she attempted to speak.

"Wait, honey," John gently lifted her head and held the pink plastic, standard-issue hospital cup to her lips. "Here, sip some water."

The cold water immediately flooded the dry cavern in her mouth and throat. "Thank you," she whispered.

"Talking may be hard for a while," Dr. Roberts said, stepping up beside John and patting her IV free hand. "She had a lot of pressure on your neck, and there'll be some residual swelling to deal with."

Her hand found its way to her throat as the doctor spoke, finding the puffiness and soreness he described. "What happened?" she whispered, trying to piece together why she was in this shape. The pain medication made everything so warped and dreamlike.

John pulled a chair up from the corner to the side of her bed. Somewhere along the way they had moved her from the ER exam room to a real hospital room. She shifted her shoulders slightly to face him, and soreness dripped from every muscle.

"Don't try to talk," John said, sitting on the edge of the hard, vinyl-covered chair. He took her hand through the bed rails. "I'll fill you in as best I can on what happened. The pink lady had stepped away from the desk in the lobby. Evelyn must have used the desk phone and called back to the ER room. She got me to come down there looking for Kelly Ann, then she came up here. When I figured it all out and got back up here..."

Katy looked as tears rolled down his cheeks. She hadn't seen him cry since the day the twins were born. Salty tears ran down her face onto her cracked lips.

"Anyway," John wiped his eyes with the back of his hand, then gently blotted Katy's eyes with a tissue. "When I got back, she was stretched across you with a pillow over your face."

That part was starting to come back. "Where is she now?" she whispered.

"Down in the ER or either the jail. I'm not sure, but the sheriff has her."

"I think they've left with her already." Dr. Roberts said. "Her shoulder wasn't fractured, just sprained."

Katy had forgotten the doctor was still in the room. She furrowed her eyebrows, trying to remember how Evelyn's shoulder injury had happened, but nothing surfaced.

"Your husband pulled her off you and she hit the floor with considerable force," the doctor said, looking at Katy's face. "But don't worry. She'll mend up just fine in prison."

She must have been completely out when that occurred. She had no recollection whatsoever of John coming to her rescue, but thanked God that he did.

"Todd's supposed to come to talk to you after while, but if you're not up to it, we'll make him wait," John said.

Katy drank more water from her pink cup. "I'm doing okay now, long as I keep sipping something wet." She sounded froggy, but her voice was fast returning. "Has anybody checked on Amanda Carson? I've been trying to call her for two days, and can't get an answer."

"I don't know," John replied, "I haven't heard anybody mention her. Why?"

"Laney stole papers, proving Miles Brown is a bigamist. I'm ninety-nine percent sure that she found these papers while cleaning up Jenna Williams' room at the Brown mansion. I think she has stashed them at her mom's place for safekeeping. Laney tried to blackmail the Browns with those papers, and that's what got her killed."

"I need to tell this to Todd." John pulled his phone from his pocket. "This mess has got to stop."

"I think Evelyn thought I had the papers," Katy whispered. "That's why she was taking me to that pond in the woods. She was planning on making me tell her where I had put them, then kill me, and sink me in that pond."

John began pacing back and forth across the brown speckled tiles on the hospital floor, his work boots clicking with each step. He relayed the information to Todd and hung up the phone before sitting back down. "Todd's going to come over and write down everything you know so he can add it to what they've found out from Evelyn Brown. He thinks that will be the quickest way to figuring all of this out."

"What about Amanda Carson?"

"They're sending someone over to her house now and making some calls to try to figure out what's going on." John noticed Katy shiver and pulled the covers up over her shoulders. "Don't worry. They'll figure this out. You just try to get some rest so we can get you home in the morning."

Katy dozed off. She didn't want to, but her body didn't ask her for permission. John stretched out on a cot an aide brought in for him and attempted to look at a magazine. Nothing could hurt her now, and there was nothing she could do to make things better. Her eyes drifted close.

❧

"This chicken is pretty sad." Katy put the pink cover back over the tray the nurse had left at her bedside minutes before. "I'm so glad you brought me some fries, Todd."

He had brought a hamburger too, but her throat was just too sore to swallow that much bulk. If she chewed the fries to a mushy pulp, and went slow, she could get them down without too much pain. She wadded up the empty silver fry container and tossed it in the white, grease-stained Burger Barn bag.

"No problem Aunt Katy." He had refused to let

her talk about 'her trip to the woods,' as John was now calling it, until she finished eating. Now that she was done, he was all ears.

"I'm ready to hear what you've found out," Katy said, as she finished a long slurp of Coke from the thirty-two-ounce Styrofoam cup. She smiled at her nephew, then winced as the cracks in her lips stretched tight.

"Well actually," one side of Todd's mouth lifted in his usual lopsided grin, "I'm here to find out what you know."

"Of course you are, but I figured since I was the one who almost got killed today, I could have the privilege of deciding who speaks first." She looked from her nephew to her husband and took a stab at playing the helpless female. "After all, I need closure before I can sleep tonight."

"Okay, you win." Todd pulled out his notepad. "Let me get to my notes and then we'll have at it."

Katy glanced at the black and white clock on the wall, almost nine. She had slept the afternoon and most of the evening away while the police were trying to figure things out. "First of all, did you find Amanda Carson?"

"Yes, ma'am. We found the whole Carson clan, and they're all fine."

"Why doesn't she answer her phone?" Katy

asked, letting out a long sigh of relief. "I hope she's not just avoiding my calls."

"I talked with Mr. Johnny, and they are on the coast in Alabama. They decided to take the grandkids out of town until their daddy had things straightened out and things settled down. Amanda didn't even take her phone. Mr. Johnny said she needed to disconnect for a while."

"You need to try to get in touch with her and see if you can get that box of Laney's papers that is hidden under the bed in their trailer," Katy said.

"You've lost me." Todd's forehead wrinkled in confusion. "What box of papers?"

She decided it would be easier to explain everything she knew before asking any more questions. She filled him in on the bigamy, the blackmail, the trip to the woods, and then let John tell about the hospital escapade.

"I got a little of what happened this morning from Mr. Byrd, Tubby, and Joe, but I ain't heard nothing about the box of papers." Todd rubbed the few sandy brown hairs on his chin. "You don't think the Carsons were planning on blackmailing the Browns too, do you?"

"No, not the Carsons, just Laney. Amanda told me the day of Laney's funeral about the box, but she didn't have a clue what was in it." She looked guiltily at Todd and her husband. "I know I should have told somebody about this before now, but she made me promise to wait until after the funeral. She was just trying to cope with the death of her only child, and I didn't have the heart to push the issue."

"That heart almost got you killed," Todd said as he jotted down some notes on his little pad.

"I know, I know. Evelyn Brown is as crazy as a road lizard. One minute she would be explaining how she bashed a woman's head in with a monkey wrench, and the next she would be complaining that she was going to be late for a country club meeting." Katy reached behind her head and adjusted her pillows. "The problem is, I know she had help doing all of this, but she didn't tell me who her helper was."

"Probably her husband Miles, don't you think?" John asked.

"No, that's the one person she said didn't do it. She said he was too lazy, and he loved Jessa. I know it wasn't him."

"My money's on Tripp," Todd said. "He's the only other person who had something to lose in all this mess."

"I agree," Katy said. "What are you going to do now?"

"I'm going to get back over to the station. Looks like it will be another all-nighter. I imagine

Sheriff Reid will want to bring Tripp in for questioning. His momma sure ain't saying anything. She's acting like she's checked into the Hilton. She's demanded a better chair to sit on, reading material, and who knows what else." Todd patted his front pocket and pulled out Katy's cell phone. "I almost forgot. I'm supposed to return this to you. They found it in the Mazda Evelyn drove over to the hospital from Brown Motors."

Katy took the phone and watched as John followed their nephew into the hall. She wanted to call and thank Mr. Byrd again for what he did for her today, but it was already after nine. She would have to think up something extra special to repay his kindness with. A peach cobbler just wouldn't be enough.

Chapter Thirty-Seven

John came back into the room after Todd left. He reached in the greasy Burger Barn bag and pulled out her hamburger. "No need to let it go to waste," he said as he clicked on the TV for the evening news.

Katy thought she wouldn't be able to sleep since she napped all afternoon, but when the nurse came by at ten to get her vital signs, she was fighting to keep her eyes open. She was just starting to doze when her phone began to buzz on the bedside table. "Hello," she said groggily.

"Is this Katy Cross, the nurse?"

"Yes, it is. Who am I speaking with?"

"I need to tell you something, and don't go

thinking I'm looney. I don't know what Evelyn has up her sleeve, but I'm not senile. Not yet."

"No, Mrs. Tellman, I know you're thinking straight." Katy recognized the old woman's voice. "What's going on?" She put the phone on speaker so John could hear.

"It's Tripp. He came in about thirty minutes ago, looking for Evelyn. I told him I haven't seen her, and he went off the deep end."

"Who's there with you, Mrs. Tellman?"

"I think it's just me and Tripp. Nelda leaves every evening at six. I got in the bed at eight like I always do, but I don't think Miles or Evelyn are here. I called upstairs for them and didn't get an answer. I even tried their phones. I don't know where they've got off to."

"Where's Tripp now?" Katy looked over at John, eyes wide. "What's he doing?"

"He's always acting a fool, that's nothing new, but tonight he's got a double dose. He came bursting into my room yelling for his momma. When he couldn't find her, he stormed off ranting and raving about jail and a bunch of other nonsense." Mrs. Tellman paused. "Then he came back in here a few minutes later with a gun."

Katy felt her heart pounding through the thin hospital gown. "Where's Tripp now, Mrs. Tellman? What's he doing?" she asked for the second time.

"He just left out of here. I heard him going upstairs. He asked me what I'd told you about the family and if you had asked me any questions about Jessa or the cleaning girl that got killed."

"What did you say?" Katy asked, swallowing hard, feeling the soreness in her throat from Evelyn's attack.

"I told him to mind his own business. That I'm sick and tired of everybody minding mine."

"My word, Mrs. Tellman, you said he has a gun," Katy whispered, her voice giving out on her. "What did he do?"

"We had a Mexican standoff for about one long minute," the old woman chuckled. "He had the gun pointed at me, and I had my cane pointed at him. I won."

John stood up and took out his phone to call Todd. "Can you lock him out of your rooms?" Katy asked, taking her phone off speaker, and raising it to her ear.

"I can lock the doors, but he knows where they keep the key. I ain't worried about me, anyway. That's not why I called." She stopped for just a second, and her voice changed from its usual bossy tone to an actual grandmotherly warmth. It sounded strained coming from this woman. "I'm worried about him, and well, you too."

"Me?"

"Yes, you." Grandmother disappeared again and boss lady returned. "He said you were going to find stuff out and ruin everything. I don't know what stuff he's talking about, but like I said, he's gone over the edge tonight."

"I'm safe, Mrs. Tellman," Katy said, glancing at John as he stood in the corner of the room talking on his cell, "but I'm worried about you."

"No need, girl. I called his bluff, and he folded. I just don't know what he has planned. I don't think he'll hurt anybody, but he might do something stupid and get himself arrested. Evelyn usually handles his stupidity, but I can't find her." The last few words were mumbled to herself, not Katy.

"Look, just lock your door anyway. Okay?" Poor woman. She had no clue that the house of cards had tumbled a long time ago. "I'm calling my nephew. He works for the sheriff's office and will be right over. He'll know what to do."

"I guess that'll have to do," Mrs. Tellman sighed. "Who knows, maybe jail is what he needs to scare some sense into him. I just hate to see the family name drug through the mud."

"I called Todd," John said as Katy hung up her phone. "Him and the sheriff are out at the Carson's place looking around. It'll be about thirty minutes before they can get there."

"Did you tell him about the gun?" Katy felt tears welling up, ready to spill.

"Yeah, and that Tripp's alone in the house with his grandmother." He squeezed Katy's hand. "Don't worry. Todd knows what he's doing, and besides, the Kevlar vest the church ladies bought for him came in."

"I'm getting more respect for grey-haired women every day." Katy smiled through her tears. "I'm still gonna pray... pray hard."

Mrs. Tellman slipped her feet over the edge of the bed and pushed her toes around in the carpet until she found her slippers. She had to lock that door, but she had to go to the bathroom. First things first. If she wet the carpet, Evelyn would have her in a nursing home by breakfast. She grabbed her cane and went into the bathroom. She had a pack of adult diapers in her dresser, but she wasn't ready to slide that far down the helpless ladder yet.

When she finished, she looked into the mirror at the old lady while she washed her hands. Something was up. It had been up for a while, but she had taken the easy road and ignored it. Now, just like a boil that had festered, grown, and become a bigger and bigger pain in her rear end, it was going to burst open and be a stinking mess. "You're slipping, ole gal," she said to her reflection. "You should have dealt with that girl when she first moved here, and none of this would be happening now." She dried her hands on the blue towel hanging by the sink, then opened the bedroom door and peaked out.

"Sit down, Nana, and don't give me no lip. I'm in a hurry." Tripp sat in the chair by her recliner, the pistol on the table at his side, and her purse in his lap.

Mrs. Tellman walked to the recliner, never taking her eyes off her grandson. "Where's Evelyn? What's going on that I don't know about?"

Tripp raked a sweaty hand through his hair and glared at the old woman. She was as hard-headed as a bulldog. He could waste time arguing with her for an hour or tell her what she wanted to know. She would find it all out in the morning, anyway. "I just got off the phone with Dad. Momma's in jail." He waited for her to cry, argue, call him a liar, something... but she didn't. She just stared. "Look, Nana, Momma got rid of Jessa then made me clean up her mess." He wiped his sweaty palms across the legs of his jeans as he talked. "If she tells them everything, they're going to come after me." He raised his voice to a shout. "I ain't got time to be sitting here. I gotta get out of town."

He put his hands back on his thighs to stop the bouncing that his legs were doing of their own accord. He needed another Xanax. He needed three more Xanax and something to chase them down with. Later. First, he needed money. He forced himself to make eye contact with his grandmother. "I need your cash."

Mrs. Tellman watched as her grandson babbled. She had suspected that he had killed Jessa, and maybe Laney too. He wasn't that bright, and killing was how dumb people took care of their enemies. But was he telling the truth about Evelyn? "Why am I just now finding out about this?"

"Why? Why? Nana, are you nuts? You don't talk about who you choked to death over the family dinner." His voice was loud, uncontrolled.

Hers was level, demanding. "No, you wait until you're buried in a self-made grave, then you give me a garden spade to dig you out with." She sighed and pushed up from the chair. He was an idiot, just like his father, but he was her only grandson. "Come on. A deputy is on his way out here. You don't have much time."

Tripp bounced up from the chair and ran his fingers through his hair again. He was doing this about every thirty seconds now as his nerves unraveled more and more. "What do you mean a deputy is on his way? What've you done? What do you know?"

She didn't answer, but walked over to her bed, and pointed to the massive family portrait hanging above the headboard. "Shut up and take that picture down."

Tripp looked at the old woman and looked at the picture. He was used to being bailed out of his problems. His momma had been doing it since he was six and got caught stealing money from the cash register at the dealership. She'd probably started earlier than that. He didn't know. He was not used to thinking for himself. He didn't question his grandmother. If she was willing to step into the role of over-protective enabler, he knew how to play the part of the helpless victim. He'd been playing it his entire life.

He moved the picture to the bed and was only mildly surprised to see the wall safe hidden behind it. He pushed the bed out just enough for the petite woman to squeeze behind the furniture and waited silently while she entered the combination and opened the door.

They would catch him. Mrs. Tellman knew this beyond a shadow of a doubt. Probably before he got out of the state. Probably before he got out of the county. All of this was a given. Still, he was blood. She had no choice. She took ten thousand out and closed the safe door. There was more in there, a lot more, but she would need that for the lawyers. One or two lawyers for Evelyn, and one for him too, if he didn't get himself killed. "Now go. Don't speed or do anything stupid to get pulled over. And whatever you do, don't start calling people and getting on that dog-gone internet."

He took the money and mumbled a thanks under his breath. The days of kissing and hugging had ended between them over a decade before.

He grabbed the gun on the way out and shoved it in his front pocket. Yeah, she thought, his days are numbered.

Chapter Thirty-Eight

The sheriff pulled into the entrance of the Browns' long driveway and waited while Todd put on the vest and put a clip in his gun. Todd was nervous. Not Barney Fife nervous, but nervous. If Katy and the sheriff were right, this guy had helped cover up one murder and assisted in another. Granny might think he was harmless, but Todd knew better.

The sheriff pulled slowly to the front of the house, lights off, and killed the engine. "Look, we're going in there blind, not knowing where he's at. He's armed, and there's a potential hostage. Our primary goal is to get the old lady out to safety."

"Yes, sir." Todd held the pistol at his side as

they walked silently passed the cement bulldogs and onto the dark front porch. He was ready.

No one came to the front door. They walked around the side of the house to the garage, which was closed. The outdoor motion sensor lights allowed them to see the backyard and the swimming pool. Thick curtains covered a sliding glass door on the back of the bottom floor, but the light was still able to peek out under the small gap at the floor. The back door, a few feet over which led to the kitchen, was locked up tight.

They stepped up to the sliding glass door. The sheriff pulled on the door latch. It was locked too. He knocked softly. "Mrs. Tellman, its Sheriff Reid. Your friend Katy Cross called us." They waited.

At first, they heard nothing, but then a faint bumping gait could be heard coming across the room. Mrs. Tellman pulled the curtain back and peered at the law officers through the glass. "Just a minute. I have to turn off the alarm." She disappeared, then returned shortly and let them into her living area.

Todd looked around the room noticing the picture laying on the bed with the wall safe exposed for public viewing. "Is your grandson still here, ma'am? We need to talk to him."

"I missed the news," Mrs. Tellman said, ignoring the question as she walked back to her recliner to sit down. "Tripp said you have my daughter in jail."

The sheriff motioned for Todd to stay with the woman as he left the room to look for the suspect. Todd came around in front of the recliner and positioned himself where he could see the hall entrance into the room and the sliding door exiting to the backyard. "Mrs. Tellman, why don't you let me walk you out to the car? You can sit there while we make sure your house is safe."

Mrs. Tellman looked up at the young man. Her eyes were sad as she stared at the officer. He was probably a little younger than Tripp, but already he was amounting to something. Tripp never would. She prayed the boy had already left, but she had not heard a car engine start or even that ridiculous motorcycle since he'd left her. "I'm in no danger. If he'd wanted to hurt me, he would have done it already." She reached down to the lever on the side of the recliner and began raising her feet. "I think I'll just sit here and catch my breath for a while."

Todd watched as the woman raised her feet in front of her and gazed at him with a look of defiance. What was he supposed to do now? He couldn't very well manhandle a ninety-year-old woman.

"Kind of got you between a rock and a hard

place, don't I boy?" Mrs. Tellman grinned, winking as she spoke.

Todd grinned back. He couldn't help it. A loud crash coming from somewhere in the house caused both of them to look toward the doorway. A gunshot rang out and Todd headed into the darkness. "Stay here," he called over his shoulder as he disappeared from sight.

Mrs. Tellman let her feet down hurriedly and grabbed her cane. She put up a good front, but she had no desire to get caught in crossfire tonight. She stood up and began making her way toward the bathroom to hide.

Before she had walked two feet Tripp came running in the doorway, gun in one hand, and a gym bag in the other. His eyes were bulging out in panic. He stopped for just a second, noticing his grandmother in his path, then continued forward, no intention of slowing down or dodging her.

Mrs. Tellman made a decision in that second. A useless grandson in prison was better than a dead grandson planted in the cemetery. She stepped to the side, out of Tripp's path, and stuck her cane forward in front of his feet. Tripp did just what she expected. His feet tangled in the cane. His arms reached out, grabbing for anything solid to stop his fall, his gun flying through the air and landing next to the sliding glass door. He face-planted flat in the thick carpet just as Todd stepped through the doorway, aiming his gun directly at Tripp's back.

He holstered his gun and put his knee between Tripp's shoulder blades, then wrestled his arms behind him and cuffed him with some difficulty. If Tripp had not fallen, there would have been a shootout right there in the bedroom. He rolled Tripp over, stepped back, and pulled the pistol back out of his holster, pointing it at the prisoner. Tripp decided to be still.

"Mrs. Tellman, get over there by your bed please." Todd's voice was shaking.

"I will, son, just as soon as I go to the bathroom." The little woman exited the room and shut the bathroom door behind her.

Todd called an ambulance for the sheriff who was in the foyer bleeding from a gunshot wound to the shoulder. He insisted he was fine, but he hadn't been able to follow Tripp out of the room. Todd also called the station and told them to send help. Finally, he sat down across from the recliner and concentrated on holding the gun steady as he aimed it toward Tripp, in spite of his shaking hands.

"In here," Todd said, hearing a vehicle drive up the driveway, assuming it was someone from the station since he didn't hear ambulance sirens.

Miles Brown slid the glass door open and

stepped through the curtains. He looked at his son on the floor and the young deputy sitting in the chair holding the pistol. He staggered across the room and sat on the bed. He had obviously been drinking.

"Mr. Brown, don't give me no trouble now," Todd said, without taking his eyes off Tripp. "The sheriff is in the next room and more help is on the way."

Mr. Brown looked from Tripp to Todd as he spoke. "I've caused enough trouble already." He ran his hands through his hair, just like his son had done earlier. "I never should've listened to Jenny. It was her idea to marry Evelyn."

"Who's Jenny?" Todd glanced at Mr. Brown out of the corner of his eye.

"My other wife," the older man sobbed. "It was her idea to marry Evelyn. Evelyn was rich. We were starving to death and going to have to give up our baby to the welfare people. Jenny said marry her and all our problems would be solved."

Tripp looked at his father with a new hate forming in his eyes. "I should've just killed you instead of that ignorant cleaning girl. I would've enjoyed that."

"I didn't have a choice, son." Mr. Brown looked at Tripp with pleading eyes. "I needed money to start up the car business. All I knew how to do was talk to people. That's all I've ever been good at. If Jenna hadn't decided to come over here and get greedy, everything would still be okay."

"Okay? Okay?" Tripp screamed. "You had another family, another child all these years that we never knew about, and you think it's okay?"

Todd stood up. "Now just calm down Tripp." He looked at Mr. Brown. "Maybe you should just be quiet until I can get you to the station."

"I need you to understand, Tripp." Miles leaned forward and put his head in his hands, ignoring Todd, his speech slurred. "I was at MSU on a football scholarship when I met Jenny. We started dating, and the next thing I knew she was pregnant, and I was married. Back then, things were different. When the school found out about it, they kicked me off the team and I lost my scholarship."

Mrs. Tellman stepped out of the bathroom while Miles continued to talk. "Why Evelyn? Why my daughter? There had to be other girls there with money. Why did you choose her?" She leaned heavily on her cane, somehow looking ten years older than she had just an hour before.

"I didn't seek her out, Mom," Miles said, looking at Mrs. Tellman, tears flowing from his bloodshot eyes. "I was working at the gas station changing oil. She showed up with a few of her sorority sisters and started flirting with me. I ignored her, Mom, I really did, but she just kept coming back."

"Did you tell her you were married, Miles?" Mrs. Tellman's voice took on the tone of judge. "Did you tell her you were a father?"

"Well, no... I didn't. I was ashamed." Miles looked from his mother-in-law back to his son. He had forgotten that Todd was in the room. "She was so happy, not a care in the world. She was finishing up her second year at Mississippi State, and was on the homecoming court. I just couldn't believe she wanted to spend time with me."

"You should have told her, Dad. You should have given her the choice of walking away." Tripp's voice had changed from rage to disgust. "She killed your daughter. You made Mom a murderer."

"I never meant for her to find out. Jenny died last year of breast cancer. I guess Jessa got to going through her mother's things and found letters I had written to her mother from this address over the years. When she showed up here demanding money, I didn't know what else to do."

"How long has my daughter known about this other life of yours?" Mrs. Tellman asked.

"I told her right after Jessa moved in with us," Miles answered. "At first I thought everything was going to work out. Evelyn was mad, but she said what was done was done. If Jessa would have been satisfied with the money, maybe it would have been okay."

Mrs. Tellman could not believe all of this had been going on right under her nose for over a year. She thought Evelyn couldn't sneeze without asking her for a tissue. She had no right to call Tripp ignorant. She had no right at all. "What do you mean satisfied with the money?" she asked. "What was she wanting?"

"She wanted to tell everybody that I was her father. She wanted to become an heir to everything here," Miles mumbled, staring at the floor as he spoke.

"Over my dead body," Tripp yelled, his face bright red with rage.

The sounds of sirens coming up the driveway brought the discussion to a close. The ambulance crew came through the back with a stretcher and continued to the foyer to check on Sheriff Reid. A couple of state troopers followed them and loaded Tripp in their car and transported him to the station.

"Mr. Brown, you're going to have to come on down to the station with me and tell all of this again," Todd said to the old man who was sitting quietly on the bed staring at the floor. Mrs. Tellman had returned to her recliner and had not spoken again. Todd walked over and squatted down beside her chair. "Can I call somebody to come and be with you tonight? I don't feel like we should leave you here alone."

Mrs. Tellman patted the young deputy's hand. "No, son. That won't be necessary. I think I have been alone for a long time now and just didn't know it."

Todd felt sorry for the spunky little woman. She seemed to be giving up. "Is there anything you want me to tell your daughter or grandson?"

"No." She paused and looked up into Todd's face. "Wait, yes, there is. Tell them I'm sorry."

Chapter Thirty-Nine

"No more ice cream ever?" John asked, eyes stretched wide.

"Nope, no more ice cream ever." Katy bit her tongue to keep from laughing.

"Woman, you have lost your mind," John exclaimed, half in jest, but half in earnest.

"Well, okay, maybe not ever," Katy said, fighting back a grin, "but it will not be every night after supper. Those days are over John Cross."

John grinned and sat down on the edge of his recliner. Katy's foot was in a 'boot' to help stabilize the break so it would heal properly. "I know we need to get in shape," he said, leaning over and fluffing the pillow under her foot as he spoke, "but can't we at least wait on all of these drastic changes until you can walk again? My body's gonna go into shock if I give up Rocky Road cold turkey."

"Okay, how about this? Ice cream only on the weekends. That's a good way to start."

"I guess I'll take what I can get." He flopped his head back against the chair and sighed.

"Just think how grateful you'll be next time you get your cholesterol checked," Katy said, reaching over to pat his hand.

"Anybody home?" Todd called as he walked into the living room, followed by Misty and Mike.

"Just us old folks," Katy answered. "Y'all take a seat."

"So how is the patient?" Todd asked, sitting down across from Katy.

"Yeah, how long before you can be back playing?" Misty chimed in. "We've got our standing date at the nursing home. Do you think I need to call the activities lady and reschedule?"

"I'm much, much better now that we're home." Katy smiled and looked at John. "He just said I couldn't drive or put weight on my foot, didn't he, John? I should be able to sit down and play the guitar without any trouble."

"Technically," John said, raising one eyebrow, "I guess you can do that as long as somebody can drive you and help with the guitar. You can't tote it while you're on crutches." He grinned. "You might want to think twice about going in that nursing home all crippled up. They might try to keep you and do a little therapy."

"Misty, I'll be at the nursing home now even if I have to call a taxi. Don't you worry." She smiled across to John as she spoke, and he winked back.

"Todd, have you gotten any time off to go home and sleep?" Mike asked. "I hear the jail's a pretty crowded place nowadays."

"Just a little," Todd answered. We're rotating twelve-hour shifts until the bigwigs can decide what to do with everybody."

"Are they going to hire some more help?" John asked. "Since somebody has to stay there around the clock with the prisoners, I would think they would have to. Even if it's temporary."

Todd nodded. "Yes, sir. They've already started the process."

"So, you have Evelyn in one cell and Tripp in the other." Katy counted them off on her fingers. "Who else is down there?"

"Well, we let the coach go home yesterday after we got a statement from Tripp. I tell you what, it was plumb crazy around there for a while." Todd paused and looked at the group. "For a while, we had Evelyn and Tripp each in a cell, Coach Finch cuffed and sitting in the corner, Mr. Brown sitting in another corner whining about his hangover, and three separate lawyers parading in and out like they owned the place."

"My word," Katy exclaimed. "I didn't realize the station was big enough to hold all of those people."

"That's the whole problem, Aunt Katy. It's not. But the sheriff was at the hospital getting his shoulder taken care of, so, I just kind of stuck people where I could until I got it figured out."

"Is the sheriff okay?" Misty asked.

"He is. He came in this morning for just a minute and laid down a few rules for everybody to follow. He went home after a couple of hours, but we can call him, and he'll come back. It's a lot more organized and calmer now."

"I don't know about the rest of you, but I'm ready for a good long run of calm and boring," Misty said.

Mike slapped his wife on the knee and started to stand. "Speaking of calm and boring, it's about time for us to go. I have to get back to work."

"Wait just a second honey," Misty said refusing to stand. "While I have Todd and Katy here as a captive audience, I want to find out a few things."

"Alright," Mike grinned and sat back down, "dig a little dirt real quick before we leave."

"So Todd," Misty said, as she poked her husband in the ribs, "I know that Evelyn Brown killed

Jessa Williams because she didn't want to share the Brown business and everything with the child of the first wife...right?"

"That's right," Todd nodded. "I think she just couldn't handle the embarrassment of being hoodwinked by a bigamist husband all these years. But the reason she's giving is about the money."

"Okay, that figures. I would just die if that happened to me too." Misty paused and looked at Mike with a raised eyebrow. "If you have any deep dark secrets, just ship me off to a tropical island somewhere and let me live in ignorance," she said, mirth dripping from her words.

"I think you're pretty much stuck in Mississippi," Mike answered.

"The thing I'm wondering," Misty continued, "is did Evelyn kill Laney Finch too?"

"No, ma'am," Todd answered. "She and Tripp set up a meeting with her to get the marriage license and pictures and stuff from Mile's first marriage. Laney told them they were in her truck and to show her the money first. Evelyn went nuts and tried to do her in, but Tripp did the choking." He shook his head in disgust. "It made me kind of sick listening to them squabble about who did what. Tripp whined about his momma making him kill Laney and Evelyn kept screaming at him like she really was crazy. Anyway, when they checked the truck out and didn't find the papers, they drove it down to the logging road and into the pond."

"And they've been looking for those papers ever since," Katy chimed in.

"Why did Evelyn think you had them, and who does have them?" Misty asked.

"I think she thought I had them because I found both bodies and was asking her mother questions all of the time." Katy stopped and sighed. "If Evelyn had found out that Amanda Carson had the papers hid at her house, ain't no telling what would've happened to that poor family."

"Thank the Lord it's over now," John said.

"Amen," Todd and Mike said in unison.

Mike stood to go again, but Misty touched his hand before she stood. "Just one more question."

Mike rolled his eyes. "One more."

"Are you going to be able to come to rehearsal Tuesday night?" Misty talked faster as she got excited about her plan. "Since you can't drive, the girls and I were thinking that we could just come here and bring the practice to you."

"I haven't thought about it," Katy said, glancing at John who was looking at her with half a scowl on his face. "The doctor said I couldn't drive and to take it easy until I see him next Friday, but I think

I could play my guitar sitting in the chair with my foot propped up."

"Great," Misty exclaimed, finally standing up to leave. "I'll set it up."

John continued to scowl at his wife. "I don't think that's what the doctor had in mind by taking it easy." He grabbed the library books from the coffee table and laid them in her lap as he stood to walk everyone out. "We'll talk about this later."

Katy grinned as she picked up the books. She knew John would give in. Besides, it would be good to get her mind off things like murder and mayhem. Reading and playing the guitar would be just what the doctor ordered. She picked up the books and read the covers.

"Now, which one to read first, Mrs. Marple or Father Brown."

Thank you for reading *Moonlight, Murder, and Small-Town Secrets*! Keep reading for a peek at K.C.'s next book in the Skeeterville series, *Music, Murder, and Small-Town Romance*.

If you've enjoyed reading this book, please consider leaving an Amazon review.

Check out my website and sign up for my

newsletter to keep up with all the Skeeterville news at:

www.kchartauthor.com

Continue reading for a sneak peek of **Music, Murder, and Small Town Romance**, Book Two in A Katy Cross Mystery Series
Music, Murder, and Small Town Romance

Book Jacket Art and Design by Moon Diva Art. Tracey Hudson Countz is an illustrator and writer currently living in Columbia, MS. To learn more about Tracey, please visit www.moondivaart.com. Follow her on Facebook, Twitter, and Instagram @MoonDivaArt.

Coming Soon

Music, Murder, and Small Town Romance
A Katy Cross MysteryBook Two

By K.C. Hart

Chapter One

Katy and Misty scooted over in the booth to let Heather and Vickie slide in. Sarah dragged a chair from a nearby table to the end of the booth and completed the party. The Burger Barn was packed like always on a Saturday afternoon.

Katy turned up the volume on her phone and hushed the other members of The Moonlighters "Alright, listen up. I've got it on 98.4 WKLL and he's fixing to announce the winners of the contest."

For the past six years several local businesses had hosted the Battle of the Bands at the Skeeterville school auditorium. The money raised from this event was used to make improvements to the elementary school playground equipment. The community called in names of local performers into the radio station all month long. The top four bands with the most votes would get to participate in the big show.

"I called and voted for Tubby and the Tubs every day last week," Sarah said.

Misty raised her pointer finger to her lips to silence the younger woman as the announcer spoke. The ladies all leaned in toward the cell phone as Rob Clay, the voice around town, began to speak.

"The time is finally here to reveal which four local groups will get to participate in the sixth annual Battle of the Bands, brought to you by Brown Motor Company, Clay House Music, Friend's Pharmacy and a host of our other fine local businesses. As you all know, the voting closed on Thursday and the votes are finally tallied up. The four bands with the highest number of votes will be participating in what is sure to be the biggest event of the year for Skeeterville. Don't go anywhere. We will count down the winners right after this brief message from the fine folks at Brown Motor Company."

Misty rolled her eyes as the announcer drug out his speech. Katy grinned at her friend from across the booth. "The man knows how to talk, that's for sure," she said, watching Misty continue to make faces at her phone. "You act like you don't like Rob Clay very much."

"Have you ever met the man?" Misty asked. "He's about as full of himself as a puffed-up rooster in the hen house."

"I don't know him all that well," Katy said, "but I've met him at his store when I've gone in for guitar strings and picks and stuff. He seemed nice enough."

Misty bugged her eyes out and younger ladies laughed. "Mrs. Katy," Vickie exclaimed, "you're one of the most naïve grown women I've ever met." Sarah and Heather bobbed their heads up and down in agreement.

"Okay girls, leave Katy alone," Misty said, looking across the booth and grinning. "Girl, Rob Clay is the biggest womanizing flirt in this town. He's fooled around with every woman that he could draw into his little spray-tanned, spiky-haired trap."

Katy's eyes stretched wide as she looked from one woman to the next. "You mean that sweet man is a," she leaned in close and lowered her voice, "a hoochie daddy?"

The four women burst out laughing again as Katy stared from one to the other waiting for an explanation.

Misty dabbed under her eyes with a napkin at

the tears of laughter ruining her mascara. "Yes girl, the biggest hoochie daddy around. I bet he hits on you every time you go in that store and you don't even realize it."

"I don't know," Katy said, shrugging her shoulders. "He just seemed very helpful to me." She looked at her friends' faces as they gawked at her in disbelief. "Okay, maybe you're right, but who cares. He's fixing to announce the winners."

The women turned their attention back to the radio. They groaned and sighed as the familiar voice of Miles Brown floated from Katy's smart phone bragging that his deals couldn't be beat anywhere in the state of Mississippi.

"Who do you think is going to make it this year?" Vickie asked. "I'm rooting for The Bluegrass Babes."

"Oh, they're a shoo-in," Misty said, brushing a strand of black wavy hair away from her face. "Everybody loves them, and they've been around for at least twenty years. The only reason they weren't in it last year is because their fiddle player was going to be out of town on an Alaskan cruise."

"Well." Katy sipped her Diet Coke. "Did any of you vote for The Moonlighters?" The four other women stared at her like she had grown feathers and was about to take flight.

"I didn't," Sarah said. The rest of the group chimed in their denials.

"Why waste our daily vote on us Katy?" Misty asked. "We've never placed before. We just aren't that well known, except maybe with the adult diaper and denture cream crowd."

"I guess you're right," Katy sighed. "But I know we got at least two votes every day from John and myself."

The women quit talking as Rob Clay's voice came back on the radio. "Now, what you have all been waiting to hear. I will be calling the winners out in no particular order. Band number one...The Bluegrass Babes."

Misty looked at the other women with an, 'I told you so,' look.

"Band number two...Tubby and the Tubs."

Sarah reached across the booth and gave a high five to Vickie. "Shush, girls," Misty said, waving her hand in their direction.

"Band number three...The Rough Edge Boys. And last, but certainly not least...The Moonlighters."

Vickie and Sarah began to squeal and bounce up and down on the benches like a couple of fish out of water. Heather, who was sitting on the end, jumped up and knocked her chair over as she began doing the happy dance.

"What happened?" Mason, one of the local teenagers sitting at the table across from them, asked. "You guys win the lottery?"

Heather, Sarah, and Vickie proceeded to tell everybody in the Burger Barn that The Moonlighters would be in the Battle of the Bands. The whole crowd began clapping and shouting out congratulations to their table. It didn't matter if they had ever heard them play or not.

Katy spewed her giant gulp of Diet Coke across the table all over Misty's face. Misty stared google eyed at the smart phone, never even blinking. Katy grabbed a wad of napkins out of the silver holder. She reached across the table and began dabbing the little brown beads of soda running down Misty's face. "I am so, so sorry." She stopped and looked at her friend who continued to stare straight ahead, mouth hanging open. "Misty, honey, you okay?"

Misty finally pulled her eyes from the phone and looked at her friend. A slow grin crept across Misty's face. "We are in the Battle of the Bands."

Katy's phone buzzed and she snatched it up. "Mom, are you listening to Rob Clay?" Kelly Ann, Katy's daughter asked. "You're in Battle of the Bands, Mom."

"Yeah, I heard," Katy said, grinning into the phone. "Where are you? Are you in town?"

"No ma'am, I'm at home. I was just curious about who would win, so I had the radio on y'all's local station. We voted for your band every day, like we do every year, but I had no idea that you'd win. You must be getting popular huh?'

"I don't think so honey. I don't know how we won. The rest of our own band members didn't even vote for us." Katy paused to think. "You know, I'm going to have to do a little snooping around and figure this out."

Kelly Ann laughed. "You do that Mom."

❧

Misty's high heeled sandals clunked out a steady rhythm as she walked beside Katy down the aisle of the high school auditorium. Two representatives from each of the four bands were scheduled to meet with Rob Clay and the chairman of the PTO to go over the rules of the competition and set up practices.

Tubby Robinson and Joe Phobs smiled as Katy and Misty walked up. Tubby had taken over The Wildcats last year after Jessa Williams died, re-naming the band Tubby and the Tubs. It turned out that Joe, who had never been in a band before, sounded a whole lot like Dwight Yoakum. He was quickly recruited to take the lead vocalist spot that had been left vacant.

Katy looked down at her black tennis shoes and then across at her best friend's clunky, stylish high heels. Last year Katy had a close call when Jessa's killer had tried to do her in. She had been in an orthopedic boot for several weeks recovering from a break caused in her struggle with the murderer. She knew that she probably wouldn't have been wearing heels, even if her ankle wasn't a little weak now. She wore tennis shoes to see her home health patients on the job two or three days a week. For some reason she just didn't see the need to change from them when she wore her blue jeans and tee-shirts on her days off.

She smiled as they stepped closer to the rest of the band winners, thankful that Misty had insisted they keep practicing through her recuperation time. The rest of The Moonlighters had come over faithfully two times a week and practiced at Katy's house until she was well enough physically and emotionally to be out and about again.

"Congratulations Mrs. Katy, Mrs. Misty," Tubby said, as both men stuck out their hands to the ladies for a shake. "Now The Tubs won't be the only new kids on the stage."

Katy and Misty shook hands with the other

participants, as well as Edna Morse, the wife of the town coroner, and head of the PTO.

"Okay," Edna exclaimed, looking around the group. "Everyone is here except Rob, who is late as usual. Everybody just take a seat here on the front row and we'll get started. If he doesn't show up soon, I'll give him a call."

The band representatives sat down in the hard, fold down chairs that had been there since Katy had been in high school a million years ago. She wondered if her name was visible in a chair on the back row where she had carved it into the armrest on the last day of her senior year. She turned her attention back to the present as Edna handed each person a pile of stapled papers with the rules of the event.

Misty looked at Katy and stretched her eyes in mock concern. "I had no idea this was such an official deal," she whispered. "We may be in over our heads."

Katy grinned. Misty had always been a notorious cut up. That's probably why they got along so well. She nodded toward Edna who was looking at them over the rim of her glasses perched on her skinny pointed nose. Misty turned toward the woman and sat up a little straighter. "Sorry, Edna."

Edna smiled at the group, like they were a class of third graders, and began going over all of the rules and regulations for the show. "Please remember that this is a family event. There should be no profanity or explicit sexual references in any of your music."

Katy held her papers up over her mouth to cover the grin that had popped up on her face. Maybe it was because she was sitting in her old high school auditorium but listening to the owner of the funeral parlor talk about sexual references struck her as extremely funny. This time Misty poked her in the side to get her attention. Edna was glaring her way. She was not smiling. "No sexual references or cursing. Got it," Katy said, lowering her papers to her lap.

Edna finished going over the rest of the paperwork with no further interruptions then glanced at her watch. "Excuse me just a minute while I call Rob. This is unusually late, even for him."

Edna turned her back to the group and put her phone to her ear. While she was doing this Tom Jones' voice began ringing out from somewhere on the stage above the auditorium chairs. "What's new pussycat, whooaaooaaoo," drew everyone's attention as it floated down from the platform.

"That's Rob's ringtone," Edna said as she turned to look toward the stage. The music stopped as the call went to voice mail.

"Call the number again, Edna," Katy said as she

stood and started going up the stairs on side of the stage. The rest of the band members followed.

Edna scowled at the group from her spot in front of the chairs, obviously aggravated with the distraction. She dialed the number again. Tom Jones immediately began serenading them as the group followed his voice toward the back of the stage to the dark green velvet curtains. Tubby lifted the heavy curtain just as the song ended for the second time.

The Bluegrass Babes screamed in harmony as the rest of the group gasped. Rob Clay, skin a pale grey beneath his fake tan, and eyes bulging, lay on the ground behind the curtain.

"Edna, call an ambulance," Katy called down to the auditorium floor. She squatted down and felt the side of his neck for a pulse, sure of what she would find. Rob Clay was dead.

She looked at the thin line mark on his neck. A wire cut deep into the flesh, and blood had trickled out forming a small pool on the stage floor behind his head. Someone had strangled him with a wire. "Somebody call the sheriff too. Rob's dead."

Katy stood and turned to the sound of heaving and retching. One of The Rough Edge Boys was tossing his cookies. "Misty, why don't y'all go back and sit down 'til the sheriff gets here."

"Good idea," Misty said, looking a little pale

herself. She gathered up the rest of the band members and corralled them back to the chairs. Tubby waited with Katy who squatted back down to examine Rob's body.

Rob's skin was still warm. He hadn't been dead very long, but his pupils were fixed and dilated, staring up blindly. CPR would do no good here. There was some purplish discoloration and swelling around one eye, like someone had punched him in the face. Katy looked at the thin wire that was still wrapped double around his neck. The end of the wire was visible from behind his head. She leaned closer to the wire, careful not to lose her balance and tumble over on the dead man. There was a familiar loop on the end of the wire.

She could feel Tubby breathing down the back of her neck as he leaned in for a closer look too. "That's a guitar string," he whispered from behind her head. "Somebody killed that poor guy with a guitar string."

Katy nodded as she quickly looked down the rest of his body. "That's what it looks like," she said. His shirt was ripped at the collar with several buttons missing down the front. The cell phone lay beside his body with the screen busted. She noticed bruising and torn skin on the knuckles of

Rob's right hand. It looked like he had tried to fight off his attacker without success.

A wrinkled piece of cloudy pink paper lay at his side, like he had dropped it from his hand when he was attacked. Katy squatted down one more time to get a closer look at the typed message on the paper. She quickly slipped her cell phone out of her pocket and snapped a picture of the note.

You are going to pay!!!!!!
EM

She turned and looked at Tubby who was still behind her. He had a strange, kind of dazed look on his face. Seeing the dead body seemed to be getting to him too. "Tubby, you don't have to follow me around. You can go down there with the rest of them if you want to. I'll be alright."

Tubby jerked his head from the pink paper and back to Katy as she stood up. "Oh, no ma'am," he said, popping out of the daze that had crept over him. "I think I'd better stay up here with you until the police get here to take over."

Katy smiled to herself. It seemed that Tubby had named himself her unofficial bodyguard. That was okay. He had rescued her in the past. Let him hang around. He might notice something that she missed.

She looked at the rest of the stage. It was a mess. There was a door frame standing a few feet away with the door missing. A raggedy dirt brown sofa was sitting to one side of the door with a wobbly side table next to it. An ancient rotary phone sat on the table. The drama team must be practicing for a play.

Katy stepped closer to the fake living room scene and noticed a square white envelope sticking out of the corner of one of the sofa cushions. "That looks like a pack of guitar strings."

Tubby, ever her shadow, bent over and looked at the envelope. "It sure is. Looks like it has been opened too. I bet that's one of the strings from the pack over there on Mr. Clay's neck."

There were a few metal chairs open around the stage as well. A couple were turned over in the far corner, like maybe somebody had knocked them over. She quickly snapped pictures of everything they saw, trying to be discreet.

"Tubby, ain't there a door back here somewhere that leads backstage?"

"Yes ma'am," Tubby answered. "I think it's to your right." He pointed in the direction of the overturned chairs. He followed as she walked that way.

Katy pulled back the thick velvet curtain. Behind it a wooden door opened to a narrow dressing room. This room was even more cluttered than the stage with props and cardboard boxes full of costumes and other discarded materials from performances of the past.

They stepped into the room to look around. Tubby had to stand behind Katy because the pathway through the clutter was just too narrow for them to stand side by side.

"Look, there's the back door behind those boxes. It goes to the rear parking lot," Tubby said, pointing over Katy's head to the back wall. "I know I don't look like it now, but I used to be on the drama team in high school."

"Oh, really?" Katy was surprised. She had pictured Tubby for a jock, not a drama geek. "What roles did you play?" she asked as she walked toward the back door.

"My junior year I was Brutus in Julius Caesar." That was kind of cool, but my senior year I was Curly McClain in Oklahoma. That was, by far, my favorite role."

Tubby squeezed around Katy and stepped toward the back door. "This leads toward the parking lot." He reached for the knob.

"Wait, Tubby," Katy said, grabbing his hand. "If the killer left this way there might be some fingerprints on the door."

Tubby jerked his hand back like he had touched a hot skillet. "Oh yeah, you're right."

Katy glanced around the narrow room at the boxes full of old costumes and props. The killer could have run through here and out the back even after people were arriving out front.

They returned to the stage just as Sheriff Reid walked through the main entrance at the back of the auditorium. "Katy Cross?" he called, walking though the mass of chairs between the stage and the entrance.

Katy lifted her hand and gave a shy wave. "Yes, sir, it's me."

The sheriff strode up the aisle toward the edge of the stage where Katy and Tubby were now standing. The other witnesses were still huddled together in the chairs on the front row. He passed them without slowing down and climbed the stairs. He stopped beside Katy and pulled out a small notebook and pen from his shirt pocket. "Tell me what you've got."

***

If you would like to read book two in The Katy Cross Cozy Mystery Series visit Music, Murder, and Small Town Romance

If you enjoyed this book please join Christian Indie Author Readers Group on Facebook. You will find Christian books in multiple genres, opportunities to find other Christian authors, and learn about new releases, sales, and free books. www.facebook.com/groups/291215317668431/

Acknowledgments

This book is dedicated first and foremost to my husband Mr. Wonderful, who always told me I could when I was telling myself I couldn't. Thank you for pushing me to be more than I thought I could be.

I am grateful to my three girls who have inspired me, encouraged me, and put up with me while I struggled to learn all the ins and outs of self-publishing a book. Emily guided has me every step of the way and answered my endless questions with patience and love for her mom and made the impossible possible. Jill read chapters and explained English rules and encouraged me to continue when I wasn't sure I wanted to. Lori listened to plot lines and twists and helped me decide whether Katy Cross could figure out who the killer was with the tools given to her in the story.

Thank you to Tracey Hudson Countz who read my very rough draft and told me it was worth keeping and polishing up into a real story. Thank you for bringing my cover design to life with your wonderful talent and for just being a dear friend during this process.

And thank you to my crazy extended family who have always encouraged a strong faith in God, a strong imagination, and a belief that every topic of discussion goes better with a little ribbing and a lot of laughter.

About the Author

K.C. Hart is an emerging author of Southern Cozies. This is K.C.'s debut novel set in a small town in Mississippi that you can only get to through the pages of her book.

K.C. resides in south Mississippi with Mr. Wonderful, her husband of thirty-plus years, where she spends her days reading, writing, playing the piano or guitar, or keeping up with her family and friends.

You can sign up for KC's newsletter at her webpage
kchartauthor.com.

KC's Amazon author link is
www.amazon.com/author/kchartauthor
You can follow KC on MeWe
https://mewe.com/i/kchart
Follow KC on Book Bub
Book Bub

facebook.com/KCWRITESBOOKS